Isaac's
Odyssey

Born in Dublin in 1980, Paddy studied film and
broadcasting after school before embarking on a career
spanning sixteen years that had nothing to do with either.
He has always had a love for story and Isaac's Odyssey is
his debut novel and is the first in a series.

Isaac's Odyssey

By

Paddy Flynn

First published March 2020

For Astrid

1

The hum of the floor buffer woke Isaac from his day
dream. Well, day dream was a bit of a stretch since it was
thirteen minutes to nine in the evening. Here he was, yet
another late shift in his disastrous job. He used the term
disastrous deliberately. He had begun by calling it "shitty"
but decided that wasn't even close to an accurate
description. Disastrous didn't just describe the job, but his
entire situation. He caught sight of himself in the office
window. His hair was getting long. Well, long for him
anyway. It was black in colour, shaved at the back and
sides, not too tight, with a slightly wavy mass on the top.
The bags under his eyes were getting bigger. He was
finding it hard to sleep after the long working days. He
was a handsome man by any standards, but it was hard to
say why. He had frown lines starting to develop on his
forehead, he was sure that his hairline was receding and he
had a scar on his chin from an unfortunate incident
involving a horse. The scar was pretty small but to Isaac it
might as well be all down his face. He liked the way he
looked, perhaps he was even a little vain. He had deep

brown eyes, with gold flecks weaved into them, but they were beginning to fade a little, losing some of their vigour. He could only put it down to one thing, this job and the fact that he had seriously under achieved since leaving college six years ago. Here he was, a degree in computer software and design, answering telephones in a call centre, for idiots with the most ridiculous problems or complaints about their newly acquired laptop. The beep for a new incoming call went off in his ear. Case in point:

"Thank you for calling the customer support helpline my name is Isaac, how can I assist you today?" Isaac rattled off the greeting from the script he had to follow, which had been drilled into his brain from day one since being hired. "I hate this place" he thought.

"Yeah listen up sunshine because I've got a big problem here and you're going fix it for me. And I don't want any fancy lingo or the techno language or none of that shite, I just want plain English and a solution, alright" barked the caller in his ear.

Isaac looked around the room he was trapped in as the man on the phone rambled on in an unending rant, a droll flat Dublin accent almost hypnotic in its rhythm. The room was a florescent cell. The lights alone were enough to drain Isaac of any self-esteem and fill him with the dull inevitability that this is, was and always will be the life that has forever been his destiny, no matter how high his hopes for himself were when he first decided what he wanted to be when he grew up. Here he was, shackled to his workstation by the head set he wore, only allowed free for bathroom breaks, a total of four in all, two minutes a piece. Any more and you would receive a pleasantly worded email from Martin in HR, reminding you that it would be greatly appreciated as well as a positive step to increasing

2

productivity if all off line times were kept inside company guide lines.

"What if I need to take a shit?" Isaac had asked in his induction, which was met by rapturous laughter by his fellow new starters. They didn't have an answer for him on the day. He was still waiting for them to get back to him.

The work stations themselves were big round desks divided into six segments. Each segment about two feet wide containing a telephone and a computer. One of the upsides to working late was that you could sit wherever you wanted, so you didn't have the pleasure of some oafish arse hole jabbing his elbows into you every few minutes.

"....so, all I can say is you better be able to help me." The voice on the line had just concluded his rant.

"That's what I'm here for sir" Isaac replied trying to sound as up-beat as he possibly could at this moment in time. "I hate myself" he thought.

"Don't get smart with me" the mans voiced boomed back.

"I wouldn't dream of getting smart with you sir, I'm only here to help." again Isaac straining as best he could to actually mean it. "Fuck you ye miserable old bollocks" were the words running through his mind though.

"Good so why don't we try that and cut out the chit chat" the man proposed. A proposition Isaac was more than happy to oblige.

"Certainly sir. So what seems to be the problem?"

The man's reply was astonishing. Of all the things that he thought this person was about to say, when he spoke Isaac was literally left speechless.

"My foot pedal is missing a bit off it."

Silence.

"Hello?" the man was obviously slightly puzzled by the absence of sound from Isaacs end of the line.

Isaac mustered up the best possible reply he could think of given what he considered to be the relatively short space of time between hearing what could possibly be the most outrageous series of words ever compiled to form a sentence and the response that was expected from him.

"I'm sorry sir could you repeat that?"

"Are ya deaf?" the man asked impatiently.

"No sir not at all. It's just, well, it sounded like you said your foot pedal isn't working and well, I suppose I have to just enquire, your foot pedal for what?"

Isaac asked this knowing full well what the answer was going to be but was still following the aforementioned script to the letter. He was convinced they had used some form of brain washing to get him to memorise it so well and follow the guides so closely. Keep asking questions. The more information they give you the easier it will be to solve their problems was the particular guide he was following at the moment. The caller however didn't fail to disappoint with his reply.

"For what do you think ye sap. The one that came with the computer."

Isaac paused for a moment taking a deep breath before he responded. He knew this was one of those times where he was going to have to take a firm stance in his retort and put this fellow in his place, because in his mind, stupidity like this must be dealt with quickly before it's allowed to spread from idiot to idiot. However, this is a situation where tact and composure are the only two words that should be weighing heavily on Isaacs mind. Yes, he must be admonished for his lunacy but at the same time, this isn't an all guns blazing moment. If you speak quickly without taking many breaths, you can get your point across and disguise any insults as poking a bit of harmless fun at the person. This man is a customer. Tact and composure. Tact and composure.

"Now you listen to me ya fucking dick head! The absolute audacity of you to actually ring a customer care line and tell them the foot pedal off your computer isn't working is just staggering. I mean how fucking thick can you possibly be. The mind-bending ignorance it takes for you to think for just one second that the manufacturer of your computer has in some way incorporated a foot pedal into its operation is just outstanding. Bravo you fucking clown!"

Too late to stop now, might as well take it home.

"So here is my official customer support advice. Why don't you return your newly acquired home computer along with your receipt to the retail outlet from where you made your purchase. Have them refund your money in full. If you have any trouble tell them I sent you, you should be fine. Then go to your nearest hardware store and buy yourself a length of rope. They sell it by the meter I suggest you get yourself about two. Then head on home, tie the rope to a secure fixture or rafter if you're fortunate enough to have one and hang yourself by the fucking neck, because sir, I'm sorry to say this but I'm afraid there's no fucking hope for you at all and you need to put an end to all our misery."

A touch over the top perhaps was Isaacs initial reaction as he pressed the button to disconnect the line.

This was confirmed when he looked around to see the cleaner who had been buffing the floor and the three other customer service operators, one of which was a duty manager, who were also working that evening staring at him slack jawed in disbelief. Isaac didn't realise that the longer he had gone on the louder he was getting and the higher out of his chair he was rising, until at the end he was standing at his work station bellowing down the phone. This one was definitely going to cost him.

2

The rain came sideways cutting across Isaacs face. Each drop felt like a razor shearing slices of his skin off as they tore past. Mid November in Dublin isn't the most pleasant time of the year. Especially on his current path, which runs directly along the coast, completely open to the elements coming in unchallenged off the sea. Isaac noted this while the wind ripped through the trees as he made his way up the Alfie Byrne Road towards Clontarf DART station car park. He was walking quite fast as he past the old traffic school. It was strange because he walked the same route from his car to work and back again every day but he never really paid attention to the place. He wasn't even sure if it was still open anymore. He momentarily thought back to the day in primary school when they were brought there to learn the rules of the road. The safe cross code put into practise on a series of mini streets, intersections and pedestrian crossings. Of course, at that age all you saw was a go kart, a race track and a series of obstacles between you and the finish line. The thought made him smile.

Isaac got to the DART station just as the rain was beginning to ease slightly. He usually parked there while in work because he couldn't manage to get a pass for the company car park. One hundred and fifty employees and only thirty parking spaces, and with ten of those reserved for the executives from the offices, he didn't even want to contemplate the amount of arse kissing required to land one. Anyway, after his latest outburst he doubted he would even have a job in the next day or two that would require a parking pass. The thought lingered with him for a moment as he entered the car park. However, once inside, a new and more immediate problem had presented itself. A big shiny yellow padlocked problem.

WARNING-DO NOT TRY TO REMOVE IT! Isaac read the sticker that appeared to have been plastered to the passenger window of his car with industrial strength adhesive. The sticker was of course alluding to the clamp on his front wheel. In his haste not to be late for work that day because he knew he was getting a bad reputation, the irony of which was not lost on Isaac, he had failed to notice the newly erected parking meter and accompanying sign requiring five euro for a maximum stay of five hours. He looked around aimlessly for a moment. Then suddenly he dropped to his knees and through sheer force of will tried to rip the clamp off with his bare hands. That was never going to work. With nothing left except pure desperation he tilted his head back, opened his mouth and let all his frustrations out in one primal scream.

"You dirty clamping bastards!" was Isaacs desperate exclamation to the universe above him.

After several moments of kneeling there on the chipped ground the little stones were beginning to push through his trousers and into the skin of his knees, so Isaac decided the best solution would be to get up off the ground, get into his car and devise a plan to get home. The easiest solution

8

would of course be to just pay the fine to have the wheel released from its yellow metal shackle. This was easier said than done unfortunately, since the grand total of Isaacs bank account was twenty six euro and thirty nine cent and the release fee was ninety euro. This was the foremost thought in Isaacs mind as he pulled the car door open and dived in, like a soldier diving for cover from an assault from overhead. A strange decision by Isaac to do this so to avoid getting any wetter, considering that he had already reached the point of saturation. Once inside he fumbled with the keys for a moment before finding the slot for the ignition. After starting the engine Isaac turned the heater on straight away. Always a bad move when it takes the engine a few minutes to heat up. A wave of cold air washed over him and he shuddered uncontrollably for a moment before that horrible, wet, cold feeling you always get once in the car after a real soaking from the rain. The windows began to steam up. Isaac pondered the few courses of action he had. He could walk. He could run. Or he could get a bus. To Isaac, this was the worst option. Like most people he hated buses, but for a particular reason.

  The last time Isaac had the burden of using public transport was one of those horror stories often heard around Dublin pubs, usually starting with "I know a guy, he was on a bus once...." with the story either consisting of crazy people, junkies or drunks. Isaacs consisted of a drunk. A few years back Isaac was on the twenty seven, the bus Route that runs from Coolock, a suburb of Dublin city where Isaacs Mothers house is, to the City Centre where he rents an apartment on Gardiner Street. After getting on and paying his fair Isaac went about the task of finding a seat. There were none downstairs, so Isaac made his way up to look for one there. The upstairs was fairly empty, apart from two rough looking teenagers about two thirds of the way to the back, an Asian guy sitting in the very front seat and a man who was fairly out of it on something, draped across several of the seats at the very back. He decided to play it safe and sit in the seat directly behind the stairs, in the middle of everyone. Plus, it happened to be the seat in the upstairs section of the bus that had the most leg room. The journey was going swimmingly until the drunk awoke from his slumber. Upon raising his head, he had decided that here, wherever he happened to be, was his stop. He bounded down the aisle towards the stairs like a gazelle that just had its back legs clipped by a lion. This was undoubtedly the reason for his complete loss of balance when he reached Isaacs seat. Isaac had turned his head just in time to see the drunks toothless gasp mere inches from his own face as he tumbled over the back of his seat towards him. The collision was horrendous. The two shared an embrace that momentarily resembled two long lost lovers, separated by continents and decades, reunited at last before crashing to the floor in a heap, like two boxers that had simultaneously knocked each other out in the last round of their fight. Unbeknownst to Isaac, most likely the drunk too, the urine stains on the heavily inebriated man's trousers were fresh. So fresh in fact, that they were still transferrable from one person's leg to another. Isaac discovered this about two stops after the drunk had got off. He was momentarily tempted to go back and find him. He knew he wouldn't have gotten far. Instead he had continued on his journey home and he swore he'd never get on a bus ever again.

Now here he was, about to break that solemn promise he had made to himself. He knew he had to. On any other night he would have walked. It wasn't that far. Twenty five minutes maybe half an hour. But on this night, he would have been frozen solid by the time he reached home. The bus stop was only around the corner and it would leave him two minutes from the lobby of his apartment block. So, the decision had been made, the bus it was. He looked around the car to make sure there was nothing in view that was worth breaking in for. The car itself was clamped so it wasn't going anywhere. Satisfied that there was nothing of value in sight he got out of the car and locked the doors. Then, turning the collar of his coat up and quickly bracing himself for the cold, he was off again into the miserable winter night.

While making his way to the bus stop Isaac had decided a fairly brisk pace was in order so as to get to the bus shelter quickly and get out of the rain. His brisk pace became crazy man running for the bus pace as a number forty two bus came up behind him while he was fifty or so yards away from the stop. He just about made it before the driver had pulled away, even though the driver had done his best to pull away from the stop before Isaac could make it. But a woman driving a large family estate car refused to let the bus just barge out in front of her, preventing the driver from leaving Isaac stranded again. He thanked God for small miracles then managed to find a seat down stairs too, another nice little surprise. No drunks this time. He sat looking out the window.

Dublin had changed. The city limits were starting to engulf some of the old suburbs. Old neighbourhoods famous around the city and its outer ring for their "salt of the earth" residents had been replaced by giant apartment blocks and office suites. He didn't necessarily think this was a bad thing, he just thought it was funny how the city you grew up in can change so much without you really noticing until you actually stop and look. As the bus went over Annesley bridge and headed up North Strand towards the Five Lamps, his mind wandered back to the days when you would look out the bus window and see a bowling alley and the building where they had the laser tag arena. Replaced by another apartment complex. Isaac couldn't help but laugh at the irony of the situation. During the good years the banks decided that the best way to fund the economy would be to provide property developers with massive amounts of money to build all these apartments and houses but now that all their money was tied up in the building side of things, they couldn't afford to give anyone the money to go and buy them. This wasn't an accurate reflection of the situation, but it was in his mind.

He caught a glimpse of his reflection in the window again. For some reason in the bus window he seemed older. It was probably just the lighting on the bus and his drowned rat appearance, but for some reason he didn't look as youthful as he had done less than half an hour ago. His thoughts suddenly turned to his girlfriend. How was he going to explain to her that he might be out of his job before the end of the week? She was his rock. No matter what had been getting him down during the day, once he got home she seemed to be able to just make him forget it all instantly. Her name was Shelly.

Isaac was staring out the window lost in his memories of when he had met his love. So lost was he, that he only snapped out of it because the driver was standing beside him tapping him on the shoulder because they had reached the end of the line. Isaac stood up and walked to the door, bracing himself one more time for the cold before this horrible journey home from work could end. As he turned the corner from Talbot Street onto Gardiner Street and walked up the road to his apartment, he noticed it had stopped raining. "One thing I can be grateful for I suppose" he thought. The wind however was still raging, blowing ferocious gusts right in his face as he fought against it. He made it past the row of hostels that during the summer would have crowds of crusty backpackers hanging outside them, usually sitting on the steps sharing one large bottle of cheap cider between them, rolling a cigarette, even though they already had one lit in their lips. Tonight the steps were deserted. There wasn't a crusty to be seen. In fact, Isaac noticed there wasn't really anyone to be seen. One lonely car drove past him on an otherwise deserted city street, narrowly missing a large puddle that would have sent a tidal wave of dirty rain water over Isaac had it connected. He turned the last corner of his journey onto Gloucester Place and hurriedly walked the few steps remaining to the entrance of his Apartment block. As he swiped the plastic fob over the box on the wall that unlocked the magnetic seal on the door with a quick beep, Isaac had never been happier to be home. The relief swept over him as he made his way to the lift. The post boxes for the apartments were mounted on the wall beside it. Isaac pressed the button to call the lift and went over to check the post. He knew this was a pointless endeavour because Shelly always got home before him and retrieved it herself but it killed a few seconds before the lift made its way down to him. Surprisingly the post, two bills, was still there. A loud chime rang out letting him know the lift had arrived at his floor. Isaac walked over to it, his mood most definitely much chipper now. He was only six floors and a few short steps away from the end of the day. A day he was more than happy to see the back of. This new happy mood was cut abruptly short when the lift doors opened and Isaac was greeted by a large steaming pile of faeces, placed perfectly in the centre of the floor. It was most definitely not human thankfully. There was no person that would be permitted in the apartments that would have been able to leave this behind them. The smell was ungodly. A deep vibration ran all the way from the pit of Isaacs stomach up his oesophagus and tickled the back of his throat. He dry reached twice before backing away to let the doors close.

"What sort of fucking animal..." Isaac began, before trailing off when he realised there was no one to actually talk to.

This created two problems for Isaac. Firstly, he now had a new image to replace the one of his aunt Jo naked from the waist down in his nightmares. This was from a trip to the beach when he was a child. He had wandered over a sand dune not realising she was behind it getting changed. The second was now he had to walk up six flights of stairs to get to his front door. He was beginning to think he had died and this was his own personal hell. He pushed the door to the stairwell open and began his assent. His feet felt like weights, because of the amount of water in his shoes from the walk to the bus stop. By the time he reached the fourth floor each step was agony, and Isaac was sure that he'd done some long term damage to his shins. Why his shins were so sore he had no idea but perseverance pays off and before he knew it, he was at the door to the sixth floor. That sense of relief he had felt in the lobby, before the incident with the lift, was cautiously making a return. He knew that the only thing standing between him and home was this door in front of him. What could possibly be hiding from him on the other side? Whatever it might be Isaac didn't care. He was too tired and practically defeated.

There was nothing more that could possibly happen to make the day any worse. He pushed the door open and prepared for whatever might be in the hallway waiting for him. He was pleasantly surprised to find there was nothing there. The hall between the stair well and his front door was clear. He walked through and didn't stop to look around, just in case. Finally, he had made it home. He looked at his watch. Twenty past ten. Shelly was probably worried about him. He had never been this late home before. Had he been driving he would have made it back long ago. He chuckled to himself. After his ridiculous trip home, he couldn't believe he was smiling. It was going to be fun explaining to her all that had happened.

3

Isaac sat on the floor of his kitchen crying. He had been in the same place for the last forty minutes or so. The Dear John letter he was holding the source of his misery. He had read it three times now. Each time brought a new flood of tears with it. Shelly had sited his lack of ambition and his unwillingness to grow as a person as the reason for her departure. She had also called him self centred, never considerate of others around him. He didn't see it coming but the fact was if he had been paying attention, he would have. The letter told him she would be in touch soon to talk it out but for now she needed to go and do some personal reflection. He was not to try and contact her. This was undoubtedly the worst day of his life so far, bar none.

He stood up and opened the fridge. There was one bottle of beer in it. He took it out, opened it and collapsed on the sofa. Lying there, Isaac began to recount the events of the day. How had it all gone so wrong? This morning he was gainfully employed, in a loving relationship and although he wasn't exactly happy with his situation, he was getting by. The day ended with his employment in serious doubt, him lying on the sofa having been abandoned unceremoniously with a letter by his girlfriend and feeling fairly down to say the least. As he lay there silently, the sound of the city six floors below rose up and crept in his window. In the distance he could hear a siren ring out as the vehicle it belonged to made its way to wherever its destination may be. Isaac speculated for a moment what it might be. In Dublin at eleven thirty on a Friday night it was either an ambulance on its way to scoop some over enthusiastic tourist up off the streets of Temple Bar, or a Garda squad car going to arrest the local who put the over enthusiastic tourist on the ground. For a split second he hoped it was Shelly, after being robbed of all her possessions on her way to wherever she had gone. Then he started to wonder, where had she gone? There were only a couple of friends she had a good enough relationship with to be comfortable enough to ask could she stay with them. Thinking about it he realised that none of her friends would have the room to put her up for more than one night. She couldn't stay in a hotel, due to the bank account being dangerously close to the letters o and d appearing beside the balance. So where could she have gone. Then it hit him. There was only one place she could have gone.

Isaac took his phone out from his pocket. Shelly had to have gone to Kevin and Lily's place. They have a lot of room and are good friends to Isaac and Shelly both. While he was flipping down through the contacts list his screen lit up with an incoming call. The caller id readout flashed Ben. Isaac was about to reject the call but decided he had time to talk to Ben before the hunt for Shelly began. Ben was funny in a strange way. He has a lot of little quirks that always make him look out of place to people who are meeting him for the first time. One of these was the way he spoke on the phone, every time, like he'd never seen one before in his life. He was always shouting down the line. Isaac remembered this and set it to speakerphone.

"Hey man, what's the story" Isaac said answering the phone.

"Hey my man what's up" Bens reply came booming out of the speaker, so loud the phone vibrated a little in Isaacs hand.

Another thing that struck Isaac about Ben was his accent. He claimed to be French Canadian, but always sounded like a Russian trying to speak Chinese. Plus, he was certain he had never heard Ben speak French once. Isaac paused for a minute before replying. He was weighing up whether or not to say anything about Shelly to Ben.

"Nothing much really, just home from work, was about to have a shower then relax for the rest of the evening" Isaac replied, deciding that for now the least amount of people that new about Shelly's departure the better. Isaac wasn't sure exactly how many people that included at the minute.

"I know it's late, but I was wondering if you had time for a quick visit, there's something I wanted to talk to you about" Ben shouted down the phone, clearly louder than he needed to be.

Isaac was in no mood for company. His day was a disaster, his face was still feeling a bit raw from all the tears and he would then have to explain the absence of his girlfriend. Tonight was definitely a night to be alone.

"Listen man any other night and you know..." Isaac had started only to be cut off by the ear drum perforating sound of Ben's voice.

"Hey man I don't want to be pushy, but I really need to talk to you about something and it can't wait til tomorrow" Ben added sounding more eager than desperate.

"Seriously man I've had a real day ya know and I really just need a night to meself ya know that way" Isaac said hoping that Ben would get the picture without Isaac actually having to be specific.

"I've got weed and beer" Ben added with finality.

"Alright, come over so" Isaac conceded.

The prospect of a joint and a few beers sounded much better than wallowing in self-pity alone in the dark all night. At least Ben would be good company.

Isaac hung up the phone. He knew it would take Ben at least 20 minutes to get there. That gave him plenty of time for him to wash the smell of defeat off himself before he arrived. First though, there was a phone call to be made. Isaac highlighted Kev's number in the phonebook and pressed the dial button. The ring tone droned in his ear several times before the voicemail message played. Isaac listened as the automated lady informed him that the customer he was trying to reach was unavailable and he should leave a message. That was exactly what Isaac intended to do.

"Kev it's Isaac" he began, "listen man I know that Shelly is there, it's the only place she could be, and since you didn't answer the phone, I can only assume it's because she told you not to." This was hard for Isaac, he was never really good at dealing with emotion at the best of times, never mind having to do it through a third party. "All I want to do is talk to her so I can find out what exactly is going on. I'm in the dark here man. Will you talk to her for me and see if you can get her to come around? Cheers, I'll chat to you later."

He hung up the phone and he felt the knot in his stomach loosen just a tiny bit. It was a start at least. He headed off up the stairs towards the bathroom.

***

There were three heavy knocks on the door just as Isaac came down the stairs. He had a towel draped around his neck because his hair was still a bit wet from the shower. He was feeling a little better now. He was feeling fresher and a little more relaxed, although he still had a small knot in his stomach over the whole Shelly situation. There were three more knocks on the door just as Isaac went to open it.

"Alright man calm down I'm coming" Isaac said to Ben as he opened the door to let him in.

The strangest thing about Ben was his appearance. He didn't look right. Isaac could never put his finger on it but there was something about Ben that when he looked at him, he always just thought, well, something's not right. It was maybe the way he stood, rigid and bolt upright. It could have been his skin tone. It had a hue of fake tan off it, but it was his natural colour. His haircut didn't look right either, it appeared, for want of a better term, lob sided. It was an off shade of brown in colour, too light to be natural but not the colour any rational human being would choose from a bottle. Ben was a little bit taller than Isaac, but Isaac was sure this was only because he stood up so straight. Or more likely it was just his mannerisms or general presence. He had a gut that stuck out a little too far in relation to his chest, which seemed to be well defined. He was something of an oddity, but he was fun to be around.

Ben patted Isaac a little too hard on the shoulder as he greeted him. He bent down to pick up the case of Heineken he had placed on the floor to knock. Isaac greeted him with as much of an enthusiastic smile as he could manage under the circumstances. Ben walked toward the living room door as Isaac locked the front door behind him. It was a few steps between doors and Ben, with both his hands occupied by carrying the beer, got to the living room door first and without breaking stride walked forehead first into it as a means to get it open. It worked, because luckily for him Isaac hadn't closed the door tight on his way to the shower. Isaac shook his head in both puzzlement and amusement as he followed him in. Ben walked over to the kitchen area and placed the beer on the counter beside the fridge. He ripped the top off and began placing the bottles in the fridge before looking around at Isaac.

"Why is it so dark in here" Ben asked noticing that only one of the lamps in the corner of the room was lit making it very difficult to see anything.

"Oh no reason I was just relaxing after work, the bright lights were annoying me" Isaac replied as he moved around to the light switch to brighten the place up. As the lights came on Ben looked around the room noticing there was something missing. He couldn't figure out what was wrong but there was something amiss. Then it dawned on him.

"Hey where's your girlfriend, where's Shelly?" he asked.

Isaac took a minute and decided whether or not to lie about it. He concluded there was no point.

"Well to be honest I'm not entirely sure," Isaac began, "you see we're having a bit of a bad time at the minute, so she's gone to stay with some friend's, I think."

Ben took his attention away from skilfully fitting all twenty of the beers into the fridge for a moment to look at Isaac and offer his most sincere and heartfelt condolences.

"Shit man that fucking sucks" was the best he could manage.

Isaac smiled as he knew this was the sincerest level of empathy that he could expect from Ben. He was happy for the effort alone. He sat down and turned on the T.V. The News was just about over and they were running a soft article about alleged strange lights seen under the water in Dublin Bay that night, which had been witnessed by two young guys and an elderly gentleman. Isaac shook his head disapprovingly at the story as Ben came over and handed him a bottle of beer.

"Man, what the fuck is gone wrong in the world?" he mused.

"What do you mean?" Ben enquired.

"Look at this shit. The news is running a story about UFO's under the water in Dublin and the only credible witnesses are dumb, dumber and Mr fucking Magoo. Surely there's better things to be worried about" Isaac spat with venom.

"I think all the real news was talked about earlier," Ben replied a little puzzled by Isaacs hatred for the fluffy news story, "there's only so much tragedy and gloom people can handle. They usually finish with a soft story. And who's to say it's not real man. We don't know what's out in the stars."

Isaac didn't want to get into a philosophical debate about the existence of extra-terrestrial life at this moment in time, so he just let Ben's comment slide. He also realised he was getting a little too irritable about the contents of the local news and realised he was worked up, so he turned off the TV and changed the topic.

"So what did you want to see me about?" he asked Ben as he took a big mouthful of his lukewarm beer, before spitting it out again and looking down at the bottle.

"Heineken? What, did they not have any piss?"

"I just picked up the first box I saw."

"Alright. Just saying, I'd rather drink piss."

22

"Well you see, I got a call last night and I have to go home" Ben replied.

Isaac was a little taken aback by this. Ben wasn't his best friend, but he was a good one. Something that was not easy to find. Another spike in the baseball bat that was this day, smashing him in the face.

"Shit man, that's, well it's shit" Isaac fumbled the words out his mouth. "Is everything alright, at home I mean. Is there something wrong?"

"No, it's just time for me to go home. I have realised everything I came here for, so I'm just ready to leave" Ben said.

The two of them sat in silence, just letting the moment take its course. It was almost like a moment of silence they shared to mourn. A moment of silence for their deceased friendship. Ben was the first to break it.

"So the reason I came over is because I have some things I want to give you. I have some things I won't be able to take with me when I leave so I would like for you to have them" he said.

"Thanks" was Isaac's initial reply. "I do appreciate that you thought of me, but I have to ask. I'm not just going to have to go to your apartment to find out I have to drag a load of crap to the dump because you couldn't be bothered to, am I?"

"No no no. I just simply can't take it with me and I don't have the time to get rid of it since I'm leaving tomorrow, it's just not feasible" Ben replied.

"Tomorrow?!" Isaac both asked and exclaimed at the same time. "Fuck man, you don't mess about do you? When you've made your mind up you just go all in."

"Well it's a little more complicated but I suppose all I can say is tomorrow is the only real opportunity for the foreseeable future to leave" Ben said.

"What the hell does that mean?" Isaac asked.

"Like I said, it's complicated" Ben replied. The only reply Isaac could see he was going to get out of him. So he decided to just let it go for now and enjoy the time that was left together.

"Right well fuck it so" Isaac smiled, "we might as well make short work of the beers and weed you brought with you."

As the night wore on, they drank the entire box of beer that Ben had brought over and rolled more than a couple of joints, laughing and joking as they reminisced about the good times they had spent over the last two years or so getting to know each other. They were having such a good time they didn't realise how late it had gotten, or how early it was depending on how you were viewing the day. Ben got up and organised himself to leave. They arranged to meet the next evening in Bens place to hand over everything he was leaving behind for Isaac and with that, Ben was off down the hall and Isaac was heading up the stairs on very uneasy legs. He made it too his bedroom at the end of the hall without any great fuss. Once inside the room he didn't even bother undressing or getting under the covers. He just fell face first onto the pillow, cracking his head on the wall. In his inebriated state he had misjudged the distance between the bed and the wall.

"Fuck."

4

The light of the new morning crept in through a crack in the curtains and illuminated the room as Isaac stirred from his sleep and back into the waking world. For a few brief moments all he could focus on was the dryness of his mouth and what felt like the percussion section of an orchestra playing a tune inside his brain. Then the memories of the previous night started to make their way to the forefront of his mind as he sat on the side of his bed and tried to compose himself. The first order of his day was to get a hold of Shelly somehow. She wouldn't answer her phone to him, but he had a fair idea of where she was. If push came to shove, he would just go to Kev and Lily's place and wait for her to come out if he had to. He also had to call over to Ben's later that day as he had to see what all this stuff he had for him was. He decided the first thing he needed was a shower. He stood up and got a towel from the wardrobe and headed off down the hall to the bathroom. As he got to the door, he heard his phone ring and dashed back towards the bedroom, stubbing his toe on the doorframe as he charged back into the room. He hopped to the bed cursing his rotten run of luck and picked up his phone. It was Shelly.

"Hello, Shelly?" he asked with a hint of expectation in his voice.

They had a conversation that lasted about ten minutes. Isaac kept angling for a face to face, Shelly doing her best to refute the idea. She was making a point about making a promise to herself, her future and some other stuff too. Isaac wasn't really listening to everything she was saying, he was just skimming her words to try and get a vague idea of what she was talking about, but really, he was just looking for an opening where he could interject and bring the conversation back around to meeting up. Yet it was still a mystery to him why she had left. Eventually she relented and agreed to meet him at eight that evening in the coffee shop in Temple Bar that they use to meet at before they were living together. As Isaac hung up the phone the tightening sensation he had felt in his gut since the night before ease a little bit more. Maybe he could still salvage the situation. She had agreed to meet him, so she obviously was willing to hear what he had to say. All he had to do was remind her of the good times. Show her that he really does care and that he was ready to make some forward steps in his life for her. At least that's what he thought she wanted. Again, he wasn't entirely focused.

As he got himself ready to go have a shower he began organising his thoughts once more. He could go to Ben's first to see whatever it was he had left for him there, then he would head off to meet Shelly and all going well she would be back home that night. She had only taken an overnight bag with her the night before. Most of her belongings were still in the apartment. As Isaac thought about it on his way to the bathroom, he realised that it was looking more and more like an attention grab than an actual attempt by Shelly to leave him for good. Maybe he had been missing the signs she had been giving him before this and leaving in a big dramatic fashion was the only way she saw left to get through to him, but he had got the message.

***

As Isaac was leaving the apartment to go to Ben's the weather hadn't really let up from the night before. The rain was still falling, but it was more of a heavy drizzle than a full on downpour. The wind had eased a little, but it still didn't make for pleasant walking conditions. It was about a twenty minute trek from Isaac's to where Ben lived. He hurried down Talbot Street towards the spire on O'Connell Street, closely inspecting his shoes, so as not to make accidental eye contact with any junkies who might be floating around and have to engage them as they pursue their never ending quest to acquire as much spare change as they can, to book themselves into the imaginary hostel they never seem to make it to. Although the weather seemed to have kept them in whatever shelter they could find. As he crossed over onto Henry Street, the main shopping thoroughfare on this side of the city, there wasn't much hustle and bustle to be seen either. There were a few people walking with a purpose to get to wherever they were going, but no shoppers browsing windows, or buskers bellowing out some Damien Dempsey or U2 cover. He walked passed the human statues who were perched outside Arnotts department store. A group of five that had started out as one, but the contingent had grown over the last few months. He admired their dedication to doing their performance, as there was no one around to put money in their bucket, yet they were still there. As he made his way

27

up Mary Street and turned onto Capel Street heading to Smithfield, he noticed that there weren't too many people around at all. The traffic was heavy enough as you would expect at that time of day in Dublin city, but there were very few pedestrians about. He walked past The Hacienda Bar, looking at the front door as he did. This place always caused Isaac to ponder. It had an unusual allure to him as it was an oddity amongst Dublin pubs. Drinking establishments had an open, welcoming type of atmosphere about them in this city. They want you to come in and feel comfortable. Not this place. There was a cage door covering the entrance, only accessible by admission from whoever was inside. Isaac always wanted to go in and check the place out but he had never found the courage to go and ring the bell. He wondered what went on inside as he continued up Mary's Lane, weaving through the cars stuck trying to drive down Church Street, all the way to Bow Street past the Jameson Whiskey distillery. He was glad of the shelter provided by the narrow streets around here as the wind had picked up a little again, though he was nearly at his destination. He hurried across the Smithfield Square past the ice-skating rink that had been set up the week before. The only people there were the staff and one middle aged man who possibly had aspirations as a figure skater in his youth, as he was trying to pull off some serious moves, given the freedom he had of being the only person using the facility.

Ben's apartment looked out over the square. As Isaac got to the entrance, he was about to ring the bell to be buzzed in but noticed that the magnetically sealed door had been left ajar, so he pulled it open and entered the lobby. He walked across to the lift and pressed the button for the eighth floor. Ben had a really nice place all to himself. As the lift stopped on the floor the doors opened and Isaac got off, turned left and walked down to the door at the end of the hall. He put out his hand, but as he knocked, he pushed the door open as it wasn't on the latch. He pushed it open fully and stuck his head inside the apartment.

"Hello," he called out "Ben its Isaac, are you here?"

He walked inside the hallway and through the door into the living area. The place was kind of a mess. There was stuff thrown around, drawers in the cabinets around the room were half open. Some were completely pulled out of their socket and were sitting on the floor. Only that Ben had told him he was leaving it would have looked like someone had been searching the place, trying to find something in a hurry. He looked around the apartment a bit more going from room to room, but Ben was nowhere to be found. Each room the same as before, with bits and pieces strewn around the place.

"Well you can say good bye to your deposit." Isaac said out loud.

He went back to the kitchen area and leaned against the counter. Across from him on the fridge he saw a note stuck to it with his name at the top. He took it down and started to read it.

Isaac.

I apologise that I am unable to be there to meet you. Unfortunately something has arisen that prevents me from saying goodbye in person. Everything I have left for you is down stairs in the car that I keep in the garage of this apartment building. I have never had reason to use it since moving to this city so it has remained idle down there for a long time. The car is leased and has six months left on it.

You can use it for that time then return it to the rental company. The keys to the car are in the drawer beside my bed. The registration number is written on the key.

Goodbye.

As Isaac read the note, he couldn't help but feel a sense of finality from the tone it held. It wasn't a see you later goodbye, it was a farewell forever goodbye. Something was strange about Ben from the get go. When Ben said he had some things to leave behind, Isaac thought he maybe meant an iPad or some drugs he wouldn't get through customs. Not a car.

Isaac was a little taken aback by the whole thing. He went into the bedroom and opened the desk drawer to find the key where Ben said it would be. He took it out of drawer and inspected it a little further and noticed that there was a Jaguar badge emblazoned on it. Ben had left him a Jaguar. A high end luxury car. Probably worth about €50,000 new. As he looked down at the key in his hand only on thought crossed his mind.

"I'm gonna drive the fuck out of this thing for the next six months."

As Isaac left the apartment he shut the door tight behind him, making his way back down to the lift and once inside, he pressed the button for the basement. As the doors of the lift opened into the buildings parking floor, Isaac looked around and realised that it was a big garage with a lot of cars in it and that finding the Jaguar was going to take some time. He looked at his watch and realised he had about 45 minutes before he had to meet Shelly, so he could spend a little time looking as she wasn't too far away and well, let's be honest, showing up to meet her in a fifty thousand euro car would be bound to leave an impression.

As he walked around looking for the car, he couldn't shake the feeling that he was being watched but every time he looked around there was no sign of anyone. He was alone as far as he could tell. After about ten minutes of walking around he decided he would have to come back and look later, as he was getting close to his meeting with Shelly and he didn't want to be late. He walked back to the lift, pressing the door unlock button on the key. Off in the distance he saw the lights on a car flash. He walked down towards the car and as he got closer to where he thought he had seen the illuminating lights he pressed the button again. The lights on the car about five spaces down flashed on and off again. Isaac looked down and sure enough there was a 2017 Jaguar XF sitting in the space with the registration plate that matched the numbers stuck to the key.

A massive grin stretched across Isaacs face as he sat down in the driver seat of what was apparently his new car for the next six months. He looked around but there was nothing else in the car. Anything else that Ben left him must have been in the boot he thought to himself, but he was pressed for time as it was and he needed to go and meet Shelly, so it would have to wait until later. So he started the car up and reversed it out of the spot. He headed towards the exit and as he got to it, there was a beep from a little plastic box stuck to the windshield behind the mirror and the barrier to the car park raised automatically. Isaac was beaming as he drove the car up the ramp towards the street. He was so wrapped up in his new vehicle and how shinny and leathery it was that he had failed to notice the car several spots down from where he had been parked pull out a few seconds after he did, follow him up the ramp and down the street.

5

Isaac drove down Queen Street and headed across the
bridge over the river Liffey. As he drove over the bridge,
he hit a bump and there was a heavy thud that came from
the boot. He thought nothing of it. Most likely some odds
and ends that Ben had left in there. His plan was to head
down Dame Street and then park in the Fleet Street car
park, then run down to the coffee shop but before he could
turn up towards Cornmarket, there was a Garda diversion in
place and he had to turn down Island Street and head
towards the Liberties. Now he was definitely going to be
late and he had to text Shelly to let her know. He would
have to pull in because he didn't want to text while driving
just after passing a Garda checkpoint. Not for safety
reasons, more out of fear of getting caught. As he pulled
in, he hit the curb and he heard the heavy thud coming from
the boot again. He also noticed in his mirror a car about
twenty metres back had pulled in too. Now that he thought
about it the car had been behind him coming across the
bridge as well. He took out his phone and sent a short
message to Shelly saying he was a few minutes behind but
would be there soon. Then he decided to check out the

boot. He opened the door and walked back to the rear of the car. As he did, he noticed that the car stopped a little further back still had its engine running and there was at least one person still in the car. He couldn't say for sure as the headlights were still on and they were preventing him from seeing inside. He fumbled around at the back of the car for a second before he realised he had no idea how to unlock the boot lid. He went back to the front and looked in around the dashboard but still couldn't see any release mechanism. Then he noticed on the key that there was a button to do it on that. He picked it up and walked back to the rear again, pressing the button as he did. The boot lid popped open and raised up as he turned to look inside.

It didn't register with Isaac for a split second what exactly he was looking at. Maybe he just didn't want to verify what he was seeing. It certainly looked like Ben. He looked different though. It wasn't just the fact that he was dead, pale, his face gaunt and his eyes cold.   The manner in which he was killed must have led to the way he looked, the way he was wearing death. There was something else wrong. Like some of the features on his face were different. All of that took about a second to pass through Isaacs head and he was now about to scream. He didn't know what to scream though. He couldn't call for help as that was a bad idea where he currently found himself. He suddenly appreciated he didn't want to attract any real attention to himself and so when he finally did open his mouth to release his horror nothing audible came out. He just stumbled backwards with his mouth open and his face frozen with a stupefied look on it. Then he heard them in slow motion coming towards him from behind. The slow heavy pound of oncoming footsteps, two separate and distinct pitches. One on the left and one on the right. That must have been the car that was following him. He wasn't crazy. The car had been following him and now the occupants were out and walking towards him. He didn't know what to do. His mind flooded with different scenarios and outcomes and his brain was beginning to overload.

Isaac didn't even notice himself closing the boot and getting back into the car. He was closing the door as the person approaching on the driver side was a couple of steps back from the rear of his car. Just before it slammed closed, he could hear the man say something but didn't get a chance to make it out clearly. He looked in his side mirror and noticed that the man had pulled some sort of identification out of his pocket. Isaac couldn't quite make out what it said. It definitely wasn't a Garda badge. He had seen a couple of those in the past. He could have sworn he saw what looked like a representation of the American flag emblazoned on the front of it, but he couldn't be sure.

The muscle in his leg twitched as he thought about making a break for it. Then the more rational side of his brain kicked in and he reasoned that if these men were figures of authority, surely he could explain the situation, spend some time answering questions and eventually the truth would come to light. Whatever the truth may be. The twitch in his leg however seemed to be his self-preservation instincts kicking in and turned out to be more of a spasm that had slammed his foot down on the accelerator. He grasped this as the man waving his badge in the mirror seemed to be getting smaller and smaller as Isaac was speeding up the road away from him.

He came too around the time he hit Ushers Quay. The last ten seconds or so had been a blur of actions as he digested what was going on. So, he was in a car, driving at reckless speeds down the south quay with the body of his friend in the boot, being pursued by what could potentially be agents of a foreign government. He checked in the mirror again but couldn't see anyone following him. At least he didn't think he could. It was hard to focus on driving forward really fast and checking to see if anyone was giving chase. He looked back one more time just as the rear window cracked right in the centre, then it exploded, then the windshield exploded and Isaac realised very quickly he was being shot at. He swung a hard right across the bridge in front of Heuston train station and then a sharp left onto Parkgate Street. As he barely missed two pedestrians trying to cross the street at the Dublin Bus depot, he realised he was doing close to a hundred up a small city street. The shots had stopped but he could see, not too far back, the other car was still in pursuit. As he ran the red light outside the new District court buildings, he decided to head into the Phoenix Park to get off the main roads. It would have little traffic that time of the evening, so he could probably get some more speed up. He broke another red light and cut across the oncoming traffic and headed up into the park.

He sped past Dublin Zoo and drove toward the House of the President, taking a couple of seconds to assess his situation. They could be some agents of a foreign government, they could be the guys who are responsible for Bens death, they might be coming for him for something that is unrelated to any of the above facts.

"What the fuck is going on?" Isaac screamed out loud to nobody. "I mean seriously man what the fuck? I have to ring Shelly."

He took his phone out of his pocket and pressed the call button to ring Shelly. She answered the phone and began shouting at him immediately about how this was exactly what she was talking about. How he couldn't even make it to get a cup of coffee with her on time. Unreliable and loser were the two words he picked out before he interjected.

"Oh my God will you shut the fuck up for two seconds" he screamed at her. "I need to tell you something. I don't know what's going on but well, Ben's dead and I'm currently being chased through the Phoenix park with two dudes who are shooting at me and I... I...hello? Shelly?"

The line had gone dead. He was about to call her back when he hit some kind of bump in the road and his phone came out of his hand and fell out through the hole that the now absent windshield had left behind. He looked up to see what was going on and swiftly realised he was no longer driving in the road but had made his way onto the grass and was now heading straight toward the cricket ground. In his mirror, not too far back he could see the lights of the pursuing car pull off the road and follow him onto the grass. Isaac was panicking and was trying to figure out how he was going to get out of this. He was doing his best to evaluate all of the options that were currently available to him. What the likely outcome would be and how he could avoid his own death if at all possible. Unfortunately for Isaac, that is when things started to get really strange.

He felt a spark coming off the steering wheel of the car. Like a static shock but a little stronger. Then it happened again. He had to pull both his hands off the wheel this time, as the second jolt hit him much harder, travelling up his arms and hitting him right in the middle of his chest. Then a strange globule of what looked like electricity caught his attention as it slid across in front of him in a fluid motion. Like a rain drop had trapped a tiny bolt of lightning as it was rolling across the dashboard. After that a flood of the fluid electricity ran over the car, from front to back like a wave from the sea slowly engulfing a rock on the shore, submerging it. Isaac looked around and he could just about make out his surroundings outside the car. He could see trees as he whizzed by them. He could hear the rush of the air flowing through the car as both the windshield and the rear window were gone. He could also feel a build-up of some type of charge permeate his entire body. It was like an accumulation of static electricity was flowing through him, having replaced the blood in his veins. He could see himself in the mirror, his hair was standing on end all over his body. So erect, that it felt like it was about to be ripped out of every follicle all at once, like a giant simultaneous body waxing. Then everything stopped dead. No wind, no sound at all. The trees were gone. All Isaac could see outside the car was white. Everything was calm.

The calmness was shattered a second later as the whiteness engulfing Isaac felt like it had imploded in on top of him. The chaos of the on rushing wind returned. The trees were gone. Isaac couldn't see anything outside the car because of the darkness, but he was definitely moving again. He was probably a second or so outside of the white void that had swallowed him when he saw the wall in front of him. It looked like a solid wall. It wasn't made from brick. It looked like a steel wall. He couldn't really see how high or how wide it was. All he could tell about it was that it was right in front of him.

He hadn't taken his foot off the accelerator since getting back into the car and fleeing. He must have been doing some speed when he entered the white. He presumed he was doing about the same when he exited it. He didn't have time to take his foot off the accelerator now, never mind trying to apply it to the brakes. It was strange. His life didn't flash before his eyes. He didn't have any profound revelation. In fact, the only thing he could think of was the oncoming wall. The car hit the wall. Isaac didn't feel anything. Everything just went black.

6

A low rumble filled Isaacs senses as he slowly started to come around. For a moment he thought he was back in his office, hearing the floor buffer again. Then he realised this wasn't the case. The darkness was still all engulfing. He was alive as far as he knew. He felt alive. He had no sense of smell, nor could he see anything around him. The only thing he knew was that he could hear the hum. A low, constant noise that was not just around him, it felt like it was in him. He took a minute to gather his thoughts. He was definitely aware of himself. So his mind was working, but nothing else seemed to be.

Sudden flashes, images of strange figures standing over him looking down, sizing him up, came flooding into his brain. He couldn't make out faces or distinguish between voices. He could just see a vision of shadows and outlines moving around him, making strange noises at each other. Communicating, but not with any language or words that he could understand. They just seemed to be making noises. It caused an intense pain right in the centre of his forehead to try and focus on the memory of what he had been seeing, so he gave up and let the images fade away.

Then something else came into focus. The blackness that surrounded him began to fade. There was a spot right in the centre of his vision that was getting brighter and brighter. It took Isaac some time to realise that he was lying down on a table, staring up at a light above his head that was shining directly into his eyes. The hum was starting to fade too. It was still there but was less distinguishable as other sounds started to make themselves known. There were beeps and pings coming from across the room. In the distance he could hear what sounded like a voice coming through an intercom speaker but it was muffled and unclear. Then he had a revelation. He was in a hospital. He must have somehow survived the crash and was coming around in the hospital.

He tried to speak but was powerless to form any words or didn't have the strength to get his vocal chords working. He looked around as best he could but couldn't see anyone in the room with him. He tried to sit up but was unable to get any part of his body to move. He stopped for a minute. Taking a second look around the limited part of the room he could see, Isaac noticed that all the machines he was encircled by were unfamiliar too him. Sure, he was no expert in medical equipment but none of the monitors he was surrounded by bore any resemblance to anything he had seen in a hospital before. It all looked very high spec. He concluded he must have been in some sort of private, high end medical centre. He tried to get up again but still his body was unresponsive. This time however he managed to get his arm to move. It didn't respond to what he was trying to get it to do. It just shot out to his right with no direction, purpose or control. He knocked over a metal tray that was sitting on a stand beside his bed. It fell to the ground and made a loud crash as it impacted the

41

floor. Then, behind him, he heard the metal legs of a chair drag across the floor as someone moved to stand up from a seated position and a female voice spoke to him.

"Oh no, please do not try to move. Your body has been through a substantial trauma and we have tried to do our best to heal you with what limited knowledge we have of your genetic structure" it said, in a soft, unfamiliar way.

Isaac still couldn't see the mystery person in the room with him. They were standing behind him out of the range that he could turn his head. The words they spoke made sense but there was something about the way she said them that didn't seem right. Something was off. More and more of the limited surroundings in his vision became focused and he could see his whereabouts a little better now. To his right there was a window looking out onto a corridor. The wall outside was steel and there were what looked like pipes running horizontally along it, red, yellow and green in colour. There was a stainless steel table in front of the window that had a gruesome pile of bloody gauzes strewn across it, with stacks of round black discs about the size and shape of a hockey puck piled up on top of each other. On the opposite side of the room were a few different shelving units with metal boxes stacked up and a few small handheld devices, with some larger screens facing towards him but he couldn't make out any of the information on them. The hum he could hear didn't seem to be coming from anywhere in the room but seemed to be coming from all around him, like the room itself was making the noise.

"Where am I?" the words leaving his mouth caused everything around him to dim and the room to become unfocused again. The sheer will of trying to speak almost caused him to pass out.

"You must not try to speak, or move, or do anything at all except lie there and rest."

As these words met Isaac's ears, they sounded soft and distant as he slipped back into unconsciousness.

***

Isaac came too for the second time with a start. He was still in the same room, but everything was immediately in focus now. He very slowly tried to move his right arm. It slowly extended out and back in again. He tried the same with his left and achieved the same result. He looked down to the end of the table at his feet, then past his feet to the wall at the end of the room. Another window looked out onto more steel walls. There was a double door outside. It was made from similar steel as the walls but each one had an opaque glass window in the middle of it, so it kind of looked like the doors of an elevator. He looked to his right again. The table that had the gauze and the medical supplies on it had been cleared and what Isaac presumed was the doctor that had tended to him was standing there with her back to him, bent forward over the table looking down and tapping away on a what seemed to be some sort of tablet device. Not one he recognised though.

Isaac tried to speak again and this time the words came out much easier.

"Thank you for saving me" he said.

"You are most welcome" the doctor replied as she turned around to face him.

Her skin had a greenish hue off it. That would be enough evidence for Isaac to know that something was strange about her. There was so much more though. Her eyes were about twice the size of any eyes that Isaac had seen before. They were blue in colour, with big pupils, about

43

the size of a penny, right in the middle of them. There were other features that stood out to him. Her nose was square across the bridge and it ran right to the tip of her top lip, to a degree where it was hard to determine where her lip started and her nose finished. She had a slightly protruding brow that turned flat down her face almost perpendicular to her much enunciated cheek bones,. Her hair was normal. It was brown, medium length and tied back in a ponytail. Isaac realised very quickly he wasn't staring at a human. She was humanoid. Two legs, two arms, ten fingers, most likely ten toes but she was most definitely not a human.

He threw his hips to the left and rolled himself off the table and his feet hit the ground. Unfortunately he didn't know muscle atrophy had set in so his legs didn't work properly. He almost fell face first but managed to grab the side of the bed and hold himself upright to look across at her.

"Who are you? Where am I? What happened to me?" Isaac shouted at her, quickly determining that these were the most pressing questions he had at the minute.

She looked back at him a little surprised. At least that is the look Isaac thought she was conveying, he couldn't tell for sure.

"My name is Sha'ala," she began, "I am the medical practitioner aboard this vessel. You are on the Sao'ise, a privately owned interstellar cruiser. We did not know you were travelling at high velocity in a vehicle when we brought you on board and you impacted the wall which caused massive injuries to your person. I have spent some considerable time ensuring your recovery."

Isaac looked her up and down. He still wasn't able to move his legs and his arms were starting to give out on him now but he gathered all his determination to keep himself as upright as he could.

"What?" he yelled at her, a mixture of fear, confusion and disbelief. "This is a fucking joke yeah. Like a sick fucking practical joke show where you've been waiting for me to come out of my coma, so you can fuck with me."

Isaac wasn't even sure what he was talking about as he could feel himself starting to hyperventilate.

"Please try to relax, I have made it my duty to make sure you don't die for some time now. I honestly mean you no harm. I need you to please lie down again on the table, you are not ready to put this much stress on your body" Sha'ala implored him.

Isaac looked at her and he was sure he could tell she was being genuine. He didn't know if he was reading her right but at this moment in time, he needed to trust her, because he was starting to feel the oncoming sensation of passing out again. He used all the strength he had left to pull himself back onto the table, lying there for a minute as Sha'ala moved towards him and stood over him looking down. After a brief exchange of glances between them he started to settle down and regain his composure. Just as he was about to ask her another question, he saw her hand move towards him and felt the sharp sting in his neck, then everything around him dissolved into a haze, before he slipped away into darkness.

7

Isaac came too for the third time in a most peculiar way. He was just suddenly awake. One minute he was unconscious, the next he wasn't. He was fully alert, but he was calm. Calmer than he knew he should be. He sat up, without any issue and saw Sha'ala sitting in a chair at the end of his bed.

"How are you feeling now?" she asked him.

"I'm actually quite relaxed. A lot more relaxed than I know I should be. It feels weird if I'm perfectly honest."

"Good. I gave you a mild sedative to remove any anxiety you may feel for a period of time so we can have a rational discussion without you losing consciousness again" Sha'ala explained to him.

"Thank you" Isaac said, not sure what he was thankful for.

"So, as I have said you are currently on board a privately owned vessel that is in transit across the galaxy. You suffered massive damage to your person and I have now tended to that damage. Is there anything else you wish to know?" she asked him.

"Why did you bring me here and where are we going?" were the next most pressing questions that Isaac had.

"You were brought here in a case of mistaken identity it would appear. I'm afraid I can't give you any more detail than that at the minute. I am limited in what I can tell you until the captain of the vessel speaks with you. The same goes for your second question. I think it would be best if you direct all your questions to him. You may stand up now and I will take you to him. I have given you a stimulant to help your legs regain their movement."

Isaac twisted himself to the side of the table and placed his feet on the floor. He moved all his weight forward and stood up off the bed. Sha'ala walked out the door to the hallway and Isaac quickly followed behind her. As he walked down the hall toward the two doors he could see through the window in the medical room, he could hear the humming sound again. Always at the same pitch, just there in the background.

"What is that constant humming noise?"

"The ships engine makes it whenever its active. You get used to it after a while" Sha'ala replied.

As he got to the doors they slid open and it was indeed an elevator behind them. Sha'ala stepped on first and Isaac followed behind her. He turned around and the doors closed in front of him. The elevator began to ascend and Isaac turned to say something to Sha'ala, but noticed she was facing the other direction just as the wall behind him opened and she walked off.

"Oh, it's one of those type of lifts is it?" he mumbled to himself as he turned around and he followed behind her.

Isaac picked up his pace a little to keep up with Sha'ala as they walked down a corridor. He became aware of the fact that he was wearing what strongly resembled a hospital gown with nothing on underneath it and suddenly he felt a little exposed. Walking down the hall Isaac was a little

47

surprised by the lack of windows looking out of the ship. He thought it was quite claustrophobic. As they got to the end of the hall there was another double door in front of them. Sha'ala got to the doors first and they slid open as Isaac followed her through. They were now in a large circular room with a table in the middle that had a giant screen for a surface. The screen seemed to be divided into four sections with what looked like different information in each one, all displayed in a strange language. There were ten chairs fixed to the floor, all spaced evenly around the table. The walls all had different work stations dotted around the room. Isaac had no idea what each station was for, but he could tell that there were differences with them. Each position had between two to four screens at them, again all had the same strange writing running across them.

After Isaac finished inspecting his surroundings, he turned his attention back to Sha'ala. She was sitting down on one of the chairs around the large table in the centre of the room. He also quickly realised that there were four other people in the room with them, all sitting around the table staring at him.

One was similar looking to Sha'ala, except this one had more pronounced masculine features. His head was bigger and he had a grizzly scar running down the right side of his face, from the corner of his eye in a crescent moon shape to his jawbone just under his ear. His features were almost identical other than that, from the protruding brow to the lack of space between his nose and his lip. Sitting directly on his right was a different species of alien. This one looked like a hairless dog, almost identical to a boxer. It had big droopy jowls, with a flat nose that turned upwards slightly and ears flopping down on each side of its head. It was massive. Even though it was sitting down Isaac could tell it was at least twice the size of him in width and was about two feet taller than the person sitting next to it. The other two were sitting on opposite sides of the table to each other. They looked like they could be the same species; the only way Isaac could describe them was that they kind of look like a bald eagle, only more human. They had flat heads and their brows ran straight across, then curved around at the sides. They both had round brown eyes that were facing forward but spread as far apart as possible on either side of their faces. The gap between their eyes was a little unsettling. Their noses were wide but short and they didn't reach anywhere near their top lip which left a lot of space between their noses and their mouths, the opposite of the green skinned folks. There were some subtle differences between them. The one on Isaacs left had skin that was red like a fire engine, with patches of lighter skin, like paint, splattered on its arms. The one on his right had a more subtle, lighter red coloured skin, with no lighter skin splattered anywhere that Isaac could see. Which was predominantly the arms and face.

Isaac was beginning to feel the anxiety he had felt in the med bay return. The sedative that Sha'ala had given him earlier on must have been wearing off. He just stood there staring at everyone, while all eyes were staring back at him, silently taking him in. Time seemed to be standing still and Isaac had no idea what to do or say, or what was about to happen. He was standing on a space ship, apparently traversing the galaxy, surrounded by a crew of aliens who were all eying him up like a fox in the hen house. Then the man with the scar on his face spoke.

"Who are you and why are you on my ship?" he asked, quite angrily.

"My name is Isaac and I he no fucking clue what I'm doing here."

"Listen very carefully. I have no time for games or subterfuge. If you hide anything from me, I will find out and I will punish you severely for it. Do you understand?" the man's voice boomed as he asked the question.

Isaac didn't say anything he just nodded his head. A gesture that his inquisitor did not understand at all.

"Well, do you?" he yelled aggressively.

"Yes," Isaac pleaded with him, "I'm nodding my fucking head amin't I."

"Who do you work for?" was the scar faced man's first query.

"We'll that's a bit of a tricky question. Right now I work for Ezra computers, but that could all change by Monday, you see I had a bit of an incident with a customer last night and…."

"Enough" the man roared at Isaac. "What did I tell you about subterfuge? Now are you an agent of the Assembly or not? Do you work for Fack? Tell me, now."

"I swear I'm telling you the truth. I don't know anything about any Assembly. I was on my way from a friend's house and I was driving his car, well my car now and next thing I know I'm in a high speed chase before a wave of electricity brought me here. Honestly that's the whole truth, that's all I know" Isaac pleaded with him.

The interrogator looked around at Sha'ala and she tilted her head to the right slightly while looking back at him. He then turned his attention back to Isaac.

"It seems you are telling the truth" he said.

Isaac looked back and forth between the two of them.

"How do you know?" he asked.

Sha'ala raised her hand up from below the table. She was holding a little device that just looked like a sheet of glass with a slight plastic rim surrounding it.

"I have been using this to monitor you since you entered the room, it has been relaying information about twenty five different parameters of you, from the pitch of your voice to the blood in your veins, if you were being dishonest, I would have known" she replied.

Isaac looked them all up and down one by one.

"Ok, can I now ask you a few questions if you don't mind?"

The man tilted his head to the side. Isaac looked at him for a moment before he spoke.

"I take it that that means yes. Who are you people? Why am I here? Why can I understand you? Where are we going and can I go home now please?"

These were all the questions Isaac could verbalise before he ran out of breath.

He stood there as all five faces stared back at him silent again. Then the scarred man spoke.

"My name is Car'esh. I am the owner of this vessel. This is my crew. You've already met Sha'ala. This is Moga," he said as he gestured to what Isaac was referring to in his head as dogman, "on your left is Niers and on your right is Taretta" Car'esh said, pointing at the two people left in the room. Niers was the bright red skinned alien with the paint like blotches on his arms and Taretta was the one with the lighter coloured skin.

"You are here because you were in close proximity, in fact, transporting the dead body of the person we were actually here to collect. You can understand us because you had a translator embedded in your ear while you were being treated for your other injuries. We also scanned your

51

cerebral cortex to find the language centre of your brain then mapped your language into the matrix it runs off. We are currently on our way to deliver you to the person who hired us to collect your friend, whose body is now occupying a cryogenic container and no, you cannot go home. We do not have the fuel cells on board to return to your world and then continue on our way" Car'esh finished.

He said all this as if it was a matter of fact. There was no malice or distain in his voice. This was simply how the situation had unfolded and this was the only option available to him. Isaac took a moment to take all of the response in. He looked around at each pair of eyes that were locked on him as he tried his best to digest his situation.

"So I'm your prisoner am I?" he asked with a hint of concern in his voice.

"No. In fact I have reservations about letting you stay on my vessel at all. You are an unregistered species and there is a huge legal entanglement and serious repercussions that we would face should we come across an official patrol" Car'esh replied. "I am tempted to just find the nearest isolated colony and leave you behind, but I would be a fool to return to my current employer empty handed. Since we don't have what he sent us for, I'm going to have to give him you instead"

"So I'm not your prisoner, but I can't go home and you are taking me somewhere I don't want to go" Isaac stated more than asked.

"If you really want, we can just leave you here and you can try and walk home" Car'esh replied.

Isaac couldn't tell but he though there was a sarcastic tone in Car'esh's reply. He didn't want to take the chance though just in case he was being serious.

"No, I think I'll stick with option A if you don't mind" Isaac said.

"Good" replied Car'esh. "I will have Niers guide you around the ship and help you get accustomed to your new surroundings."

Everyone else got up and departed the room and Isaac was left alone with Niers just sitting down staring at him.

8

Isaac stood there staring at Niers and Niers just sat there staring back at him. The silence seemed to last an eternity and Isaac couldn't take any more.

"So…I…Um…"

Niers interrupted Isaac before he could figure out anything else to say.

"Would you like me to show you around the rest of the ship?" he asked.

"Yes, please" Isaac answered.

Niers stood up and walked out of the room and Isaac followed swiftly after. As they boarded the lift Isaac noticed they were pretty much the same height as each other.

"We might as well start at the bottom and work our way back up. If you have any questions, I'll do my best to answer them as we go."

"Sounds good" Isaac replied.

He pressed a button on the console just inside the door and they slid closed. Isaac could feel the carriage move down as they descended into the bowels of the ship. The journey took less than 20 seconds to complete and as the doors opened he found himself looking into a large open space. They exited the lift and walked out into it.

"This is the cargo bay" Niers informed Isaac as they entered.

Standing in this particular area was the first time since waking up that Isaac didn't feel like the walls were closing in on him. The space was quite expansive and he guessed it was probably half the size of a basketball court. The ceiling was about twice the height of him above his head and there was another big steel door at the far end of the room. This door, Isaac assumed, was used to load and unload the ship. As he looked around he noticed that there was very little cargo in the cargo bay. Just a few crates here and there. He then noticed some serious damage to the wall behind him. This was obviously where he had impacted it with the car. He stopped and stared at it for a minute.

"You hit it at quite the velocity. You are very lucky to be alive. If it wasn't for Sha'ala, you most certainly would not be. She spent almost every moment she could tending to you" Niers informed Isaac.

He didn't acknowledge him and just kept staring at the damage to the wall for another minute before they moved on, walking back to the lift. Once they boarded it, the door behind them closed and the one in front of them immediately opened.

"That is the med bay down there, but you've already seen that."

The door closed again and the carriage started to move up. As they stepped off the lift on the next floor Niers led them down a hallway. It was lined with doors. There were four on either side of the hall. Each one was about ten feet apart. At the end of the Hall was a double steel door with a window in each one starting at the top and going half way down.

"These are the crew quarters. The ship can accommodate eight crew members" Niers informed him.

"How many crew members do you have on board now?" Isaac asked.

"There's currently five crew aboard the ship. This is the communal kitchen and dining area" Niers said as they walked through the double door at the end of the hall. They entered a room that looked pretty much like a kitchen come dining area. There was a cooker; surprisingly enough it looked exactly like a modern cooker you would find in any home on Earth. Four hobs and two compartments one on top of the other, most likely the oven and grill. A sink sat next to it with some dirty dishes piled up in it. There was a table in the middle of the room and two benches that were both fixed to the floor that ran along either side of it.

They turned and walked back up the hall and once again boarded the lift. The doors closed behind them and the lift started to climb again. The doors opened and they were back in the hallway they started from. As they walked back into the room Niers informed Isaac that it was their main operations hub. This was where they all met for daily briefings and everybody on board had a workstation where the entire ship could be run from. They then continued on through the room to the other side. A door slid open and in front of him, Isaac could see the cock pit of the ship.

Car'esh was sitting at the controls, piloting the vessel.

"Have you shown him around?" he asked as they entered.

"Yes" Niers answered.

Car'esh gestured to Isaac to take a seat in one of the empty chairs in the room and Isaac duly obliged him. He looked around the cockpit as he sat down. There were

56

consoles and screens lining the wall at the front where you would expect a windshield to be located. Car'esh momentarily turned the steering column to correct the ships course and then presses the screen in front of him. There were still no windows anywhere to be seen so Isaac couldn't see outside, which was a shame as he was now curious about what travelling through space actually looked like. Isaac turned to Car'esh and waited for him to begin speaking.

"I have good news for you. I have spoken to my employer and it would seem that he is satisfied that the body of your friend we have is enough for him. He won't require us to turn you over to him" Car'esh informed Isaac.

Isaac felt a massive weight lift off his chest. At the very least he wasn't going to be just brought to an alien planet and left there.

"So are you going to take me home then?" Isaac asked with a glimmer of hope in his voice.

"Yes we are" was Car'esh's reply.

Isaac jumped out of his seat and punched the air in front of him. Car'esh jumped up and grabbed Isaac and twisted his arm around behind his back forcing his face into the seat of the chair he had just leapt from.

"You attempt to attack after I have granted you safe passage home" he screamed.

Isaac struggled to twist his head to the side out of the seat to try and catch his breath. He put all the energy he could muster into a response.

"Happy…Free…Not threat" was all he could manage to get out.

Car'esh released his grip a little to let Isaac free his head enough to speak clearly.

"It's a gesture of joy. It just means I'm elated you came to that decision" he pleaded with the captain.

Car'esh loosened his grip and allowed Isaac to sit back down in the chair.

"I'm sorry," he offered, "I'm not familiar with your kind's body language."

"No problem," Isaac replied rubbing his arm trying to get the feeling to return.

"So are we heading back to Earth now?" Isaac asked expectantly.

"No" Car'esh replied bluntly.

"Why not?" Isaac demanded.

"Fuel." Car'esh began. "We just don't have enough to take you back then return home. We only carry enough for the job at hand, with a ten percent reserve. You will simply have to wait until we have finished our task and then we will figure out what we will do from there."

Isaac began to protest but realised very quickly that his objections were falling on deaf ears.

"So what do I do until then?" he asked.

"You may use one of the crew quarters to rest. You will be confined to those quarters except for meal times" Car'esh said.

"So I am a prisoner" Isaac bemoaned.

"You are an unregistered species. It is a very serious crime to transport someone who is not a citizen of the Galactic Assembly. If we were found with you on board, I would be stripped of my license and imprisoned. As would my crew. Be thankful that I am allowing you to stay on board at all" Car'esh stated.

Isaac stood up and turned to leave.

"I will take you to your quarters" Niers said as he stood up and followed Isaac out of the room.

They boarded the lift once more and descended back down to the crew quarters they had been to earlier. They walked down to the end of the hall and stopped outside the last door on the left side. Niers tapped the console on the wall outside and the door slid open.

"Once you go in, I will lock the door behind you as the captain has instructed. There is a console in your room that carries a connection to all of the stored information on record for the Galactic Assembly if you want to inform yourself. I will check on you periodically each day and let you know when there is food to eat" Niers told him.

Isaac turned and walked into the room. The door slid closed behind him.

9

Isaac sat on the end of the bed in his quarters. He wasn't sure exactly how much time had passed. He was guessing a couple of days at most. He hadn't left the room once since Niers locked the door on him when he first entered. Niers had come back four times now to tell him there was food available for him to eat in the canteen but Isaac had refused the offer every time. He was anxious, he was scared and he just wanted to be left alone. The third time Niers came back he had brought what he called a protein block and some water. The protein block he explained, had all the required nutrients in it to keep a person alive. It was grey, solid and flavourless. It reminded Isaac of tofu but with a harder consistency to it. It wasn't really food. It was more just survival, which was all Isaac really needed right now.

He glanced around his room, estimating it was about ten feet by ten feet square. There was a drab, greenish hue to the walls that surrounded him. Isaac wasn't sure if it was the natural colour of the metal the walls were made of or if it was a colour that someone had chosen to paint it. He hoped it was the former. He didn't like the idea of sharing a confined space with anyone who would pick this dank and dreary shade. It was soulless. There was a bed fixed to the wall on the left side. There was also a monitor built into the wall at the opposite end of the room from where you entered, with a table and a chair situated in front of it. To the right of the table in the corner of the room, there was a cubicle containing a shower that when you pressed a button on the wall, the shower disappeared into the floor and a toilet came down out of the ceiling. Isaac had hygiene concerns about the toilet being on top of the shower but there wasn't much he could do about it and it seemed to work fine thus far. All down the right wall of the room were cubby holes. Storage space for any personal items you might bring on board. It was useless to Isaac as all he had in his possession were the clothes he was wearing.

He had been given a jumpsuit to put on by Niers since his original clothes were ruined in the accident. It resembled a flight suit that a fighter pilot would wear, only it was black in colour. There were elasticated cuffs on the arms and legs that kept it tight around the wrists and ankles. He also had a pair of shoes that had been given to him. They were kind of like loafers but had more of a tennis shoe appearance to them. Isaac had a feeling everything he was wearing belonged to Car'esh, as it was all slightly too big for him in length so it was a lot looser than he would like and the shoes felt about a size bigger than he would normally wear.

He turned his attention to the console in his room. It was on standby, so the screen was black. There was a control panel on the table that sat in front of it. The controls by their very definition, were alien. On one of his visits Niers had given Isaac a crash course on how to navigate through certain sections so at the very least, he could get himself up to speed on the current state of the galaxy that was out there. Then he had an incredibly belated revelation. Humans had always wondered if they were alone or not. Isaac now not only knew that there were aliens out there, but the bastards had kidnapped him too. He figured he better get some sort of information on what he was in for once they reached their destination, which, according to Niers was going to take close to another week at least.

Isaac stood up and walked to the chair and sat down, looking at the control panel on the table in front of him. It was laid out similar to a keyboard on a laptop for the most part, but the symbols on the keys didn't make any sense to him. He pressed the first key that Niers had told him to and the screen lit up. There were dialogue boxes popping up on the screen with all different types of what Isaac assumed were launch commands. After a couple of seconds the dialogue boxes disappeared. The sign in screen loaded up and Isaac waited a minute as Niers said he had programmed it to log in automatically, so Isaac wouldn't have to remember usernames or passwords in an alien language. After a few seconds this happened and Isaac was looking at the home screen. Niers told him he had also added a program to the software that would let Isaac just tell the console what he wanted to see and it would display the information in English so he could read it.

"Galactic Assembly history" Isaac spoke to the console.

The screen changed and paragraphs of writing started to scroll down the screen. After a few moments Isaac realised that he had pulled up the entire history of the galactic Assembly. He attempted to refine his search.

"Concise galactic history" Isaac tried again.

This time the screen had only a couple of paragraphs of text.

The Magalians:

The Magalians are the first known race to have mastered galactic travel in the modern era. Approximately ten millennia ago they were going through an industrial revolution when a group of their scientists accidently stumbled upon element drive technology. Unfortunately, the group of scientists vaporised themselves and half a city in the resulting explosion. While investigating what happened it was discovered that they were trying to stabilise a new element to be used as a power source. The amount of energy created from the microscopic amount of the element used led the Magalians to the element drive discovery 50 years later.

They spent a thousand years exploring the stars looking for extra-terrestrial life but found only empty planets which they quickly colonised. After all the years of exploring the star ways they had colonised 10 planets in different solar systems but had found no intelligent life, until they discovered what they thought would be the 11th planet of their empire, which it turned out was called Tal.

Initially the Magalians were met with fear by the Talanites who thought they were an invading force from outside their solar system, but over the course of 2 years they earned their trust by helping them develop their own element drives and starting them on the path to interstellar discovery. They found, thanks to the Talanites, many ancient and dead libraries of information that belonged to a society called the Karlal in a language that died out eons ago. This was a great and exciting revelation to the Magalians, as they had not found any other historical signs of civilisation in the galaxy previous to this.

The Garians and the Talanites:
 Although the Talanites were the first civilisation discovered by the Magalians on the planet Tal, it was not their ancestral home. Originally, they came from their sister planet in the solar system called Gar. The Talanites were the descendants of the original founders of the Tal colony who came from Gar 300 years previous. Gar and Tal are two planets in the same solar system that have the capability to support life. A mere 650,000 kilometres separate these two worlds. They both have breathable atmospheres and moderate climates, Gar being slightly warmer as it is closer to the sun.

 Once the Garians, discovered interplanetary travel their first stop was the neighbouring world that was visible to them day or night with the naked eye. For millennia their imagination was captured by the close proximity of another world so close to their own. There were myths and legends of the beings that lived on it. All of which were fallacies. But it did spur them on to try and get there as soon as they could to see for themselves. Once they arrived, they found that there had once been a civilisation living on the world. But they had long since departed the world or died off. It was exciting as it proved that life did inhabit other planets.

 After 100 years of effort the Talanite colony became too much of a financial burden on the Garian government, so they decided to end their support of the venture. They cut off all financial investment and told the citizens of the colony to return home. But at this stage several generations of people had been born there and considered

64

Tal their home. Only 20% of the population returned to Gar and the other 80%, approximately 1.2 Million people were left to fend for themselves.

On Gar things vastly improved. Since the government was no longer pumping money into an extra-terrestrial colony the planet enjoyed a golden age of prosperity. Tal however suffered incredibly. The main industries on the planet were agriculture and relic hunting. Many of the citizens took to searching the ruins for anything valuable to trade to artefact collectors. The most valuable of these were ancient writings, or any sort of personal possession. With a century of distain built up amongst the Talanites over their abandonment by the Garians, they launched an offensive attack on their sister world in a bid to highlight the suffering they were experiencing. This ignited interplanetary hostilities, mostly from the Talanites, aimed at the Garians, who endured almost seventy years of killing and terrorism.

After so much death and destruction both sides determined it was time to find a peaceful resolution, so they decided that the Garians would trade aid and financial support for the colony once again in return for access to the historical ruins, due to a renewed interest in what they were. After 30 years of peace the Magalians arrived at Tal and both Garians and Talanites were guided to the stars and the Galactic Assembly was formed. There are currently 7 Colonies belonging to what is referred to as the Gar/Tal dominion.

The door to Isaacs room buzzed and slid open and Niers was standing on the other side. This was the first of his daily attempts to get Isaac to come down to the mess and eat with some of the crew. Strangely enough, even to

65

Isaac, he was more open to the idea this time. He still said no, but mainly because he wanted to read more about the history of the people surrounding him.

"Next time" Isaac assured Niers.

Niers accepted Isaacs refusal as he had the several other times previous, closed the door and locked it again. Isaac realised he was actually hungry and took a piece off the protein block that was sitting on the table beside him. He took a bite and turned his attention back to the screen.

Ilians:

Ilians are a race of people from the planet Aeroen. They have only been a part of the wider galactic community for the last 3000 years. Although 3000 years have passed the Ilians have yet to colonise a single planet, beyond resource purposes. The majority of the population prefer to stay on their home world than traverse the galaxy. They are of the opinion that there is nothing out there that they can't have on their home world. There are some Ilians that have ventured off their world but the vast majority have opted to stay. This of course is all relative to the fact that seven thousand years ago they were

Suddenly the ship slammed to the side like it had hit something. Isaac was thrown from his chair and landed on the floor about five feet away as vibrations rattle through the walls and all the lights went dim. A loud noise rang out all around him. Isaac was only getting use to the alien's ways and customs, but he knew an alarm when he heard one. The intercom buzzed and crackled on the wall above his bed but he couldn't make out what was being said. He ran to the door and pressed the button to open it but nothing happened.

"It's still locked" Isaac muttered to himself.

He ran back over to the intercom above his bed and pressed the button to talk.

"Hello. Can anybody hear me? Hello. What the fuck is going on?" Isaac screamed into the mic.

There was no reply. Isaac sat down on the end of his bed and listened. He could hear a rumbling sound. Then there was a second vibration that ran through all the walls around him again. He started to panic. All sorts of thoughts were bombarding his paranoid mind. Had the ship crashed? What if the hull had been ripped open? He sat there for a few more moments as the sounds of banging, grinding and the low rumble that was running through the ship's walls all built up and then suddenly, they all stopped. There were still some sporadic bangs and clangs but the crescendo of noises had ceased. He walked back over to the door and put his ear up against it. He could hear murmurs and what sounded like heavy footsteps moving around, but it was all distorted and he couldn't really make the noises out. As he was intently listening to the door, the release mechanism unlatched and the door slid open. There were two figures standing outside the room. They were wearing, what looked to Isaac's untrained eye, like space suits. They were jet black. Tightly fitted to the wearer's body. They looked like they were made out of a rubber type of material but had plates of a more solid type of substance fixed to them covering all the vital parts of the body, like an armour. Their helmets were about the size of a gas mask and they had jet black glass visors that ran from the forehead to the chin and covered their face.

"Found him" one of them said.

"Found who?" Isaac asked.

They didn't reply. The one standing directly in front of Isaac lifted the butt of the rifle he was carrying and

67

slammed it into his forehead, knocking him back into the room and onto the ground. Isaac looked up and could feel a trickle of blood run down his face to the tip of his nose. He wiped it off and looked at his hand.

"Fucking dick head. What the fuck did you do that for?"

The assailant again said nothing, he just stepped forward into the room and lifted his rifle, pointing it at Isaac. Isaac put his hands up like lots of people do when someone is pointing a gun at them, in the hope that they will be the first person in history to ever stop a bullet with either their hands or telekinesis. He looked past his attacker to the second intruder behind him, who suddenly disappeared. He was there one second and was gone the next, like he had just vanished into the ether. The assailant lowered his gun and looked around at the commotion behind him to see that his comrade was inexplicably gone.

"Vash," he called out, "where did you go?"

He turned and walked back towards the door, just as Moga charged around the corner and into the room towards him. The intruder tried to raise his rifle but by the time he got it waist high, Moga was on him. He slammed into him with the force of a small car, sending him hurtling into the console screen on the wall, several feet away at the far end of the room, smashing right through it and landing face down on the floor. Moga charged again and as the man in black got to his feet, he looked up and saw the big fist of Moga flying towards his face. It was the last thing he saw. The impact shattered the visor of his helmet into pieces. It also snapped his head back at such a velocity that it severed his spine from the neck down and he fell to the floor, dead. Moga stood over him looking down.

"Ilian" he growled to himself.

Isaac looked down at the lifeless body on the floor. The face was a little mangled but he could still make it out. It was jet black. There were big bulbous yellow eyes looking off lifelessly into the distance. His skin was smooth and hairless. There was no nose to speak of, just two slits that ran vertically down his face.

"Follow me" Moga said as he walked out the door.

They made their way towards the lift but Moga took a left before they boarded it and Isaac followed. There was a hatch open in the wall beside the lift. It wasn't very big and Moga had to squeeze his way in and he started to ascend a ladder. Isaac followed him closely. He climbed about twenty five feet behind Moga until they reached another hatch that led out onto the deck above them. When Isaac emerged he was standing in Operations. All of the crew were there, each one of them standing at a station assessing what was happening.

10

"What's going on out there?" Car'esh asked, demanding a report from his crew.

"It's an unregistered transport. Modified. I have a visual on high yield missiles on each side. No markings. It's not giving off any I.D signatures" Taretta said looking at an image on her stations screen.

"Put a visual on the main screen" Car'esh ordered.

Taretta tapped a couple of buttons on her console and a big screen in the middle of the room lit up with an image of the attacking vessel. It was long and slim. It was almost conical in shape from back to front, except the bottom seemed to be flat. There were small wings on either side with 2 missiles mounted on each one. The attacking ship was side on with theirs and there was what looked like a tunnel running between the two ships connecting them together.

"They're Ilians. Special ops based on equipment, not Assembly" Moga informed everyone in his low gravelly voice.

"Why would Ilian special forces be boarding us on an unregistered ship?" Niers asked.

"I don't know, but I imagine it has something to do with our new passenger here" Car'esh said, pointing at Isaac.

"Me. What would they know about me?" Isaac replied.

"I don't know, but I have every intention of finding out" Car'esh answered as he moved around the room to a station on the far side.

"What are our options when we break free?" he shouted to the room.

"We have an uninhabited planet close by. We'll get there in about thirty minutes at top speed" Niers replied looking up from his screen.

"Chances are that's where they were waiting for us and that's where they want us to go" Taretta warned.

"Well it's not like we have much of a choice. Once we get separated from them, we're going to have a pretty big hole in our ship. We'll need to fix that before we can try to properly escape" Car'esh barked back.

"Plan captain?" Moga enquired.

"Niers, if we hit them with a death charge will that disable their missiles?" Car'esh asked.

"Yes it would. But we would still be connected to them through the bridge they've attached. We wouldn't get very far. We could run, but we'd just take them with us" Niers responded.

"Ok. So we need to go down to the cargo bay and blow that thing off the ship" Car'esh pondered.

"It's very likely they have already moved more people on board. They will be waiting for you" Sha'ala said with a hint of concern in her voice.

"Well we don't really have much of a choice. Moga, you and our new travelling companion come with me. Niers be ready to strike them with a charge. Taretta, When I say so

71

you hit it and head straight for that planet as fast as you can" Car'esh ordered.

"Me? What the fuck am I gonna do?" Isaac demanded.

"You're my distraction and I want to know what they want from you. You're going to ask them" Car'esh informed him.

Isaac looked around the room in the hope that someone would tell Car'esh it was a bad idea to bring him. None of them seemed to think that though.

Isaac followed Moga back through the crawl space that ran between the decks. They were going down this time instead of up. They had gone down three ladders and were stopped at a hatch. Car'esh had followed them in but had taken a left earlier at an intersection while Isaac and Moga had taken a right.

"I'll open door, you go see what they want" Moga instructed Isaac.

"Excuse Me? What if they just shoot me?" Isaac probed back.

"Hope they don't" Moga replied before opening the hatch and pushing Isaac out through the hole.

Isaac fell a couple of feet and landed hard on his chest and face. He stood up and shook himself off before surveying his surroundings. He was back in the cargo hold. He glanced around the open room. There were 4 intruders, all wearing the same suits as the first ones he had encountered, standing with their backs to him. He noticed across the cargo hold, there was an opening that had been blasted into the side of the ship and a large, sealed walkway extended from the other vessel and was anchored into his.

One of the four intruders looked around and spotted Isaac standing behind them. He raised his weapon and walked right at him. The other three took notice and did the same.

"Where is the scientist?" the leader of the group demanded.

"What scientist?" Isaac pleaded with the trespasser.

"Where is the one that you collected from the Earth?"

"That's me," Isaac insisted, "I'm the one they took from Earth."

The armed invader looked him up and down for a moment taking Isaac in from head to toe. He seemed to relax a little but still kept his weapon aimed at him.

"The genetic modifications are getting better and better it would seem. Do you have it?" The intruder asked, a little calmer now.

"Do I have what?" Isaac replied, a little mystified.

The interloper tightened his grip on his weapon and tensed up again.

"Do you have the package, what I was sent here to retrieve?" he demanded.

Isaac raised his hands up to surrender.

"Don't shoot man please. If you tell me what you're here to retrieve I can tell you whether I have it or not" he insisted.

The intruder wrapped his finger around the trigger of his weapon and prepared to fire.

"You're not who we're looking for" he said.

Isaac closed his eyes as every muscle in his body tensed up. What seemed like an eternity passed, still nothing happened. Then Isaac felt wet across his face, hands and neck. It took him a moment to open his eyes as he was terrified that when he did, he would see his insides on the outside. Or maybe he had already tried but since he was dead it just wasn't working. Eventually he did manage to pry them open and he looked down. There was indeed what looked like blood all over him. All down his front from his face, which had splatter on it to his chest, which was saturated, there was a thick red liquid dripping off him. Strangely there was still no pain. He stood there waiting for his body to give out, expecting to fall to the floor but nothing happened. He looked in front of him where the invading soldier was still standing with his weapon raised, prepared to fire. He brought his eyes level with the intruder's mask but the mask was gone, shattered into a thousand pieces. He didn't quite understand what he was looking at initially. His brain was confused and it didn't really register with him what he was now observing. There were bits of what looked like skin hanging off the jagged edges of glass that were still attached to the helmet and there was a steady stream of thick red liquid flowing out of the hole where his face use to be. That face was gone now, replaced with a crimson mass of bone, skin and glass.

The grisly image caught Isaac by surprise. He had never seen the inside of someone's head up close before and he felt his legs go weak at this sudden and unwelcome visual atrocity.

He wasn't sure what had happened. He didn't even notice the other three armed invaders simultaneously point their weapons toward him at first. Before he had a chance to raise his hands or open his mouth to protest his innocence there was a pop that rang out in the room. The intruder to his rights helmet exploded, out to the side this time. Again, another splatter of red shot across the room, this time covering the wall just beside where the other ships makeshift gangway had entered the Sao'ise. The two trespassers that remained turned to look behind them, baffled, to see where the shots had come from as three more heavily armed invaders came rushing in to the ship from the extended walkway. They must have been there the whole time, unbeknownst to Isaac. Then he felt himself moving backwards under some force other than his own power. Before he knew it, he was back in the crawl space, in the wall and Moga was closing the hatch to seal him in.

Isaac could hear the commotion outside. There was shouting, loud blasts, things were being slammed around, then there were what sounded like screams of agony, followed finally by an eerie silence. For a moment Isaac thought about trying to open the hatch to see what had gone on, but quickly realised this was not a good idea. The quiet lasted another moment or two but was then shattered by a massive explosion that shook the walls around him and seemed to reverberate through the ship to its very core. Another moment of silence followed before the hatch in front of him flew open. Moga grabbed Isaac by the arm and helped him out of the crawl space back into the cargo hold. As Isaac looked around he could hardly see because of all the smoke now in the room. There were also the scattered bodies of the people who had boarded them, littered all around. The floor beneath him freshly painted with the gory remnants of the encounter that had just taken place. The walkway that had been connecting the two ships was gone and there was an immense hole in the side of their ship that seemed to open out into space. A black veil, a shroud of darkness was all that Isaac could see outside the wall.

"How are we not dead?" Isaac asked, standing right in front of the hole, his nose inches from what should certainly be his demise.

"Electronic barrier," Moga Replied, "in case of hull breach."

Isaac reached out and touched the empty space, causing green ripples of energy to float up the wall, in the way a pebble would cause undulation if dropped in a puddle.

"Who are you really?" Car'esh asked Isaac.

"I swear this has nothing to do with me" Isaac responded, still looking out into the emptiness, mesmerised by what he was seeing and certain he was telling the truth.

"Then why…" Car'esh began before being cut off by a voice coming through the ship's intercom.

"Car'esh we need to move now. Niers has activated the death charge so we need to head for the planet" Taretta's voice said through the speakers.

"Alright" Car'esh replied as he moved towards the door of the Cargo hold. As they got outside into the hallway he turned to a key pad on the wall and punched a few buttons on it.

"Niers, I've sealed the cargo bay off. Disable the shield before you head to the planet to flush the mess out. All the other cargo is bound to the floor. Then see what you can do about masking our signal on approach. They will be waiting for us down there. Whoever they are."

As they moved down the hall towards the lift, Isaac felt a sudden shift underneath him as the ship accelerated forward. He couldn't help but feel he was being ushered through the ship by Moga and Car'esh. When they entered the lift, he could almost sense the two of them tensing up during their ascent towards the top deck. Once the doors opened he was marched into the operations room and sat down as Moga and Car'esh stood over him looking down.

"Who are you?" Car'esh demanded of him.

"We've been over this," Isaac answered, amazed at the confidence he could hear in his own voice, "this is not my fault."

76

Moga leaned forward and Isaac swore he could hear him growl a little.

"Ever since we brought you on…" Car'esh began, but Isaac cut him off before he could finish.

"I never wanted to be here in the first fucking place. You took me up here by mistake, remember?" Isaac insisted to them as they continued to stare down, looming over him.

Car'esh was about to say something when Taretta's voice came over the intercom again.

"We're about to begin our approach to the planet. I need you up here Car'esh."

Car'esh looked to Moga and said something that Isaac couldn't quite make out, then he ran through the door at the end of the room and disappeared onto the bridge of the ship.

"This is fucking bullshit," Isaac insisted to him, "you heard the dude in the cargo bay, they weren't even here for me."

Moga looked at him with what Isaac could only assume was confusion. He couldn't tell what Moga was thinking any more than his mother's Labrador.

"I heard nothing" Moga retorted.

Isaac looked at him. He was angry now. He had been taken from his home against his will, almost died twice and now, finally, he'd had enough.

"For something that looks an awful lot like a dog you've got pretty shit hearing so" Isaac snapped.

Moga looked down. He wasn't sure what Isaac had said but he was pretty sure it was an insult. Caninans had developed their communication to not just include words but to pick up on the tone in a voice and also specific inflections in speech patterns way beyond what a human could detect.

"What is dog?" he asked.

"You're a fucking dog. You walk on two legs and you have weird little hands but you've got a wet nose, big floppy ears and a permanent stupid look on your face, just like a dog" Isaac bit back.

Moga looked down at his hands.

"What you mean little?" he asked with a disapproving grunt in his voice.

Isaac held himself back from saying anything else. He had a penchant for losing his temper at the wrong moment and saying the wrong thing and he realised that this was neither the time nor the place to be alienating himself.

"Nothing, I don't mean anything by it" he said with a hint of sarcasm in his voice.

They both sat there for a few minutes in silence before Taretta broke it with an announcement through the comm.

"Alright everyone, we're just about there. With the hole in the hull it's going to get a bit rough so strap in" she ordered.

The vibrations in the ship started just as she finished her announcement. At first it was just a little shaky. Then there were a couple of heavy bumps in a row as the slight shakiness started to turn into more of a constant bounce. Isaac looked to Moga to see if he was nervous or had any worry at all expressed on his face. He could have for all Isaac knew. There was just no way he could tell. Suddenly there was what felt like a huge dip in their altitude, like when a plane drops for a second in turbulence and then suddenly levels off, except this was a much sharper drop and a more sudden halt. If Isaac wasn't strapped in, he was sure he would have flown though the roof. He felt like his stomach was pushing its way up his oesophagus and trying to escape out of his mouth. The severe rocking seemed to start subsiding and the shaking seemed to stop. Isaac looked around at Moga again.

"Cleared atmosphere. Should land soon" he growled as he got up and headed towards the lift.

For a few seconds Isaac sat in his seat, still waiting for the adrenaline to level off in his system so he could stop shaking. Then there was a slight thud from below him. They had landed.

11

Isaac sat in his chair, waiting. He wasn't sure what he was waiting for as he had no specific role to play in the crew and they all knew what they were doing. Since they had actual jobs on the ship, in an instance like this they would automatically know what was expected of them now they were grounded. All he could do was just sit in his chair in the operations room, waiting.

After a couple of minutes Niers and Taretta walked in. They were wearing what appeared to be space suits. They were white in colour, not to dissimilar to what a NASA astronaut would wear, just a little more streamlined. On closer inspection they were pretty much identical to the outfits worn by the intruders that had put them in this situation, only these were white and the visor on the helmets they were holding were more transparent. Niers was carrying an extra one under his arm.

"Put this on" he said to Isaac as he threw the extra suit towards him.

"Where are we going?" Isaac asked as he looked for a zip at the back.

"Car'esh has ordered us to fix the hole in the hull of the ship" Taretta said, as she took the thing back off Isaac.

She placed it on the ground in front of him and spread the neck of the suit out as wide as it would go. The hole now seemed to be big enough for him to get in. Isaac rolled it down towards the legs and stopped at the waist, before sliding his legs into their place in the ensemble and pulling the waist up so it was tight. The bottom of it had what resembled a pair of booties, like the kind you would see on a baby's onesie attached to them.

He was surprised at how soft and fragile the material felt. It was like silk, only coarser. He pulled it up and he slipped his arms into the sleeves, which had gloves for his hands to go in. He slid his fingers into place and let the rest of the suit hang off his shoulders. As he did this, he felt the front of the uniform touch off his chest. The chest plate in the suit was harder than the rest of it. It seemed to be heavier than the rest of the material that it was made of. Isaac was a little alarmed at just how flimsy the suit felt.

"You want me to go outside in this? It doesn't really inspire confidence in my well-being if I'm going to rely on it to survive" Isaac said.

Niers stepped forward and slid his finger across the neck of it. Immediately the outfits material became stiff. Isaac ran his glove covered hand across the exterior of the part that was covering his arm. It felt more like rubber when he pressed against it now, only sturdier. The booties that were at the end had hardened even more. They felt like a proper pair of boots on his feet. He was also surprised at the freedom of movement he had, considering how rigid the material now felt to the touch.

Niers and Taretta turned and walked back to the lift as Isaac scurried along behind them. Although the suit

81

provided ease of movement to Isaac, for some reason it didn't seem natural, so it took him a couple of steps to get used to it and he just made it in the doors before they closed.

As the lift doors to the cargo bay opened Niers and Taretta stepped out and Isaac followed behind, now more comfortable with the feel of the material on his body. He still had questions though. Everything was new to him after all.

"Sorry Niers, Taretta if you don't mind, I'd really appreciate a little information. If it's all the same to you."

"Of course" Taretta replied seeming genuinely eager to help.

"Cool. What am I to do when we get outside and how necessary is this suit I'm wearing to," he pondered for a second for the best way to ask the question, "to my being alive?"

Niers was rooting around in a container looking through what Isaac presumed were tools and material needed for the task at hand. He picked up a long shafted device with a square on the end of it that looked like a spanner, without the groove that the bolt would fit in, and tossed it towards Taretta who turned and caught it, then placed it in a smaller box beside her.

"What we are about to do is a three person job" Niers began, "unfortunately for both you and us, you are the only other person on the ship who is able to assist us at this time. Car'esh and Moga have both gone ahead to scout out the area and keep a watch for anyone who might be hiding on this planet lying in wait for us."

He continued as he walked over to the box beside Taretta and placed a couple more things in it.

"Sha'ala must stay at the controls of the ship in case there is an immediate need for us to depart, and she cannot contribute as she is the only trained medical practitioner on board, so she is the only one who can help should any of us need immediate assistance" he finished, as he pulled what looked like a roll of leather, out of another shipping container.

"Cool" Isaac said, genuinely happy to be of use to them.

"Very is the answer to your second question" Taretta said as she picked up the small box they had put all the tools in and handed it to Isaac to carry.

"Excuse me?" Isaac asked.

"The suit you are wearing is very important to your survival" she explained. "This planet doesn't look very hospitable. Our readings of the atmosphere show there is a very high concentration of carbon dioxide. Your environment suit will filter this and give you a supply of oxygen to breath. If you weren't wearing the suit you would asphyxiate in approximately one minute. Also the radiation it's star is giving off would be lethal without the shielding it will provide you."

Isaac looked at her with his mouth open, shock and apprehension now etched on his expression.

"One minute. Right so" he offered, trying to sound as brave as possible, but not succeeding.

Niers and Taretta slipped their helmets on and Isaac did the same. Taretta then came over to him and fixed his helmet so it would activate. It made the sound of an air tight seal locking into place. The seal created an isolated environment inside the suit, so now all Isaac could hear was his breathing.

He followed Taretta and Niers to the doors at the opposite end of the ship from the lift. These doors, he had correctly assumed earlier, were the exterior entrance to the cargo hold. They past the hole in the hull and he tried to peek outside at the world beyond it but he couldn't get a good look. Taretta walked up to a console on the wall and she tapped a few buttons in quick succession. There was a low beeping noise that began to ring out around the compartment, then she tapped a few more buttons and the big doors in front of them slowly began to separate from each other, sliding along the walls as they did so.

When the doors were far enough apart, Niers walked out of the ship and Taretta followed behind him. Isaac took a second and then walked out the doors after them.

"One small step" he thought to himself as made his way out into the natural light.

When he got outside, he walked down a small ramp that had extended from the back of the ship to the ground. As his feet touch the surface, he stopped for a second and looked around to survey what was the first alien planet that any human had ever set foot on.

Soft, fluffy golden clouds drifted high across the backdrop of a ruby red sky. Way in the distance he could see jet black mountains, tall and flat at their peaks, rising out of the ground, almost giving the impression they were painted on the crimson canvas that offered itself behind them. He looked directly down at his feet. The ground beneath him was jet black too. It was cracked, and there was a loose top surface like gravel, though it was quite sturdy despite its loose appearance. Solid under his feet. He felt a sudden sense of awe. This was incredible. He was actually standing on an alien world and it was most definitely alien. He looked around the sky until he found the star that was this planets sun. It was a large red beacon, much bigger than the sun on Earth appeared in the daytime sky. He could see ripples moving across its surface and erupting out as solar flares. Unexpectedly he heard a voice talking directly into his right ear.

"Isaac when you are ready we need your assistance to get this fixed" Niers said to him from the side of the ship.

Isaac snapped back to reality, as crazy as reality had become and followed them around to the side of the ship they were on. He walked up behind them and put the small tool box he was carrying down on the ground. He could hear them talking to each other, through what he now knew was a communication head set that was obviously built into the suit he was wearing. Niers was pointing to the edge of the hole and was saying something about the diameter of something, while Taretta had a device in her hand and she was entering information into it and telling Niers what information was being returned to her. They were speaking English, but Isaac still had no idea what they were talking about as it was way beyond his comprehension. He stepped back and looked up again, this time at the ship. He realised this was the first time he was seeing it from the outside.

Isaac's first thought was how big it actually was. It didn't feel as big inside as it looked outside. From the tip of the front of the ship, were the cock pit was located, all the way back to the rear doors at the end of the cargo bay covered at least a hundred feet. The belly of the ship from the ground up to the top was at least sixty feet. The design of the ship seemed a tad clunky. It was essentially a large rectangle shape sitting on top of a smaller one, with the nose of the craft rounded off at the front. He could pretty much make out the different areas of the ship from the outside. The square section on the bottom was the cargo hold and the med bay. That was about sixty feet from front to back.

The larger rectangle shaped part that sat on top of that was everything else, the crew quarters with the engine room, control centre and cock pit all in there somewhere. What Isaac could only compare to a kick stand from a motorbike seemed to be extending out of the nose of the ship, supporting the front, holding it off the ground. There was a wing extending out from the side of the craft, more towards the rear, in between where the cargo hold joined on to the decks above it. Another stand was extending down from that, holding the bottom of the ship off the ground. There was also a giant engine attached to the wing. Isaac didn't know if this was the space engine, or the engine for inside the atmosphere of a planet, or even if it was an engine at all. It just looked like an engine to him. The ship appeared to have a steel look to it in both the appearance of the material it was made from and the colour of it. Worn and weathered, it didn't give the impression it was a new vessel. He could tell it had seen its fair share of voyages and had been involved in more than a few skirmishes. There were quite a few dents and more than a couple of impact marks on the hull.

"Can you come over here and hold this in place?" Niers asked Isaac once again bringing his focus back to the task at hand.

Isaac walked over to where Niers was and placed his hand on what he was indicating he wanted Isaac to hold. It was a piece off the roll of material he had brought with them, now cut to cover the size of the wound in the ship's exterior. It felt a little soft and not fit for purpose in Isaacs mind. After what he had seen with the suit he was wearing though, he wasn't going to jump to any conclusions. It was about four feet wide and about six feet from the ground up.

Pretty much the exact size of the runway the other ship had smashed through their hull and used to board them.

Isaac was easily holding the top left hand corner in place, but Taretta was struggling to hold up her side as she only stood just about five and a half feet tall. Niers looked like he was applying some sort of adhesive to the back side of the material before pressing it up against the hull. He made his way around the entire rectangle shaped hole, applying the material and making sure it was completely sealed. When he was satisfied, he turned to Isaac and handed him the adhesive to place back in the container, then bent down to pick up something else off the ground.

"You are concerned about the strength of the material I am using to fix the hole are you not?" Niers asked of Isaac, like he could read his mind, or just his general manner.

"Not concerned, more curious" Isaac replied honestly.

"It is a very versatile material," Niers began to explain, "once you have it in place you simply apply a pulse to it, and it will take on the structural properties that you require. The suit you are wearing is made from a similar material. It is quite reliable."

Isaac relaxed a little. Just having that explained to him, even though he didn't fully understand it, told him that although it was strange to him, it was something that was fairly standard to them.

"Yes, the material is never a concern," Niers continued, "it's my calculations that provide the worry."

"Excuse Me?"

"Well the material will always do what you tell it to do. The problem is whether or not you tell it to do what you want it to do correctly."

He turned and looked directly at Isaac and Isaac could swear he was smiling at him.

"I have to match the material to the exact frequency of whatever I am trying to bond it with. Too much or too little would prove disastrous. Too much and…"

"Hey. Hey." Isaac cut him off as he could feel all the colour rush from his face. "I really don't need to know all this. There's a hole in the ship. The material will fix the hole. I'm good. That'll do."

Niers turned around and started to input some more data into the little tablet that Taretta had been working with earlier. He ran his fingers over the outside of the material one more time to check it was sealed correctly and then pressed the screen on his pad. The sheet of material vibrated and morphed into what seemed to be the perfect replacement for the missing hull. Isaac looked on once again in amazement.

"So is that it? Is it fixed?" he asked.

"For now I believe so yes. It's not a permanent solution by any means but once we get to our destination it can be properly replaced. I just have to make some final checks to ensure it will get us to where we're going" Niers said as he ran some more numbers through his data pad.

Isaac stepped back and left him to his work. He walked along the ship towards the front, looking up as he went, taking in the size of the ship again. He could see up into the bridge. He could actually see the shape of someone on the bridge looking out the window down at him. Which was strange because when he was on the bridge himself, he didn't remember there being a window. Then he noticed a blast shield that had been protecting it had been raised up to reveal the interior. He looked closer and he could make out that it was Sha'ala. She was so far away he could just about identify her, but it looked like she was signalling to him. After a couple of seconds straining his eyes to focus, he could definitely see she was trying to tell him something.

He looked over his shoulder to where he thought she was pointing to but couldn't see anything, then turned back to her and tried to make out what she was gesturing. He turned around again but there was still nothing there he could see.

"Niers, Taretta. I think that Sha'ala is trying to tell us something from the bridge of the ship" Isaac said into his environment suit.

"What are you doing all the way over there?" Taretta asked Isaac.

"I was just checking out the ship and I looked up and she was signalling down to me. She's pointing off into the distance, but I can't see anything."

"Why would she be signalling down to you? She can just use the comms" Niers said.

"I'm telling you she is definitely trying to tell me something."

"Sha'ala, what is the problem?" Niers asked to no response. "Sha'ala, can you hear me."

"Sha'ala" Taretta tried, still nothing.

"The remote uplink that connects the ships coms to the suits must have been damaged" Niers pondered. He looked around on the ships exterior until he found a panel, then he popped it off and began to work away on whatever components that were hidden in behind it.

Isaac walked back down to the front of the ship and looked up again. Sha'ala was still there but now she was frantic in what she was trying to relay. He looked around over his shoulder off into the distance to try and see anything but there was nothing obvious there.

"Car'esh or Moga. Can you hear me?" Isaac said into his helmet.

As he waited for a response, about ten feet in front of the ship, the ground silently erupted, and a large animal burst out from under the surface. It stood for a second looking directly at Isaac. Isaac tried to take the animal in as best he could from where he was. It was big. About the size of a large dog. It had four legs with massive claws at the end of each one. It looked like it was covered in scales rather than fur, with a long tail extending out from its back, that somewhat resembled that of a rat. It had small eyes, but huge ears that stood up straight and formed a point on either side of its head. It also had what looked like giant whiskers pointing out from both sides of its face, with fangs protruding straight down from out of its mouth, that reminded Isaac of a sabre tooth tiger.

As Isaac was eyeing up the animal, he felt some slight vibrations in the ground beneath his feet and he immediately got the urge to turn and run. Just as he took his first few steps the ground behind him tremored violently as another one of the animals burst out of it, right where Isaac had been standing. Isaac looked back over his shoulder at the animal not five feet away from him as it swiped its giant claw towards him, missing by inches. A quick glance showed that just as Isaac had though, the creature was covered in scales that seemed to move independently from each other.

"Guys we have to move" were the words Isaac tried to scream into his helmet, but it just came out as "Aaaarrgh!"

Niers and Taretta turned around to see what was going on. As Isaac ran towards them, they could see the animal about to make a move towards him. In an instant, both Niers and

Taretta had their side arms off of their hips and were pointing them directly at Isaac.

"Get down on the ground" Taretta shouted at him.

Isaac dropped as quickly as he could and Niers and Taretta both started to unload their weapons into the creature. Energy blasts whizzed over his head toward the unwanted visitor. After they shot it with maybe fifteen direct hits, it just flopped over onto its side, lifeless.

"There's more of them and they're in the ground" Isaac screamed as he picked himself up and ran towards them.

Niers looked past Isaac and saw the second creature burrow its way back down below the surface and disappear.

"Let's go" Niers said to Taretta and they turned and ran back towards the cargo bay, looking back to make sure Isaac was still behind them.

Isaac rounded the corner to the entrance but was stopped in his tracks as he bumped into Niers who had pulled up short of boarding the ship. He was about to ask what the problem was but before he could, he saw the problem sitting just inside the doors. One of the animals had made its way onto the Sao'ise and was blocking their way in. It was staring right at them, probably assessing the threat they posed and waiting for its time to pounce. Niers and Taretta both lifted their weapons to fire, but neither seemed to work and the animal shifted its weight, in a move that suggested it was about to strike. Before either could do anything, the animals chest ruptured and its back blew out, spreading the contents of its innards all over the floor of the cargo bay. Niers, Taretta and Isaac all looked behind them and to their collective delight, saw Car'esh and Moga walking towards them from about thirty feet away. Car'esh was holding a rifle type weapon to his shoulder and it was clear that he had taken the shot that saved them. They walked past their three companions and straight onto the ship.

"We need to get moving" Car'esh said as he pointed to the animal's carcass and directed Isaac and Niers to dump it off the ship.

"Readings we took suggest that the people that attacked us were staged on this planet so it's very likely there's more of them here waiting for a report back. We need to be gone before they realise that report isn't coming."

Isaac and Niers each grabbed an end of the animal. It was heavy and awkward to lift because of the dead weight. They walked it down the ramp, blood dripping from its wound all over the floor of the ship and dropped it on the ground just outside. Niers turned and walked back into the cargo hold but stopped when he realised Isaac was still looking out. Isaac was taking a final moment to look around his first alien planet before he joined him. Niers stood beside him in silence.

"It's wild. My first visit to a different planet. It's pretty beautiful for a barren wasteland populated by monsters" Isaac told him.

"Come on. We must move" Niers replied.

He walked down to go close the doors, when the ground exploded a couple of feet away from him. Isaac saw the rubble fly and watched as another one of the creatures leapt out of the hole. The way it moved, effortless, akin to a great white shark propelling itself up and out of the sea. Isaac reacted on instinct. He reached out and grabbed Niers, pulling him back onto the ship out of the way of the vicious creature, its bite barely missing Niers' arm. Niers fell over and landed on the ground behind him. The creature turned its attention to Isaac and lunged at him. He put his hands up to try and stop the animals advance but it just pushed its head through his arms and sunk its teeth straight into Isaacs left leg. A large spray of blood fired out of him and straight up into the air. The animal lunged again, this time sinking its teeth into Isaac's stomach. Another large spurt erupted from his abdomen firing in several directions, splashing onto the wall just to his right. Isaac was lying on the ground with his hands covering his wounds, watching helplessly as the animal moved forward for a third attack. Its face was met with one of Moga's boots that sent it back a couple of feet out onto the ground, then several blasts hit the animal dead on and it stumbled around for a moment before it slumped over.

Isaac saw the cargo bay doors start to close. He looked down and moved his hands. He could see a mass of bloody strips hanging off his suit but he couldn't distinguish from the hanging scraps what was part of the getup he had on and what was part of his body. He let his head fall back onto the ground so he was looking straight up at the ceiling. Moga, Taretta, Niers and Car'esh were all hovering over him. Car'esh was kneeling down beside him, trying to keep Isaac's intestines inside his body. His hands were a bloody mess. Niers had his helmet off and seemed to be calling for help. Isaac couldn't hear anything. Everything was silent because of the air tight seal the helmet he was wearing had created. The only noise that accompanied the scene he was watching play out over him was a slight ringing in his ears that seemed to grow louder as the seconds passed. He felt what was now the familiar sensation of darkness closing in on him. Then he was gone.

12

Isaac shot up off the table into life from unconsciousness with a start, in what was now the familiar surroundings of the medical bay. He involuntarily shouted something as he rose but wasn't sure what it was. The noises of the machines around him were somewhat comforting now. He glanced around the room and saw Sha'ala was there monitoring his life signs again. She looked over to him as he shifted in the bed.

"This is becoming a bit of a habit for you Isaac" she said with a smile on her face as she walked to his bedside taking readings on her tablet.

"How long was I out?" Isaac asked as he lay back down on the bed.

"It has been a little over twenty four hours. We had to shut your body down to minimum function so it could heal itself. Who is Shelly?"

Isaac wasn't sure how to answer. That must have been what he shouted when he woke up.

"A friend" was all he said.

There was a sharp stinging pain in his side as he shifted his weight, that forced him to re assess his efforts to move.

Then he remembered what had happened to put him back in a medical bed. He moved the blanket to the side that was covering him from the chest down and as it came to rest on his waist, he could see his stomach. There was a large gap in his skin that ran across most of his mid-section. He could see the muscle tissue of his abdomen through a transparent goo that was covering it. It was soft and slimy to the touch. There were little pads attached to him at different areas on his body that bore a resemblance to EKG nodes. Every so often he could feel a tickling sensation emanating from the pads into his body.

At this stage Isaac was beyond panicking about all the new stuff he was seeing every time something happened to him. He was just going to relax and leave it all in the hands of the professionals.

"So what exactly is going on here?" Isaac asked gesturing to his stomach.

"We have applied a medical gel to the open wounds you had. It is not dissimilar to the material we used to fix the ship actually, only this gel contains biological agents as it's used to heal people, not things" Sha'ala told him.

The plural of wounds reminded Isaac that he had also been bitten on the leg, so he moved the blanket down to his knee, exposing a similar picture to his stomach on his upper thigh, only smaller.

"So how long am I looking at before I can get up and move around?" Isaac enquired.

"You should stay immobile for at least one more day, to allow the healing to complete and the gel to set. You will still be required to keep the electrodes attached to you for one more day after that but there will be less strain on your body by then" she told him.

"Ok, so another day of R and R for me it is so."

"R and R?" Sha'ala asked.

"Rest and relaxation. It's a term used on Earth for people who are not allowed to do anything strenuous" Isaac explained to her.

"Ah. Very good. It's a shame Niers is not here as you awaken," Sha'ala said as she moved back across to her desk at the end of Isaacs bed, "he has spent most of his time off at your bedside."

"Why?" Isaac asked as he settled back down under the blanket.

"Well because of what you did to prevent him from injury. It is an incredible thing to put yourself in harm's way to protect another. It would be expected of the crew to do this for each other, but you did it for someone you barely even know. It did not go unnoticed by Car'esh either" she explained to him.

"I didn't even think about it to be honest," Isaac revealed as he lay his head back down and closed his eyes, "I just kind of reacted."

"Well even so, we are all very grateful that you did" Sha'ala said as she walked back to Isaac's bedside and injected something into his arm.

"What's that?" Isaac asked as he could feel his senses getting blurry and his consciousness becoming heavy.

"It's a mild sedative to let you rest a little easier to try and allow the healing process to finish" Sha'ala informed him as he slipped back into slumber.

***

Isaac came too again. He lay there for a minute allowing all his surroundings to come into focus. He immediately became aware that there was someone sitting at his bedside.

96

He looked to his left and saw Niers there, quietly staring at him.

"Hello" Niers said, smiling at him with the broadest smile Isaac had ever seen.

"Hi" Isaac replied as he sat up in his bed.

"I have spoken to Sha'ala and she says that if you wish you may get out of the bed and go for a walk around the ship" Niers told him with a barely concealed note of expectation in his voice.

"Sure," Isaac replied, "it can't hurt to stretch my legs I suppose."

He shifted to his left and moved his feet out of the bed and placed them on the floor. He looked down at his stomach. It was still not fully healed but the muscle tissue was no longer visible. It was now more like skin, just a lighter shade than his own.

"The material will take on the properties and pigmentation of your natural skin colour, you just have to give it time." Niers assured him.

"Hey, I'm just glad not to have a giant hole in my abdomen anymore. Everything else is a bonus" Isaac replied.

"Would you like to get something to eat?" Niers asked Isaac.

"Yeah, all I've had is that protein stuff for over a week now. Some real food would be nice" Isaac said as he picked his new jump suit off the end of his bed and slid it on.

They walked down the corridor and entered the lift. When it reached their desired floor, they got off and walked into the kitchen.

Taretta and Moga were there already eating some food. There was a big pot in the middle of the table which had steam emanating out of it. Isaac sat down in the empty chair beside Moga and smiled at him as he did so. Moga just looked back at Isaac with the usual inexpressive face. Niers placed a bowl in front of Isaac that he had filled with some of the contents from a big pot that was sitting on the table.

"Mana assortment" Niers informed Isaac.

The bowl was filled with a clear broth that seemed to have a medley of different things in it. Most of it looked like different forms of vegetables.

"What's it made from?" Isaac asked.

"It's mostly just whatever plants that we have left over in the stores," Niers informed him as he placed another bowl on the table in front of himself, "whatever we have left in the stores that is about to spoil."

"Well in lieu of a burrito I'll give it a go."

"What's a burrito?" Taretta asked.

"It's a type of food from a place called Mexico. It's like a load of different things, vegetables, meat, guacamole and a couple of other things wrapped up together in a tortilla. It's awesome" Isaac told them, as he thought fondly of his favourite burrito place back home for a minute.

"You miss it" Taretta said.

"Yeah. To be honest I hadn't really thought about it in a while but now that I do, I really want one. My favourite was a place called Taco Taco, but it's gone now. There's a few places that do them that are really good but they're just not the same."

"I miss frab shanks" Taretta told them.

"What are those?" Isaac asked.

"A frab is an animal. They are wild and very elusive which makes them extra tasty. My father used to take me to hunt them on weekends during the summer. We'd always catch a few to bring home, but the first one was always ours to eat. We'd roast it over a pit fire on skewers. It's more about the memory of the time spent with my father and the good times we had than the actual food. But they were delicious."

"Sun cake," Niers said, "My mother was an expert at them. So soft and sweet. They were the reason I was so fat as a child."

The thought of Niers as a fat child drew chuckles from Isaac and Taretta.

"What about you Moga?" Isaac asked.

"Food is fuel. Not pleasure" Moga answered.

"Spoken like a true cocker spaniel" Isaac said in jest.

Niers took a big spoon of the food from the bowl in front of him and emptied it into his mouth.

"Since we are nearing the end of our journey it is prudent to use all the food have on board. It's simple, mainly it's the spices I use that give it its flavour. It's my mother's old recipe."

Isaac lowered his head to take a sniff of the contents of the bowl. It smelled familiar but he couldn't place what it reminded him of. He took a spoon of the stew and was surprised that his immediate reaction wasn't to just spit it back out again. He could get an unusual taste from whatever he was eating. It was something new that he had never experienced before but at the same time there was a familiarity to it that he couldn't pin point.

"It's really good" Isaac exclaimed as he took a second spoonful from the bowl.

"I am glad you like it" Niers said.

"Wait, did you say we are nearing the end of our journey?" Isaac asked with a mouthful of food.

"Yes" Niers replied.

Isaac looked around the table at the three faces staring back at him.

"In three days we will reach Magaly. Once we have finished our business there Car'esh will set about finding the best way to get you home" Taretta informed him.

"Wow," Isaac said, "excellent."

Isaac realised Niers was looking at him from across the table while he was eating. He looked up and put his spoon down.

"What's up Niers?" he asked.

"You seem so eager to leave. You have yet to see what is really out here in the galaxy."

"I don't belong out here man. I have no understanding of how anything works. I'm lost" Isaac told him with sincerity heavy in his voice.

"Do you have people who you left behind?" Taretta enquired.

Isaac sat back and thought about that for a second. His parents lived in France these days. They had retired early a few years ago and moved away. He didn't see them too often anymore but his mother did phone him now and then to check up on him. He and his friends had drifted apart over the last few years too. He would see them at the usual times, Christmas and that but he had no friends he saw on a regular basis. Shelly was it really. He had lost contact with almost everyone he had known and the one person he saw regularly had now left him. It took a second for him to realise that he had become something of a loser.

"One or two." Isaac replied, not wanting to expose his loneliness. "But it's not just that, I'd be lost out here. Where would I go, how would I survive?"

"Well you can live with me until you establish what you want to do" Niers offered.

100

"Look, it's just…" the door opened before Isaac could finish and Car'esh walked in. He sat down beside Isaac and looked him dead in the eye. Neither of them said anything for a moment, they just looked at one another.

"Can I help you?" Isaac finally asked.

"I'm going to ask you this one more time and I want complete honesty from you"

"Of Course" Isaac replied.

"Are you in anyway associated with the corpse in our cargo hold beyond what you have already told us?" Car'esh asked.

Isaac looked around the table and once again everyone was looking at him waiting for him to answer. Before he could speak Niers interjected.

"I believe that Isaac is genuine in all he has told us thus far."

"Let him answer the question please" Car'esh snapped back.

They all looked back at Isaac again and waited one more time.

"I swear to you, I have no association to that man beyond the fact that I met him about two years ago and we became friends. That's it. I don't know anything about his mission. I don't know anything about his allegiances. I don't know anything about him being from another planet. I only ever knew him as Ben. The incredibly awkward but oddly endearing human he was pretending to be" Isaac answered.

Car'esh kept his gaze fixed firmly on Isaacs pupils for a moment longer.

"Follow me, all of you" he said as he stood up and left the room.

101

They all got up and followed him through the ship to the bridge. As he entered the room Isaac saw Car'esh and the others standing next to a monitor and he walked over and stopped in front of it. Car'esh tapped a couple of points on the screen and the display changed to show a picture of another Maglian.

"Observe" Car'esh said as he tapped the centre of the screen and a video began to play.

"Car'esh my friend, I hope you are well. There has been some commotion around here the last few days. I was sent some data to comb through and as I was searching, I found several references to your ship in it. Apparently, you are at the top of a list that some very important people are anxious to find. Something to do with a missing scientist and his odd companion, something called a human. They are supposedly involved with each other relating to something to do with the Ilians and the Assembly are keen to find them. You keep popping up for some reason in the communications. Whatever you are into its trouble. Stay safe."

The message ended and the screen went blank. Isaac looked around at all the faces staring back at him, again lost for words.

"Now hang on a minute. I mean who the fuck is that guy? Why should we believe him? Where's he getting his information from?"

"That is Ran'gis. He's a fellow privateer like myself. We go back a long time. I trust him implicitly" Car'esh answered.

"Well shit man. I mean, fair enough but he's letting the side down here because everything he just told you is wrong. That can't be anything to do with me. Nobody would know who I am. Look whatever this is clearly

102

involved Ben, but I have no connection. I was just in the wrong place at the wrong time after associating with the wrong person."

Car'esh, Taretta, Moga and Niers all looked round at each other.

"Well it would seem the answers we seek can only be found by asking questions of a dead man" Car'esh said as he turned and headed back out the door towards the lift and once again everyone followed behind him.

13

Isaac and Car'esh descended into the lower deck of the ship together. Car'esh had sent everyone else back to their post while he, Isaac and Sha'ala all tried to get to the bottom of their mystery. They travelled in silence. Car'esh seemed to be deep in thought and Isaac didn't want to disturb him. Then the silence got the better of him and he just had to speak.

"So who was the guy in the message?" Isaac blurted out.

"An old friend of mine. He passes on information he receives that I may find useful sometimes and I do the same for him when the opportunity arises" Car'esh replied.

"Where do you think he would have got this information from?"

Car'esh looked at Isaac and for a second Isaac thought he saw a hint of uncertainty for the first time in Car'esh's eyes. Like as if he hadn't considered that before. He turned back to the doors of the lift just as they opened on the med bay deck. They walked out and down the corridor to the space that Isaac had become so familiar with. As they entered Isaac could see that Sha'ala had Bens body out of storage and he was lying on the examination table. He looked more like his natural self now. Some of the human gene treatment was still present but for the most part he had reverted back to his Magalian appearance. His skin was an off shade of green. His eyes were larger, not as big as Car'esh and Sha'ala's, but greater in size than a humans, like they were stuck somewhere between his disguise and his true appearance.

"He will never fully revert back to his original form" Sha'ala said to Isaac like she could read his mind.

"Why would anyone do that to themselves?" Isaac asked her.

"Who knows," Sha'ala replied, "everyone has a different circumstance that forces them into dire decisions. Surely you have people on your world who do drastic things when they find themselves in desperate situations. It's hard to say without knowing."

She turned her attention back to the device in her hand and tapped on the screen inputting information into it.

"So what is it you want me to do?" Isaac asked Car'esh as he turned to face him.

Car'esh was standing at the foot of the table that Ben was on just looking down at him with an expressionless face.

"I'm not sure right now. Sha'ala is going to run some tests on him and I want you here to answer any questions she may have while she is working I suppose" Car'esh informed him.

"Ok, whatever you need" Isaac replied.

Isaac looked down at Ben again. Even though he looked vastly different he could still see his friends face lying there. He felt a little sad about the whole situation. He was looking good for a dead guy to be honest. Isaac had seen a dead body before. The eyes were all sunken in. The skin was much paler. He could make out who the body was but

105

they looked different. That wasn't the case here. Ben didn't look dead, he just looked like he was asleep. Aside from the lack of life signs and the open lifeless eyes looking up at him. This suddenly caught Isaacs attention and he couldn't look away now.

"Can we close his eyes please. The deadness of them is freaking me out a little" he asked.

Sha'ala turned to look and used her fingers to close them over.

"So what have you found Sha'ala? Do you know anything at all new about him?" Car'esh asked.

"Well I only conducted cursory examinations when he and Isaac first came aboard. But now I am running a full audit of the body to try and determine if anything is out of place. So far, apart from the genetic tampering everything seems to be in order."

Sha'ala was cut off by a noise coming from the tablet in her hand. There was a beep followed by a whistle that came from it that drew the attention of everyone in the room.

"What is it?" Car'esh asked her.

"I'm not sure," she replied, "but whatever it is it's in the base of his skull."

She ran the device over Ben's face and then turned to Isaac and Car'esh.

"I'm going to need you to turn him over so I can get a better reading."

Isaac looked at Car'esh to see if he shared his sense of apprehension about what they had just been asked to do but Car'esh was already putting on what looked like a pair of surgical gloves.

"Well come on" Car'esh said as he threw a pair of the gloves at Isaac.

Isaac caught the gloves and put them on. He put his hands under Ben's shoulders while Car'esh grabbed him by the waist. They lifted him up and turned him over so he was face down on the table. Sha'ala came over and ran her hand held tablet over the area she had gotten the signal from and the readout on it changed and displayed a new message.

"There is something giving off a signal inside his body, just below his skull that has remotely connected to my network, it's asking me if I want to activate. What should I do captain?"

"Do you have any idea what it wants you to activate?" Car'esh asked.

"None, it just says activate" Sha'ala replied.

Car'esh pressed a button on a panel on the wall.

"Niers I need you in the infirmary now" he said into it, then returned back over to the table.

"Do you notice anything else out of the ordinary?" he asked.

"Nothing. If it wasn't for this signal that connected to my pad automatically, I wouldn't have known anything was unusual at all."

They all stood there watching the screen as the scanner ran up and down Ben's body. After a couple of moments it stopped and Sha'ala began to relay what the scanner had picked up to Isaac and Car'esh.

"There is a subdermal implant at the top of his spine. That is obviously what's connecting to my network. Other than that everything seems to be normal. I have initiated a full examination of him for everything, down to the cellular level. So that should give us a full understanding of what's going on" she explained, as Isaac sat there not fully understanding much of anything that had just been said.

107

"Subdermal means below the skin right?" Isaac asked, trying to fit himself in to the conversation so he wouldn't appear stupid.

"Yes" Sha'ala replied looking at him and waiting for him to add more to the question.

After a moment Isaac realised she was waiting for him to contribute more but he didn't have anything else to say.

"No, that's all. I was just making sure" he said.

She looked at him a moment longer then turned her attention back to the screen that the scanner was reading out on. As they were watching the readout Niers came into the room behind them.

"Niers I need you to have a look at this information and see if you can tell us anything about the device that's buried under his skin" Car'esh said.

"It's lodged just at the base of his skull if that helps" Sha'ala added.

Niers walked over to the readout and began to comb through the words that were on the screen. He sifted around the data while Isaac looked at the monitor over his shoulder. There was a lot of information on it and Niers was running his finger over certain passages as he read them.

Isaac walked back over to the table and looked back down at Ben. He was remembering the times they had spent together in the two years he had known him. They were good times. Isaac realised they were the only really good times he had had over that whole period. Ben had been a friend. The best one Isaac could remember in recent years. He felt his sadness well up again. This time it lodged in his throat like a ball and Isaac had to do everything he could to choke it down and not have it explode out of him into a fit of tears. His attention was brought back to the room as Niers spoke.

"I can't be certain but it looks like a data storage device. Only it seems to be way more sophisticated than anything that is commercially available. There seems to be 100 times the amount of storage space on it than your high end data disc and from what I can tell, it's very close to capacity" Niers told them.

"Any idea what it's storing?" Isaac asked.

"I can't tell. It's encrypted. This is military grade encryption Car'esh. But the strange thing is, from what I can tell, the activate prompt that we are getting will decrypt it so the only way to know for sure is to turn it on" Niers said, as he looked away from the screen to them.

"Why would something have military grade encryption but then be accessible by just turning it on?" Car'esh pondered out loud to himself.

"Anything that you've seen before?" Niers asked him.

"No. It's very strange."

"Well it sounds like the most obvious trap ever concocted but I suppose the only way to find out is to turn it on and see" Isaac offered.

They all turned to look at him, and then back to each other.

"That sounds like your eager to have me activate it. Why? What will happen if I do?" Car'esh asked Isaac, eying him up suspiciously.

"You know what man. Turn it on. Don't turn it on. Bring this dead body home with you, or fire it out into space. I don't give a bollocks what you do" Isaac replied, frustrated by the continuing display of distrust being constantly levelled at him.

109

"I think it's strange that it wasn't there before but now it's asking us to connect to it, but at the same time we need to figure out what's going on. So we must activate it" Sha'ala told Car'esh.

Car'esh looked around at them one more time then back to Ben lying on the table.

"Alright, let's see what it has to say for itself. Niers, isolate this room from the network in the rest of the ship. I don't want any surprises that will leave us vulnerable" he instructed.

Niers tapped a couple of things on the screen in front of him.

"Ready" he said once he was finished.

Sha'ala looked at the pad in her hand one last time, going over the material that was on the screen in front of her. As she did this Isaac walked over to the table and stood beside Ben. He looked down at him for what he knew would be one last time.

"Ok, here we go" Sha'ala said as she pushed the button on her tablet.

The information started to stream to Niers' screen immediately. It flashed down the monitor far too quickly to read.

"Wow," Niers said, "look at all this."

"What is it?" Car'esh asked.

"I'm not sure, it's all different types of material from what I can gather, completely sporadic. Species population estimates, topographic maps, general observations and suppositions. There is a lot of it though."

They all stood around looking at the data as it transferred onto Niers' work station. Instantly the flow of information stopped and a warning flashed on the readout.

"What's that?" Isaac asked.

"I'm not sure," Niers replied, "but I don't think it's good."

Like the living dead, Ben shot up on the table into a seated position and looked directly at Isaac.

"Ben!" Isaac exclaimed as a big broad smile crept across his face, then a narrow frown swept across his brow.

Ben just stared at him cold, with no emotion expressed in his demeanour at all. The rest of the room turned around to look at Isaac not realising that Ben had returned to the living, as they had been distracted by what was appearing on the screen. As they did Isaac felt a hand grab him around his throat and squeeze. It didn't instantly register with him it was Ben's until in a quick singular movement, Ben seemed to slide his legs around from behind him and somehow wrap them around Isaacs neck. This was especially troubling to Isaac as he realised, just as Ben moved toward him, that he was still naked and the Magalian male anatomy appeared to have a striking resemblance to the human one. As Ben bound his legs around Isaacs neck and forced him to the floor, his well-endowed penis poked Isaac in the eye. Isaac felt his back hit the ground but he couldn't see what was going on around him. All he could see was Ben's member sliding up and down, back and forth across his face, while his testicles rubbed on his chin.

Isaac could hear the commotion going on around him intermittently. Every few seconds he could hear a shout or a scream from one of the crew, then his ears would be plugged by Ben's thighs as they closed tighter around his head. The pressure seemed to loosen for a moment and Isaac opened his mouth wide and drew in a deep breath of air but unfortunately he couldn't get it closed in time before Ben's testicle came plunging down and slid straight inside.

As Isaac lay there gaging, he realised he faced a choice that no man wishes to face. He closed his eyes, braced himself and bit down, hard.

He held on with his teeth for what seemed like a solid ten seconds. The crushing pressure of Ben's thighs around his head grew and grew the more he bit down. Isaac was close to passing out when suddenly he felt Ben's weight move upward off him and he let the grip his teeth had on Ben's scrotum go. What were the muffled sounds in the room, now became clearer as Ben's thighs were no longer restricting Isaac's hearing. He could hear a loud scream echoing around the room. It took him a second to realise it was Ben making the noise.

Isaac stood up and looked around at everyone. Car'esh and Niers were holding Ben down on the floor. Sha'ala was behind him lying on the ground. She was conscious but was clearly hurt. Isaac realised she must have been knocked down during the commotion that had been going on while he had been trapped. He got up and ran over to her.

"Hey, are you alright? What can I do?" Isaac asked her.

"I'll be fine," she assured him, "just a little shaken up."

Isaac turned back to Car'esh and Niers just as Moga came running in the door. He looked down at the three men who were wrestling with each other on the floor and dived down and on top of them.

After an epic struggle that could have went either way due to Ben's seemingly excellent ability to remain elusive from restraint, the three of them manage to subdue him. Isaac was impressed by Ben's ability to almost handle three people at the same time, especially Moga. While Car'esh held him in a choke hold from behind, Moga and Niers managed to get him back down onto the table and Sha'ala activated the restraints attached to it, which lassoed around his shoulders, chest, waist and thighs and held Ben in place. He continued to struggle against them for a moment before realising it was a futile endeavour.

"Release me fools" Ben demanded.

"Ben, it's me," Isaac said to him as he put his hands on Bens shoulders, "do you recognise me? It's Isaac. Your friend."

Ben jerked and moved around reacting to the touch of Isaac's hands.

"Take your hands from me vermin, I am not Ben and you are not my friend. You were a tool I used to complete my mission."

Isaac let go and moved back a couple of feet away from the table. His shoulders slumped down and he just stood there staring at the floor.

Car'esh looked at him and then down at Ben on the table.

"Then who are you," he demanded, "and why are you on my ship?"

Ben began thrashing around on the table again trying to release himself from his restraints. After a few hopeless attempts, he stopped and turned to look at Isaac once more.

"I am the herald of the new rulers of you pitiful fools and I bring evisceration to the humans of Earth" he said as he began struggling against his restraints again with another attempt to free himself.

"What the actual fuck does that mean you absolute psycho?" Isaac shouted at him.

As this was happening, Sha'ala came up behind him and injected him with a sedative that made him pass out instantaneously.

14

Isaac and Niers unstrapped Ben from the table and lifted him into a chair that was fixed to the floor beside it. Then Sha'ala placed some medical restraints around him to hold him in place. Isaac took a step back and leaned on the table looking down at Ben.

"So, I have a very obvious question. How is he not dead?" Isaac asked, still shaken.

"There are black market devices that you can get a hold of. They can put your body into a hibernation like state that would simulate the appearance of death" Sha'ala told him.

"Yeah. That's cool and all. I'm sure there's all manner of nifty gadgets for all sorts of fucked up shit available. But what I mean is, he was in the boot of the car when I crashed into the wall. I was wearing a seatbelt, he wasn't. How did that not kill him?"

Everyone in the room looked at each other but nobody offered an answer. None of them had one. Car'esh had been rooting in a box of the medical supplies and he came over to stand beside Isaac, placing some equipment on the table that could have been ear bud headphones, except they had little antennas sticking out of the bottom and a little interface that connected to them.

"Are you alright?" he asked turning to Isaac.

"I suppose so. I mean it's a bit crazy all that's going on but to be fair him being a nut job pretending to be my friend is actually not the craziest thing that has happened to me recently. So I suppose that's a plus" Isaac replied as he turned to Car'esh and forced the best smile he could muster.

"Good, at least now I have the answer to whether I can trust you or not" Car'esh said picking the equipment up off the table again.

"Yay, good for you."

"Now we need information from him and there is only one way I think we can get that with what we have available to us, but it's quite crude."

"Car'esh no, you can't" Sha'ala interjected, but Car'esh just shot her a look that suggested there was to be no objections at this moment, it was happening.

"Fine" she said trying to hide the emotion in her voice as she walked past them and out the door.

"You may leave too if you wish Isaac," Car'esh said as he reached down and attached a node to each one of Bens testicles, "this man was your friend and this won't be pretty."

"No," Isaac insisted, "I'll stay if it's all the same to you."

"Very well." Car'esh replied, as he tapped away on the screen of the device he was holding in his hand.

"So what's the plan here then," Isaac asked, pointing to what Car'esh was doing, "are you going to shock his balls to get him to talk?"

"Shock his balls?" Niers asked.

"That thing you just attached to him. Are you going to send electric shocks to his testicles to get him to give us information?"

"No," Car'esh replied as he and Niers exchanged glances, "it is like that but a bit different."

"Oh, different how?"

"Well first of all I'm going to wake him up" Car'esh said, striking Ben across the face with the back of his hand.

Ben's head turned abruptly with the force of the blow and he snapped into consciousness, immediately surveying the room around him.

"You are all dead already fools" he snarled at them.

"Now what?" Isaac asked.

"Now I'm going to melt his genitals" Car'esh roared.

As the words left his lips everyone looked down between Bens legs, just as Car'esh pushed on the screen in his hand. There was a brief but intense flash. Bens penis and testicles disappeared and were now just a puddle of slime dripping off the chair and onto the floor. He screamed out, but to Isaac it seemed to be a scream of rage rather than agony. He couldn't look away from the mess that was formerly Ben's genitals oozing over the side of the chair and his stomach started to churn. Once the smell of it hit his nostrils he couldn't keep control of his faculties and he threw the entire contents of his stomach up, right into Ben's face.

"Nicely done" Car'esh said as he turned to look at Isaac with a smile on his face.

"What the fuck?!" Isaac screamed.

"Put them back. Put them back now you desta" Ben demanded.

"What the fuck?!" Isaac repeated.

"What?" Car'esh asked Isaac.

116

"You've melted his dick. You're supposed to start off light and work your way up to dick melting, not go all in with it up front."

"He knows what we want and once he gives it to us I will fix him" Car'esh replied.

"How? You've flash fried his cock and balls into soup."

"The system automatically saved the genetic schematic of his, dick, as you say, in the ships medical memory core. Once he tells us who he is and who he works for all with be righted, isn't that correct, Ben" Car'esh said with a sneer.

"I will kill you slowly desta if you do not fix this now" Ben said staring at Car'esh.

"Who are you," Car'esh demanded, "what is your name?"

"Isaac," Ben said looking away from Car'esh towards him, "as we are familiar with each other I will reason with you. Stop this now and I will do my best to have you spared."

"Spared from what?" Isaac pleaded with him.

"From what is coming to you all" Ben hissed at him.

Car'esh walked over to the table and picked up another node. He walked back to Ben and stuck it to his left shoulder. Without saying anything he just tapped the screen again and in a flash, so to speak, his arm was now in the same state as his penis, running down his side. This time Isaac held it together.

"What is your real name?" Car'esh demanded of Ben again.

"Desta" Ben snapped at Car'esh.

"Tell me now or I will do it" Car'esh warned him.

"Do What? Is this not enough? There's an it to follow all this mutilation?" Isaac asked.

"As of now I have muted the neural pathways in his brain to the pain receptors in his body. If he does not simply tell

117

me his name I will turn them back on. Can you imagine what that would feel like?" Car'esh asked as he turned away from Isaac to stare straight into Ben's eyes.

"No thanks" Isaac said.

"Because I know what it feels like" Car'esh added.

"Jesus," Isaac offered as he too turned to look at Ben, "I'd tell him your name if I was you."

"I have no name that would mean anything to you," Ben screamed at them, "I was freed of its burden when I was gifted with a celebrated purpose."

Car'esh looked over Ben's shoulder at Niers who was looking right back at him. They both had a similar puzzled expression on their face.

"What purpose?" Niers asked from behind Ben.

"What are you rambling about?" Car'esh followed up.

Ben turned away from Car'esh and looked at Isaac.

"Listen to me. I will say this one last time. You set me free or I swear to you, once I have liberated myself from your ship I will return to Earth and I will visit unspeakable horrors onto the girl you love. I will tear her heart from her chest and eat it raw in front of her as I fuck the hole that I rip it out of."

Isaac felt the blood drain from his face. At first he thought it was fear but he soon realised it was anger that was welling up inside of him. He turned to the table and he grabbed a node from it and marched over to Ben. As he did, he snatched the device from Car'esh's hand.

"How does this work?" he asked him.

"You place the node on his body then you press that button there" Car'esh said as he pointed to the device.

"Last chance you absolute shit heap," Isaac said as he looked at Ben, "tell us what we want to know or I'm gonna put this last one on you and then turn your pain back on."

118

"Desta" Ben said as he spat in Isaacs face.

Isaac didn't even hesitate. His fury reached a climax inside his head as he felt the warm saliva running down his nose and drip onto his bottom lip. He slapped the node right in the middle of Ben's forehead and slammed his hand down on the button on the device. He raised his eyes back up to meet Bens, just in time to catch a look on his face that conveyed a combination of both confusion and terror, as once again the flash of brilliant light ignited in the room and Bens head disintegrated into a puddle of ooze, that ran down his chest onto the chair, before combining with the mess that was his genitals and overflowing onto the ground below.

"Oh My" Niers exclaimed.

"What did you do?" Car'esh asked, stunned.

Isaac looked around at both of them as they stared at him in disbelief.

"What? Just do your advanced space whammy on him and grow him back" Isaac instructed them.

"The brain is a complex organism. Too complex to be stored on a simple ship core" Niers explained to him.

"It only works on limbs and organs" Car'esh interjected.

"There is no space whammy to fix him" Niers continued.

"You've killed him" Car'esh finished.

Isaac looked at them both with the anticipation that they would start laughing or something to show they were joking but they just stared at him in shock.

"I killed him?" he asked as he looked back down at the half man half puddle that was Ben.

The three of them stood in silence for a minute before it was broken by a tinkling sound of something metal hitting the floor.

119

Car'esh and Niers looked down to see what had caused the noise but Isaac continued to stare off into space. Niers saw a gleam out of the corner of his eye and spotted the small metal object sitting on the floor with blood covering most of it. He bent down to pick it up.

"What is it?" Car'esh asks as he rose back up from the floor.

"Well, at the very least it looks like you have gotten us the subdermal implant" Niers replied.

"Do you think you can get us into it?" Car'esh asked.

"I'm not sure. But I will certainly try" Niers answered.

The two of them walked out of the room and left Isaac standing beside what was left of Ben. He stood there, contemplating. He had just killed someone. Not by accident either. Well technically it was by accident because he didn't realise the consequences of what he was doing but all the same, it was he who had directly caused the expiration of another being. How could his conscience process this? He was a murderer. As he was thinking all this Niers popped his head back in the door of the med bay.

"Come on Isaac, let's go" he urged.

Isaac looked up at him, snapping out of his vacant stare.

"I killed him" he whispered.

"Yes, but it's ok," Niers said trying to ease Isaacs guilt, "he was, as you've said before, a shit heap."

"I suppose" Isaac nodded in agreement.

He took one last look at Ben and then followed Niers out of the room.

They walked towards the lift where Car'esh was waiting for them. As they got in and the doors closed behind them he turned to Isaac.

"Is that the first person you've killed?" he asked.

120

"Of course," Isaac replied, a little taken aback by the question, "I've done a lot of firsts since I came aboard this ship."

"You will get over it, particularly since he was not a nice person to begin with. In time, you will see" Car'esh offered as consolation.

"I take it you've knocked more than a few people off in your time?" Isaac asked Car'esh.

"Of course," Car'esh replied nonchalantly, "I served in the MOA for years when I left my planet."

"What's the MOA?"

"Military of the Assembly. It's a joint military peace keeping venture between the cooperative nations of the Assembly. Everyone who lives on this ship has taken the life of another in some way."

"Except Sha'ala" Niers interjected.

"Yes except Sha'ala," Car'esh agreed, "her aim is to save lives, not take them."

Isaac felt a cold shiver run down his spine. He had never thought of it before but he was surrounded by a bunch of rogues and killers and now, without even trying, he had become one of them.

15

As the doors to the lift opened Car'esh got off first and headed straight to the cockpit. Niers got off and walked over to a station in the control centre and sat down. Isaac followed Niers and sat in the seat beside his. Niers was already frantically typing into the console as Isaac joined him. He was furiously tapping away at the keyboard and watching the readout intently.

"So like, how many people have you killed?" Isaac asked him tentatively.

"Oh a few, not as many as Moga though" Niers replied with a smile.

"Right, and…." Isaac started.

"Sorry Isaac but this conversation will have to wait I'm afraid. I need all my focus on the task at hand" Niers said as he cut him off.

"Sure, sure. No problem." Isaac replied backing off a bit.

"I sense you have a problem with it but let us just say that everyone I have killed were far from innocent" Niers offered as he continued to try and crack the device they had gotten from Ben.

"Yeah, no, totally get it. No problem" Isaac said.

"Oh no" Niers said as he looked away from the screen for the first time since sitting down.

"What's up?" Isaac asked him.

"Car'esh, we have a serious problem," Niers said into the intercom not answering Isaac, "you need to see this."

Isaac turned to the entrance to the cockpit and saw Car'esh come steaming out the door and walk right up behind him. He stood there looking over Isaacs shoulder at the screen in front of him.

"What is it?" Car'esh asked Niers.

"The device was activated for a reason" Niers began.

"What?" Isaac asked.

"Since it was dormant when we took him aboard there was no signal to read, but once it was activated, either by the initial crew that attacked us or by Ben himself, after we woke him it has started broadcasting" Niers explained.

"Broadcasting what?" Car'esh asked with a concerned tone in his voice.

"It's location."

"Well can you turn it off?" Isaac asked him.

"No. I still can't access the device. It is still sealed with military encryption. There is no way I can get into it to turn it off. All I can do is read the signal its broadcasting."

"So why can we read some of the data on it then?" Car'esh asked Niers.

"The file that transmits the signal they are most likely trying to track is in one of the devices directories. Whatever else is in there must have to be decrypted for the tracker to work. So once we accessed the drive the signal was activated. But most of what is in the file is just random information. Maps of urban areas, population estimations and other random things. Nothing that would mean anything without seeing the full contents of the device.

123

I've managed to scramble the signal for now but it's a complex algorithm that's constantly adapting, eventually it's going to find a way around the enclosure I've fenced it into and start to transmit a location" Niers explained to them.

Car'esh moved away from the console and took a couple of steps back to sit on a ledge behind him. He seemed to be taking all the information in, unfazed as far as Isaac could see. A couple of moments passed before he offered them his thoughts.

"Can you find out who is tracking it?" he finally asked Niers.

"No," Niers responded immediately, as if he had anticipated this question, "like I said the entire thing is locked behind military encryption. The best thing for us to do would be to eject it from the ship now before we move on any further."

Car'esh pondered this for a moment as he walked around the control centre looking off into the distance.

"No, I think that's a mistake. This is obviously very valuable to someone. The crew that attacked us would have at the very least sent a transmission that would have identified us to whoever they are working for. I think that no matter where we go now in the civilised galaxy, once we hit atmosphere we'll be identified" Car'esh said as he pondered some more.

"Well who hired you to retrieve it? Surely they're the one tracking it. Why don't you just pay them a visit?" Isaac asked.

"We were hired through an agent. They wouldn't even know who the job came from" Car'esh answered.

"So what do we do?" Niers asked him.

124

"We need to get ahead of this thing. We have become involved in something big but we're flying blind. We have no idea what it is and that puts us at a disadvantage. We need information" Car'esh decided.

"So how do we get that?" Isaac asked.

"I need to make contact with an old acquaintance and see if he can tell us anything" Car'esh explained.

He turned towards the middle of the room and walked over to another console. Niers walked after him but stood off to the side a little. Isaac followed and did the same. Car'esh tapped at the keys on the console and the screen if front of him flashed into life. A single word appeared in the middle of it and Isaac just stood there waiting to see what was about to happen rather than ask. Then the screen changed and a Magalian appeared on it. Isaac couldn't be sure but it seemed to be male and if he had to guess he would say that this Magalian was older than Car'esh.

"Aba'dal" Car'esh said in a tone that would suggest they were friendly with each other.

"Car'esh," the other Magalian replied in a less friendly tone, "as good as it is to see you, I'm afraid I know why you are speaking to me. Is the line secure?" Aba'dal asked.

"Of course," Car'esh replied, "how much trouble am I in?" Car'esh said, half-jokingly but with genuine concern present in his voice.

"Far more than the last time we spoke I am afraid" Aba'dal replied.

"What can you tell me?" Car'esh enquired.

"Some, but not a lot and certainly not over this channel, as secure as it might be. What is the nearest colonized world you can make it to from where you are?" Aba'dal asked.

Car'esh looked over to Niers who was already looking through the navigation system on a different console.

125

"Tuchan" Niers said to Car'esh.

"Tuchan" Car'esh repeated to Aba'dal.

"I'm sending you a location. I will meet you there in fifteen hours. Be safe my friend" Aba'dal said.

The screen went blank and Aba'dal was gone. Car'esh pressed the intercom button.

"Taretta, get us to Tuchan a soon as you can" he said into it.

"Ok we'll just about make it with the fuel we have left" Taretta said back through the intercom.

"It would seem that Aba'dal was concerned" Niers said to Car'esh.

"I know," Car'esh replied, "that is a worry."

"So what now?" Isaac asked them.

"Now we get to Tuchan early see what we've gotten ourselves into" Car'esh replied.

16

Isaac sat in his room at the desk looking at the screen. He had been spending his last few hours going over the state of the galaxy he now found himself in. The different players in the top roles, the public opinion of them and just getting a sense of what was going on. From what he could tell the Galactic Assembly was comprised of three delegates who rotated every few years and were appointed, not elected. Each species was free to make their own laws and govern themselves on their own world and any colony that was initially settled by them. Any colony that had been settled as part of a galactic initiative was ruled under the defined galactic code and laws. Tuchan was one of those worlds.

Most governments followed the Galactic Assembly laws nowadays as it made things more uniform and produced less administrative red tape in terms of dealing with the other species. There did however seem to be a growing movement in each society to have less interference form the Assembly in domestic affairs and to move a little back to their own customs and traditions. One group in particular that stood out to Isaac was Kassai Faith, a growing group of Ilians with an ethnocentric position who had taken to violence recently to try and segregate any non Ilian on their home world.

From what Isaac could tell Tuchan was initially settled as a mining colony. There was a gold rush type situation on the planet a decade ago, when a large cache of mineral deposits was discovered. It turned out that this came from a falsified report from the company who did the initial scan, as they were trying to garner interest in the planet. There had been a flurry of settlements developed around the main spaceport on the planet's surface that have since been occupied by less desirable types after the truth about the report came out. Now the planet is known for having one of the highest crime rates in the settled galaxy.

The low hum that permeated the ship changed in tone going lower and Isaac felt his bodyweight shift outside of his own control. He knew this meant they had entered the atmosphere of the planet. He got up from his console and left, heading towards operations. He boarded the lift and began his ascent to the top deck. When the doors opened he was met by Niers, who was standing at the entrance and almost appeared to be waiting for him. Niers stepped into the lift and put his hand on Isaacs shoulder to stop him from stepping off.

"I need you to help me load the transport before we land" Niers said.

"But I was gonna go down to watch us land on the bridge. I've never seen another settled world before" Isaac replied.

"You can see it when we land. I need your help now" Niers said, with a little tone of annoyance in his voice.

"Aw!" Isaac bemoaned as he slumped back against the wall in the lift, while Niers pressed the button to descend back down to the cargo bay.

Isaac hadn't missed the tone in Niers voice. He also couldn't help but notice the awkward silence in the lift on the way down. He didn't even shift in his position so as not to break the stillness, then he became aware of his efforts to remain absolutely motionless and couldn't help but feel more and more uncomfortable. The lift doors opening on the cargo bay was a sweet relief and Isaac rushed off passed Niers.

"Is everything alright?" Isaac blurted out almost involuntarily.

Niers looked up at him with what seemed like a slightly puzzled look on his face.

"Fine. Put that box that's right at your feet there in the rear of the transport and then lock it up please" Niers said and he turned to pick another box up himself.

Isaac did as he asked, getting the hint that he was not going to get anything more out of Niers even if there was something wrong. He picked up the box and carried it over to the back of what Niers was referring to as the transport. It was a vehicle that had been covered by a tarp in the corner of the cargo bay, which was obviously going to be used in ferrying them to their destination. It looked kind of similar to an old Range Rover, that had its wheels and roof removed. There were two seating compartments, like the front and back seats of a car. The back storage compartment was long and flat, with all the equipment they were bringing with them now fully loaded in it. Isaac couldn't help but notice that the space was predominantly occupied by guns a couple of boxes, the contents of which were a mystery.

"Are they going to fight a small war here?" Isaac asked jokingly as he looked up to where Niers was but he was alone. He looked around in the silence. He couldn't shake the feeling that something was off.

The lift doors opened and Car'esh, Moga and Taretta came walking off and headed straight towards the transport. Car'esh threw a jacket at Isaac as he climbed into the vehicle.

"Put that on and get in" he said as he started the ignition.

The engine flashed into life as the bottom of the vehicle lit up and it raised itself off the ground by about twenty inches. Moga climbed into the seat in the front beside Car'esh and Taretta got into the seat behind Moga. Isaac put the jacket on and climbed in behind Car'esh.

"Why exactly am I coming with you?" he asked as he sat down.

"We'll explain when we get there" Car'esh answered as he slammed down on the accelerator. Isaac heard a roar of engines fire up as the transport kicked into life, flying forward, sending Isaac backwards into his seat. They exited the Cargo bay and sped out into the space port of Tuchan.

The city flew past Isaac too quickly at first for him to get a sense of his surroundings. All he noticed was the sky above him. It was getting dark. They must have arrived in the evening. The hue in the sky was a mixture of dark blue and light pink, the two colours entangled with each other in all directions, like someone had spilled two vials of ink across it and one was bleeding into the other. A flock of birds flew overhead high up, changing directions several times in unison, like a murmuration of starlings back home. As he settled down into his seat the city came into focus. It wasn't spectacular by any stretch of the imagination. It was mostly two and three story buildings lining the street they were travelling down. They passed several turns, each one lined with similar structures to the ones they were speeding past. In fact, the word city was being generous Isaac thought. It was more like a town. One from the old west in nineteenth century America. The path they were driving on was pretty much a dirt track. There was no paved road. The buildings, although sturdy looking, reminded him of the old saloons and haberdashery you would see portrayed in a Clint Eastwood spaghetti western. Some of them had flashing signs on the front. The street they were driving on was relatively empty and seemed to be heading in a straight line away from the space port. It was something of a disappointment for him. He had been expecting Blade Runner, or something similar at the very least. What he was seeing was more like Blackpool. Run down and tacky looking. Isaac leaned over to Taretta.

"Where are we going?" he yelled above the noise of the open top vehicle as they whizzed through the sprawl.

"Our meeting place is in a drinks establishment just on the edge of the city" she shouted back.

"Are we expecting much trouble when we get there?" Isaac asked, gesturing to the back of the car that contained all the guns they had loaded on.

"No," Taretta smiled, "that's just Moga being paranoid."

Isaac sat back and watched as the rest of the city pass him by. Eventually they slowed down and pulled off the main road into a smaller side street that led down to the intergalactic equivalent of a car park. They pulled up alongside another transport not too dissimilar to theirs and got out.

Car'esh and Moga lead the way towards the door of the bar while Isaac and Taretta followed behind. Isaac had pulled the hood on his jacket up over his head on the instruction of Taretta to hide his appearance. Not only had everyone in the place they were about to enter not seen a human before, they didn't even know they existed.

Just as Moga was about five feet from the door it burst open from the inside and an inebriated Magalian came stumbling out in front of them. He took a minute to steady himself before looking up at the oncoming foursome. Moga and Car'esh stopped for a moment as he was blocking the door. The patron eyeballed them one last time before he reached around and pulled a gun from some concealed location behind his back and raised it, pointing it directly at Car'esh.

"That's them," the drunk man shouted, now seeming a lot less worse for ware, "all positions move in."

Immediately, they were surrounded from all angles. On top of the bar four armed men stood up from behind a parapet and pointed their weapons at them. Another crew of about seven or eight came in from all sides out of what seemed to be nowhere, surrounding them.

Car'esh and Moga both made moves to draw their weapons when a voice called out from behind them.

"Don't be foolish, we have you" it said.

All four turned around to see where the voice had come from. They were met with the sight of an Ilian, wearing a very official looking military uniform walking towards them. Isaac had seen an Ilian on the Sao'ise after they boarded them, when he first came aboard. Although the one he had seen before was expired so it wasn't a perfect example of the race. His skin was black. So black that it seemed to absorb the light around him. He had big bulbous eyes, golden yellow. His head was quite round and his neck was quite slim, like a golf ball sitting on top of a tee. He had no hair to speak of and no nose either. Just two small slits in his face that ran down between his eyes. There were no real discernible features to him other than that. But still he looked different to the one that Moga had killed inside Isaacs quarters. Car'esh, Moga and Taretta all had a look of recognition on their face. Well Car'esh and Taretta did, Moga just did the thing where he turned his head sideways like a confused dog.

"Lower your weapons please. Let's not make this a bigger incident than it already is" the uniformed Ilian ordered.

Four of the armed attackers moved forward towards them while the other four stayed at a distance with their guns pointed firmly in the direction of Isaac and his crew. They reached out and disarmed them. One approached Isaac and when he realised he didn't have a weapon in his hands he started to search him.

"Get your fucking hands out of there!" Isaac demanded as the soldier rooted around under his jacket.

He pushed the soldier's hands away, so the soldier raised his gun and put it right in Isaacs face.

"He's not armed" Taretta pleaded with him.

The soldier didn't budge. He kept his rifle pointed right between Isaacs eyes. Isaac wasn't sure where it was coming from, but he felt a surge of defiance swell up through his body and he just stared the soldier down.

"Alright, that's enough," the uniformed man commanded, "all of you, into the empty building over there."

He gestured to an open door about thirty feet away. Car'esh and Moga headed off towards the door in silence and Taretta grabbed Isaac by the arm and lead him away after them.

"What's going on? Isaac asked Taretta.

"I don't know, but I believe we will be not long waiting for answers" Taretta replied.

133

Isaac followed Moga through the door and once Taretta came behind him it slammed, closing them in. They were in complete darkness for a moment before the room illuminated. It was just a big empty warehouse and once again the four of them were surrounded by the armed posse that had ambushed them. The uniformed man was standing in front of them staring at Isaac with a bemused look on his face. The sound of Car'esh's voice pulled his attention away from Isaac.

"Sir, with all due respect, what exactly is going on here?" Car'esh asked.

"Sir?" Isaac said, confused.

The uniformed man just stared at Car'esh for a moment without saying a word.

"Sir?" Car'esh said again.

"Sir?" Isaac echoed, but Talking to Moga.

"General Olan'ko," Moga said looking at Isaac, "military leader for Ilians. Sometimes he work with our commander."

"Your commander?" Isaac yelled.

"Yes. One of" Moga said.

"I thought you were a group of misfits who just got together to find work?" Isaac asked completely shaken.

"No, military task force" Moga answered.

Isaac looked around the room at his three companions. He was stunned, confused and hurt. They had been lying to him all this time. He was just coming around to accepting them as allies, people who were going to help him get home and now he was finding out they hadn't been who they had claimed to be all this time. They were probably complicit in his abduction in some way.

"Alright, that will do" General Olan'ko said to Moga.

"We are under instructions from Commander Aba'dal to bring the human here to meet him and await further orders" Car'esh said to the general.

"Over ruled" Olan'ko said bluntly.

"Why?" Car'esh asked.

"Chain of command" Olan'ko said looking at Car'esh, a little surprised at the insubordinate tone in his voice.

"With all due respect sir, I don't answer to you" Car'esh started before being cut off.

"With all due respect, you had orders from a commander, now those orders are being superseded by a general. This is an Ilian matter and will be treated as such" Olan'ko hissed.

"So what now?" Car'esh asked.

"Now you are to relinquish your prisoner and turn him over to me to be transported the rest of the way" the general commanded.

"We weren't aware he was a prisoner" Taretta interjected.

"Perhaps that is why you are being relieved of your mission" the general snapped back at her.

"But…" Taretta began.

"You have your orders," Olan'ko bellowed, "relinquish the human and report back to your commander for a new assignment."

Car'esh, Moga and Taretta all looked at each other before turning to look at Isaac.

"All yours sir" Car'esh said stepping back and walking out the door of the warehouse. Moga and Taretta followed him without saying another word and the door closed behind them as Isaac looked around the room at the soldiers surrounding him. He had only just begun to get accustomed to being on the ship with the crew he knew and now he was being sent off with some military people to God knows where against his will.

"So, where to gentlemen? Know any good spots for a night on the town?" Isaac asked light heartedly.

He felt his arms being pulled back and before he knew it his hands were being cuffed together. He tried to protest but before he could utter a word, he felt a sharp sting in the back of his head, then he lost consciousness.

17

Isaac came too, slowly. It started with sounds he could hear around him that seemed to be leading him back to sentience. His head was cloudy and he couldn't really focus. His vision was hazy and as he looked around all he could make out was the difference between the bright patches of the room and the dark ones. He could hear some voices talking now but couldn't make out what they were saying. They sounded like they were in the distance and there was an echo to them that made it hard to focus on the words. Then he felt a pressure clasp around his arm. He strained to raise his head but all he could make out was the outline of someone standing in front of him. Their voice was closer sounding but it was still imperceptible, it was just louder. Then he felt a slight sting in his wrist. A second later the whole room around him exploded into focus and he was immediately mindful of everything surrounding him. The walls were a crisp white, a sterile colour. There was a table about five feet in front of him with all sorts of implements and needles lying on it. There were several screens off to his right and he was fastened securely by his wrists and his sternum to some form of table, that was standing vertically. The two people who were in the room talking to each other were standing beside the table in front of Isaac and they had now both fixed their gaze firmly on him.

They had white lab suits on, a one piece type of overall which had a white hood attached to them that was pulled up over their head. They were both wearing masks which were the same white colour as the suits, that covered the bottom half of their faces and completed the ensemble, so basically all Isaac could see was their eyes. Even so, he could easily tell that they were Ilians. It was the bulbous yellow eyes that gave them away. The one on his left spoke.

"Yes, that adreno shot has worked alright, he's fully conscious and alert" it said, a distinct soft female sound to it.

"Good job on estimating the dosage too. I was worried we might have over compensated and blown his respiratory system to pieces" her anonymous colleague replied. Isaac could tell it was a man.

"Blown my what to where?" Isaac asked.

"We should start with a full dissection and then go from there" the woman suggested.

"Yes, I agree" the man concurred.

"Start with dissection?" Isaac shouted in horror.

He tried to move again, struggling in vain. The woman approached him and plunged a needle into his arm, without any hesitation in doing so. Isaac felt a stinging sensation run up his left side. It became unbearable. It burnt like napalm, working its way through his veins, spreading all around his body and before long it had completely consumed him. He felt like he was boiling from the inside out. He started to convulse and his jaw clenched so tight he thought it might break. The sensation persisted for another few moments before it eventually began to subside. It didn't completely disappear but it just became more bearable. He began to feel it tickle the back of his eyeballs, which then felt like they were slowly sinking back several feet into his head. The muscles all around his skull relaxed so much his forehead now felt like it was occupying two different time zones. His brain became two separate entities. One side was leaning up against the inner wall of his head, flaccid and sweaty, the other was trying to make its escape out through his ear canal to go and try to find Olan'ko to negotiate a peace treaty. The rest of his body seemed to have abandoned him, as he was in no way cognisant of it.

"What was that, what did you give me?" Isaac asked, slurring his words like a drunk.

"It should have taken effect by now" the man in the in the lab coat said, ignoring Isaac completely.

"Ok, time to get this started, I have plans this evening" the woman replied as she pressed a button on the side of Isaacs restraints.

The table he was secured to elevated vertically about three feet. It came to a sudden halt, then began to rotate until Isaac was horizontal. The ceiling was the same sterile white as the walls. The table then began to descend until it stopped at waist height of the two people in the doctor's scrubs. Isaac was now staring up at them and they down at him. One at either side of the table. The man was on the right and he lifted a scalpel and put it to Isaacs chest. Without any explanation or reassuring words, he sunk it into his flesh and slid it from the top of his chest all the way down to his pelvis. Isaac was frozen in terror. He could feel the blood running out of the wound, across his shoulder blades and pooling in the centre of his back, but that was all he could feel. There was no pain. No agony. He waited, thinking that he must be in shock and that at any moment the pain would kick in and he would feel it all. The seconds ticked by but still nothing changed. Just the subtle burning sensation from the injection they had given him and the uncomfortable wet feeling from the blood that had gathering on the table behind him.

He was snapped back to the moment with quite a jolt as he felt a new uncomfortable phenomenon. It was the feeling of a hand reaching into his chest and sliding one of his lungs over to the side. Isaac suddenly found it very hard to breathe. He gasped for air but could barely get any into his lungs. Then the pressure released and he filled his lungs to capacity.

"What the hell are you people doing to me?" Isaac pleaded as he struggled to catch his breath.

"That is so strange" the man said again completely ignoring Isaac.

"His entire cardiovascular system is backwards" the woman replied in agreement.

"He has some very interesting looking organs in some very interesting location too. I wonder what they do?" the man added.

"Yes, and just look at that gastrointestinal tract. It's so primitive looking" the woman finished.

"Hey," Isaac screamed, "what the fuck is wrong with you people?"

A new sensation took over. A crushing grip tightened around his wrists, then he felt strings crawling inside his fingers and coiling around his bones, up into his arms and continuing all the way around his back. He looked down at his right side to see a contraption strapped to him. It was

140

floating about six inches above his hand and there were cables flowing out of it that had pierced the tips of his fingers and made their way up inside his body.

Then he looked at his chest and saw that clamps were holding open his sternum and all his organs were on display. He could see his heart beating. His lungs rose and fell with every breath he inhaled and exhaled. He could see his ribs sticking out like two gates that had been blown open in a storm. Isaac started to freak out. He could feel himself losing it as his mind began to release its grip on the present. He began to shake uncontrollably, spasming so hard that he was rocking the whole table. He opened his mouth and a roar from the debts of his being erupted from inside him. It lasted for a good few seconds before Isaac exhausted all the oxygen in his body and he had nothing left to exhale. As he breathed in again, he could feel himself recapturing his senses. He was still shaking from the adrenaline spike his body had just released but he was able to slow his breathing down and recompose himself after a brief moment of hyperventilation. He looked up again at the two people in the surgical outfits and they looked back down at him.

"He is very loud and annoying though isn't he" the woman said looking back up at the man across from her.

"Yes, he is" the man replied returning her gaze.

"Maybe we should think about sedation" the woman suggested.

"No, we need him conscious for this part, but maybe I could disable his vocal ability some way so we can work in peace" the man responded.

He leaned down to take a closer look at Isaac and he fixed his gaze on his throat. Isaac just saw an opportunity to do something. There was no thought process involved in his next move. This guy had sliced him open, ripped apart his organs and had ignored his pleas for them to stop. As the man leaned a little lower, Isaac raised his head as fast as he could and smashed his forehead right between the eyes of his tormentor. He heard a very distinct crack as he connected the flat part of his forehead with what he assumed was the bridge of the nose, or in the absence of an actual nose, where the weak point of his face might be and the man fell backwards crashing onto the floor and out of Isaacs sight.

"Ha. That's a broken nose anyway. Or a broken face slit, or whatever it is you have on there. Enjoy that you fucking ball bag" Isaac gloated, as he rested his head back down on the table.

He looked up at the woman, who was staring at the man on the ground. She rushed over to help him, disappearing out of Isaacs sight as well. He stared up at the ceiling feeling quite delighted with himself for a second before he looked down at his chest again and reality kicked back in.

"Can you hear me Hal'ack" the woman asked.

Isaac didn't hear a response.

"Any chance you could stich me up here?" Isaac smugly enquired.

"Help," the woman cried out, "I think he's killed him."

"Not again" Isaac said, worried that he may have committed his second murder in quick succession.

The woman got up and ran to a door that was located off to Isaacs right.

"Help" she said again as she ran off down the hall.

Isaac lay there for a moment in silence. He couldn't hear a sound except for the ambiance in the room. Then he heard a pain filled groan rise from the floor beside him.

"Thank God for that, I thought I'd killed another one" Isaac said with a sigh of relief.

He could hear the sound of multiple footsteps coming running up the hall towards them. The woman had returned and she entered the room with two armed guards following close behind her. They were Ilian too. She went straight to the injured Hal'ack and disappeared out of Isaacs sight again. The two guards ran straight to Isaacs table and stood either side of him, pointing what looked like hand guns at him less than an inch from his face.

"Hal'ack can you stand?" Isaac heard the woman ask.

"Yes" Hal'ack groaned as she helped him to his feet.

Isaac could see them now positioned just off to his right. Hal'ack had taken his mask off and there was a steady stream of blood flowing out of his face from a gash right between his eyes. It was also pumping out of the two slits on his face that must have been his nostrils, where Isaac had connected with the headbutt. His white lab suit was stained heavily across his chest with the blood. He looked at Isaac and his eyes narrowed. The woman looked around at him too.

"Sedate him" she hissed at one of the guards standing at Isaacs bedside.

The guard disappeared out of Isaacs sight for a minute then returned with a syringe full of a dark brown liquid.

"Wait" Hal'ack ordered.

The guard stopped beside Isaacs bed with the needle in hand. Hal'ack walked over and put his hand on Isaacs arm, yanking what looked like an I.V needle out of Isaacs wrist. He stood over Isaac looking down into his eyes.

"We had been providing you with pain relief during the procedure. I have just removed that. Now you will feel

143

every single bit of what it's like to have your entire insides cut out" Hal'ack said with a smile on his face.

Isaac could feel the pain starting to build up almost immediately. His entire chest felt like an exposed tooth cavity with the air rushing in to aggravate the nerve. This built and built until it reached its peak and Isaac began to scream in agony. He noticed that Hal'ack had leaned in lower again.

"I'm going to make it last as long as I can" Hal'ack whispered to him.

Isaac once again lunged his head upward off the table, but this time he opened his mouth and sank his teeth into Hal'ack's cheek. He could feel his teeth slide deeper and deeper into his face and the warm blood wash over his tongue. Isaac could still hear screaming but this time it was Hal'ack.

"Sedate him! Sedate him!" were the last words he heard Hal'ack shout before he lost consciousness again.

18

Isaac came too in complete darkness. He must have fallen
asleep again. Ever since he bit Hal'ack's cheek he had
been confined to the room he currently occupied. There
was no light. Even after his eyes adjusted to the room there
was nothing to see except complete darkness. He wasn't
sure how long he had been there. There was no sense of
time, day or night, or anything to give him his bearings.
That was probably the idea. He was fairly certain that it
was somewhere between four to seven days but he couldn't
be sure. He knew he was starting to lose his mind a little
bit, so he had taken to talking to himself to pass the time.
  "So what have you been up to today Isaac?"
  "Not much, just chilling out in total darkness without a
clue about what's going on" Isaac replied to himself.
  "That's cool, that's cool. So how's the chest?"
  "Oh fine, fine. Well as fine as can be for someone who
was cut open while fully awake. I mean I haven't seen it
since I've been in complete blackness for a while now, but
it feels fine and I don't seem to feel any scarring or
anything so I'm hoping for the best" Isaac answered his
own question.

He stood up and raised his arms out in front of himself, with his hands open and pointing up. He took a few steps forward until he felt the wall of his cell in front of him. It was cold like always. Probably some form of steel. Once he had his bearings he took a few steps with his arms outstretched again. He walked tentatively forward since he couldn't see. After eight steps, he had reached the other side of the room, indicated by another cold wall that he couldn't see.

"Where the fuck am I?" Isaac shouted into the darkness.

Immediately there was a sound. It was like an electric engine starting up. Low but audible and distinct. Slowly he could see the light level rise in the room. At first it was barely noticeable but became more so every second, then he realised that it was the walls that were changing. They had been completely solid walls of blackness that light was unable to penetrate, now they were transitioning to a slightly opaque look before becoming fully transparent. He could see the outline of two figures starting to appear standing outside the wall. Then, unexpectedly, he noticed that there was someone else in the room with him, sitting in the opposite corner to where he was. Isaac jumped, startled by the presence of this other person.

"What the hell?" he exclaimed, "Who are you?"

"Sato" the other cell occupant replied. He appeared to be a Garian. He had a very slender face and his nose was quite long. He also appeared to have tufts of hair that resembled sideburns on either side of his head.

"How long have you been there?" Isaac asked.

"Longer than you" Sato replied.

"Why didn't you say anything?"

Before Sato could answer the wall in front of Isaac started to shimmer and then it disappeared completely, as if into thin air. The two armed guards who were standing outside the cell gestured for Isaac to walk out. He obliged them and then the wall seemed to shimmer back into place.

"Move" the guard on the left instructed Isaac while raising the rifle he was holding a little.

Isaac raised his hands and walked off as the two guards followed behind him. He took a moment to survey his surroundings. The room he was in was a long corridor. It seemed to run for several hundred yards. Every ten feet or so there was another cell. Each one with a black wall at the entrance. He walked along in silence.

"Turn" one of the guards ordered from behind him.

Isaac looked to his right and noticed that there was a corridor leading off to a double door. He turned and walked toward it. When he got there, he stopped and the door shimmered, similar to the way the cell did and disappeared. On the other side was another long hallway that ran so far he could barely see the end. One of the guards behind him stuck his rifle into Isaacs back and pushed him forward. Isaac didn't rise to the provocation and just walked through the door and along the corridor. Again the walls were lined either side with cell doors. After a long slow walk down the corridor that seemed to go on forever, they eventually came to a double door on the left.

"Stop" one of the guards behind him ordered.

Isaac stopped right beside the doors. The guard that was behind him on the right walked around him and pressed a button on a panel on the wall. Seconds later they slid open and revealed a lift. The guard behind Isaac again jammed his rifle into Isaacs back and he walked forward into the lift. The two guards walked in behind him and the doors closed. Isaac was now standing in front of them and they were behind him with their rifles half raised, ready to fire at the slightest provocation. The lift began to ascend and Isaac noticed that it had windows that were looking out onto the walls of the elevator shaft. After a few moments they passed through a gap and the outside of the facility was suddenly visible to them.

Isaac gasped. The facility seemed to go on for quite a distance. He looked to his left and then to his right out the windows and the buildings outside extended as far as he could see in both directions. It was like a massive industrial complex. There were numerous chimneys and vents spewing smoke out of them, up into the cloudy sky above. He could see a couple of towers in the distance in both directions. He could see some mountains dotted around the rocky landscape but there was no sign of any other structure apart from the facility he was in. He felt the lift slowing down and eventually it came to a gentle halt and the doors opened and led out into a small reception area. There was a desk with a female Ilian sitting behind it just outside the lift doors. Isaac stepped out and the guards followed behind them. They approached the desk and the woman looked up at them and pressed a button in front of her and the doors behind her desk slid open. The guards walked through them and Isaac followed. When they got inside Isaac was a little surprised by what greeted him. It was like a CEO's office. The room was curved. There were no corners. The wall seemed to be completely glass, all the way around looking out over the complex. There was a giant desk facing the door and there were what seemed like two sofas in front of it, on either side, facing each other. Other than that, the room was sparse. There wasn't really anything else in it. After a moment Isaac stopped looking around and turned his attention back to the desk. He hadn't noticed at first but now he realised there was someone sitting behind it. A familiar face.

"Hello again Isaac" Olan'ko said as he raised his head up from the screen he had been looking at.

Isaac looked at him with distain.

"General."

"I imagine you are a bit confused as to what exactly is going on here" Olan'ko said as he stood up from his desk and walked towards Isaac.

He was tall creature. He stood about six inches over Isaac. Considering Isaac was six foot three that made the general quite intimidating as he looked down on him. He had a wiry frame but the way he moved gave you the impression that he knew how to handle himself. He stopped a couple of feet away and looked Isaac up and down.

"I hear you have been a bit of trouble since you arrived" Olan'ko said through his teeth.

"I'm sorry if that's the case, I just don't know how else to react when someone guts you like a fish" Isaac answered.

"What's a fish?"

"It doesn't matter."

"Yes, I suppose not"

He took another moment to appraise Isaac from head to toe, almost sizing him up. Isaac stood, paralysed by fear for a moment. The general vibe he was picking up from the room was he could be attacked from all angles at any second. He tensed up. Then the general gestured for Isaac to join him on the sofa, as he himself walked over to sit down. Isaac obliged and he sat on the sofa across from Olan'ko. The tension he was feeling didn't subside. They remained silent, just staring at each other. The general was the first to speak.

"I suppose you're wondering what it is you're doing here."

"The thought has crossed my mind."

"Well it's quite a long tale. I'm part of an organisation you see. An old institution that sits outside our governments oversight. In fact, it predates our involvement, our necessary but undesirable cooperation with the Galactic Assembly by quite some time. We safeguard knowledge not widely possessed on our world. We discovered that we were not the first sentient species to live there. Before us were the Karlal. A race of beings who came to our world, like many other worlds, resided there and then departed again. This society I belong to was established to further the discovery and to align our way of life with the blueprint they left behind for us to follow, finding the remnants of this civilisation was our only purpose."

"A secret organisation you say. Well that's not quite what I was expecting." Isaac interrupted.

"No. I don't imagine you were. I expect you are oblivious to a lot that goes on. You strike me as that kind."

"What kind?"

"The kind that talks when they should be listening. The kind that absorbs themselves with their own unimportant needs, rather than that of the greater good."

"Is this why you remain an isolated species even though you are aware of and affiliated with the Assembly?" Isaac asked, ignoring the insults that had just been thrown his way and flexing on Olan'ko a little, sending him a message that he shouldn't underestimate him.

"Well aren't you a clever creature. Yes it's part of our isolationist ways. We have a couple of members of the order in high positions of government who, cautiously and discreetly try to steer the will of our people towards our agenda" Olan'ko replied.

"Do you wear long flowy robes and chant mantras?" Isaac asked.

Olan'ko looked at him perplexed.

"No. Anyway, recently we came across information that would make my ancestors proud. We found the Karlal home world. Or at least the coordinates to where we believe it to be."

Olan'ko paused for a moment looking out the window of his office. A smile crept across his face. He seemed to sit up straighter as he said it. He drew his shoulders back and pushed his chest out. Isaac could tell that this was quite an achievement for him and an immense source of pride.

"This is all fascinating. I mean that, genuinely fascinating. What does it have to do with me though?"

"I'm glad you asked," Olan'ko said turning away from the window and back towards Isaac, "because you will play the most important part in my people claiming this world."

"How's that now? How am I, a human from a world that has no involvement in any of your galactic affairs, the most important part of your seemingly nefarious plan? And where are we anyway? What is this place."

"This is the biggest Ilian mineral refinery. We use it to process raw materials into usable ones. Or at least that's what it was built as, what it's officially registered as. Really it's a place where we can conduct our affairs away from the Assembly's prying eyes."

"This is fucked up man. Only I could get whisked off into space and end up in some super villains' evil lair. I mean, there are bad cycles of luck and then there are monumental shit hurricanes. I'm at passing through one of those right now I think."

151

Olan'ko sat looking at him, completely mystified by his relentless absurdity. "Are you finished?" he finally asked. "Yes, sorry continue, sorry. Why am I here?"

"Well quite simply put, it's your world that we are seeking to take hold of."

Isaac sat there for a moment in silence processing all the information he had just been given. His first thought was, this was quite cool actually. An ancient civilisation had evolved on Earth tens of thousands of years ago and had departed for space, leaving the world behind. Humans were not the first sentient species to live there. What this meant for humanity was immense. All the scholars were wrong. There was so much to disseminate his mind started to work overtime. Then his thought process came to a screeching halt and he was thrust back into the present.

"You're gonna have to spell this one out I'm afraid. What does this have to do with me, specifically?" he asked warily.

Olan'ko smiled again. Not like the smile he had a few minutes before. That one seemed like a genuine expression of happiness. This one was more sinister. It sent a shiver down Isaacs back.

"Well," he began, "we had sent an agent there to gather information about your species. I believe you knew him as Ben."

Isaacs brow furrowed with the thought of Ben and what had happened.

"Yeah, I knew him."

"Well it was his job to establish contact with you humans. To blend in among you. Examine and study you. To see what you were like as a species and to determine the best course of action to proceed with claiming the planet. He found you to be violent, destructive and quite inflexible.

He came to the conclusion that the planet would have to be taken by force if we were to proceed. Of course, this is not an option. Although we are not officially part of the Galactic Assembly, we do have certain requirements of them, so to invade the planet of a primitive species and take it by force would be problematic. Also, our undertakings are secret from both the Assembly and the vast majority of our government, so to do this would also expose us to the public. A new idea was formed. We take the planet in secret. A fully fledged military invasion would be noticed but if your species were to befall some sort of biological catastrophe, well that would just be a tragedy. Since nobody is aware of you nobody would miss you. We would simply then lead an expedition to your world, discover your dead race and claim it."

Olan'ko turned to look at Isaac directly in the eyes as he spoke. His glee at the thought of this was quite evident.

Isaac felt himself go weak. All the colour was draining from his face. If he had been playing poker he would have given his game away. He was terrified.

"But there are over seven billion people living on my world. How would you even do that?" he asked, his voice quivering with dread.

"Oh, it's a much bigger problem than just disposing of seven billion people. There is also the problem with cross contamination. We need to create a synthetic agent and make it look natural, that will quickly exterminate your kind, while at the same time refrain from eliminating more than forty percent of the wildlife, leave the flora and vegetation intact and also not have an effect on any of the current species that are a part of the Assembly. That is where you come in my friend. We need your genetic code to fabricate an agent that will do just that. Why do you

153

think I've been so eager to get my hands on you? You should be honoured really."

"Fuck you."

Isaac shot to his feet. He didn't really have a strategy, he just wasn't going to sit there and let this guy threaten his home planet like this.

He didn't even see Olan'ko move but just as the words came out of his mouth he was on him. He grabbed Isaac by the throat and began to squeeze, cutting off his air supply. Isaac was acutely aware of the fact that his feet were no longer on the ground. He was at least a foot in the air, his legs moving backward and forward trying to get some purchase on the floor that wasn't there.

"I am not some feeble medical practitioner who you will attack by surprise, I am a decorated senior military officer. I would crush you with a thought."

He held on to Isaacs throat for another moment until he was close to passing out, then he released his grip and Isaac fell to the floor gasping for air.

"You're a monster" Isaac wheezed at him, trying to breathe.

"Maybe" Olan'ko replied emotionless.

"Why though? Why do this? I mean, we're fairly sound in general. You can just ask can you come in and check the place out. I'm sure we'd let you."

"I'm building a utopia. A place that emulates the type of society that the Karlal lived in. Where better to do that than in the place where it all began? You're in the way."

He gestured to the two guards and they walked over to Isaac and grabbed him by an arm each, then dragged him out of the room.

19

Isaac sat in the darkness of his cell in silence. He knew Sato was there, he could sense him. Every now and then he would hear him exhale a slow breath. If he had of been paying attention before, he probably would have heard him breathing and known he had company, or maybe now that Sato knew he knew, he wasn't trying to keep up the charade of pretending he was alone. He didn't want to speak to him as he was angry that someone was in the cell with him all that time but had remained silent. Then he thought about what Olan'ko had revealed to him. His whole planet was in danger from a madman, hell bent on extinction. He realised that he was the only hope that Earth had. This also led to another realisation. If that was true, then Earth was fucked. He shifted in his sitting a few times at the thought of this reality before he became so uncomfortable that he had to speak.

"So how long have you been in this place?" Isaac asked out loud.

"You talk too much" Sato replied from somewhere in their cage.

"I haven't said anything in nearly a day."

"Yes, but you didn't shut up for the entire first week talking to yourself."

Isaac didn't know what to say. He was right.

"Ok, fair enough, but I didn't know you were here" he said.

"Too long" Sato replied to Isaacs original question.

"Why are you here, where are we?" Isaac asked.

"I'm here because I was in the wrong place at the wrong time. I have no idea where we are. That's the point of this place I imagine"

"Ok" Isaac replied.

The two of them sat in the silence and darkness.

"What are you?" Sato eventually asked Isaac.

"I'm a human."

"Never heard of them."

"No, I don't imagine you have. We're not as advanced as you folks are. We're still primitive in comparison to you and the rest of the Assembly species."

"Advanced?" Sato Scoffed, "Technology doesn't equate to enlightenment. Look around. The races of the Assembly still act like savages when they need to. Caging people up, testing and experimenting on unwilling participants for the greater good that they claim to represent. All the time it's really only for personal gain as far as I can tell."

"Well, one race, but yes. I have been circling around that conclusion myself since I got here. What have they been doing to you?" Isaac asked.

"What do you mean, one race?"

"From what I've seen this is an Ilian operation. No one else. I copped a couple of Garians a while ago but for the most part its Ilian."

The hum of the cell began to increase and Isaac knew that someone was about to open the door. The light level began to rise and he could see the surroundings of his cell a bit more clearly. Sato was still in the same corner that he had been before. It looked like he hadn't really moved. The door shimmered and two guards walked in to the cell. One turned to face Isaac and the other to Sato. The one facing Isaac just stood there looking at him through his visor. The other removed his helmet and poked Sato with a baton he was holding.

"Olan'ko is unhappy with the lack of information you have been providing recently" he said.

"I can only tell him what I know. I could make up a story or two if that would satiate him."

"You would be wise to hold your tongue unless it is something important you have to say."

The guard stuck the baton into Sato's midsection. The baton lit up and an electric like charged slammed Sato in the stomach and caused him to gyrate in pain. The guard stopped and Sato just lay there motionless. Isaac expected him to react in some way at least. Throw a punch. Maybe lunge at him to try and take him down.

"You're fortunate that they turned off the biochip that works my legs" Sato snarled at the guard.

He shoved the baton back into Sato and turned it on again.

"Stop" Isaac shouted as he leapt to his feet, but the other guard was ready for him, slamming a fist into Isaacs stomach, sending him down to one knee to catch his wind.

Isaac took a moment to regain his composure. Then he saw an opportunity. He didn't really take time to put much thought into his next action, he just did it, a common theme in Isaacs life lately. He wrapped his arms around the guard's legs and picked him up off the ground, turning him

157

upside down, slamming his head into the floor as hard as he could. Before the other guard knew what was going on Isaac was behind him. He kicked at his knee bending it forward and knocking the guard off balance. Then he took the guards baton off him as stuck it into his throat.

"Move and I'll fry your nose holes closed" Isaac shouted.

The Guard lay there for a moment looking up at Isaac, with a broad smug grin, taunting him.

"You have no idea how that works, do you?"

Isaac squeezed his fingers around the baton. His knuckles looked like snow-capped mountains they were so white due to the tightness of his grip. Then he raised it up and began to slam it down viciously and repeatedly into the guard's head.

"Does it work like this?" he shouted as he pounded away on the guard, smashing his face into oblivion. He hit him so hard with it, that a couple of times pieces of skin and chunks of flesh came loose and stuck to its tip.

"Look out" Isaac heard Sato shout.

He didn't have time to turn around and just felt a blow hitting him on the back of the head. It knocked him senseless but not unconscious. He became woozy and lay on his back on the ground, staring up at the two guards standing over him. He saw the one he had attacked with the baton. He had made a terrible mess of him. The part of his face that was his nose was gone, instead of two slits there was now only one hole. There was a lot of blood leaking from some open wounds too. Isaac saw him raise his foot, then the foot came slamming down onto the top half of Isaacs head. He heard the crack of his nose but didn't feel the pain. He felt the blood running into his mouth and down his throat and he choked on it a little, coughing and spluttering. The guard raised his boot again

158

and slammed it down into Isaacs chest. This time he heard his ribs crack and felt the pain too. He gasped for air but found it very hard to fill his lungs. This coupled with the steady flow from his already broken nose meant he couldn't breathe properly, to the point where he was beginning to drown on his own blood. A third boot came slamming down onto his forehead, the heel of it cracking the back of his head onto the ground beneath him.

Isaac came too and passed out several times over the next few minutes. He could tell he was moving but that it wasn't under his own power. He was being dragged by his arms, face down along the floor. He still couldn't breathe properly and was unsure of exactly where he was. Then the movement stopped. There were muffled sounds coming from the room around him. He could hear voices. In the distance or close up, he couldn't really tell but it didn't matter, they were there. The voices seemed to change. They became more frantic. A few moments passed and then there was silence.

As Isaac was lying there face down, he noticed a small shadow start to creep into his field of vision from the left side. He was still not entirely with it and was finding it increasingly hard to breathe. He summoned all the wherewithal he could muster and focused on the shadow as it started to take shape. He realised that it was getting bigger and bigger. He strained to see it and his vision focused enough for him to realise that it was a puddle that was forming below him. He also realised he was on a table a few feet above it. It was a thick liquid flowing across the floor. He rallied all the strength he had remaining in him and turned his head to the left. His eyes locked onto the eyes of the guard that had beaten him in his cell. They were looking upwards, rolled back, really far into his head.

There was a look on his face that had a certain familiarity to it but at the same time he wasn't sure what it was. It took him some time to realise that it wasn't changing. It was permanently frozen, with an element of pure horror about it. His mouth was agape, his tongue was hanging out, drooping to the right. Eventually, after looking at the scene intently for a while, it registered with him that the liquid was blood and it was streaming from the head of the guard, that was no longer attached to his body. The look he was seeing was the last expression the guard would ever make. His terror at being decapitated, forever etched across his features. The look he was seeing was his last. His eternal face of death. It shook Isaac to his very core.

It sat there on the floor, unmoving. Isaac tried to look away but had used all the strength he had to turn and look at it in the first place. There was nothing left in him to reverse his position. Movement beside the head drew Isaacs attention and he could see Olan'ko standing beside him, his clothes covered in his cronies blood. He was talking but not to Isaac, there was someone else in the room. He strained to listen to what he was saying.

"I need what I asked you for" he said.

The reply came from elsewhere in the room and Isaac couldn't make out who was speaking or what they were saying.

"Well if you are seeking inspiration then look no further than the last person who disappointed me."

Again, the muffled voice spoke, out of reach of Isaacs ears.

"Very good" Olan'ko replied as he made his way out the door.

20

Isaac was back in his cell. At least two more days had passed. He could remember Hal'ack, the doctor who had dissected him, working on healing him after the guard's assault. He smiled at the idea of Hal'ack having to save his life. He had also spent the day after being poked, prodded, cut open and being almost drained of blood. Each time they took him apart they carefully put him back together. They obviously needed him still. This also made Isaac smile.

"Can I ask you something human?" Sato's voice came from across the cell in the darkness.

"Go for it."

"Why did you intervene to stop the guard from beating me?"

Isaac took a moment to think about the question. After a brief reflection he realised he didn't really have any answer. Not anything that would make sense anyway.

"Honestly I just seem to throw myself into ridiculous situations" he said.

"You don't know me, nor do you owe me anything" Sato replied.

"It's a character flaw I apparently have. One that I only recently discovered the extent of believe it or not. If I see someone in trouble or if I see someone pulling a dick move, I somehow always seem to involve myself. I don't like to see people getting picked on or abused I suppose. Especially when it's some big meathead picking on someone who can't defend them self" Isaac answered, a little surprised by the revelation he had just come to.

"What's a meathead?"

"Oh, it's an expression. It's like a person with big muscles but little intelligence."

"Is this a character flaw for all of you humans?" Sato enquired.

Isaac let out a laugh involuntarily.

"No, not all of us, only the stupid ones. Some humans are good, some are bad, some are oblivious to most of the shit that goes on around them. We're always fighting with each other about some trivial nonsense."

"I feel it is not stupid nor a flaw that you would do this. I think it's genuinely noble that you would do a thing like that. Although I would not be so helpless had they not sabotaged my implants" Sato said.

"Yeah you said that before. Your biochip. What exactly is that?" Isaac asked.

"I am an invalid," Sato began, "I lost the use of both my legs and my arms while serving my government. I was caught in an explosion while I was on assignment that severed my spine. I was lucky to be extracted. I had a biochip installed after. It uses impulses to stimulate somethings and make connections to other things, to be honest I'm not sure how it actually works, I'm not a doctor. All I do know is that when it's on I can fight and when it's off I can't do a simple thing. And as you can tell from the fact that I haven't moved an inch since you first came here, it is currently disabled."

"Damn, that's fucked up. How did you end up here?"

"As I have said before, I was simply in the wrong place at the wrong time."

Isaac realised that was all he was going to get from him on the matter.

"What about you Human?" Sato asked.

"My name is Isaac."

"Isaac, and what about you? How is it that a person from a planet that is not part of the Assembly races, or from a species not capable of interstellar travel, found their way into a cell on the most secretive installation in the known galaxy?"

"That, is a long story."

"I believe we have time. Unless you have some place to be."

"No, I suppose not. Well it started a few months ago when I was on my way to meet a friend in his home. When I got there he wasn't about but he left a note for me. Long story short, I picked up his car from the garage. I noticed I was being followed so I took off. Next thing I know I'm on a space ship flying across the galaxy being chaperoned by Car'esh and his merry band of misfits. After a few stops I ended up getting kidnapped by Olan'ko and his goons then I woke up here and they started to experiment on me."

"Do you know why they are experimenting on you?" Sato asked.

"Yes, I do actually. Olan'ko was kind enough to share his master plan with me, or at least the fundamentals of it. They are trying to create a disease that will wipe out my species while not affecting any Assembly race species, so they can claim a natural disaster killed us off and then they can take over our planet without the Assembly interfering. They believe it's a world they have been searching for, for a long ass time, as part of some order who worship an ancient race called the Kajal or the Kerhal or something like that."

"The Karlal" Sato said.

"That's them" Isaac replied, acknowledging Sato's help.

"Do you have any idea why they want to do that to your planet?"

"According to Olan'ko he wants to build a utopia or some such bollocks."

"A utopia? Give me strength. The idea of a utopia is ridiculous. I've been on thirty six planets. Every one of the Assembly worlds. Not one of them is a Utopia. Most of them are far from it in fact. I'm assuming your world doesn't fit the description of a Utopia?"

"Nope. Definitely not" Isaac agreed.

"That's because everyone disagrees. There will always be people who fundamentally disagree with how you live your life or the virtues you subscribe to. Because there will always be someone who subscribes to the exact opposite of what you believe. Some will be genuine in their belief. Some will disagree and say you're wrong, just to argue with you. But at the end of the day people will always disagree. Then what do you do with those people? Force them to live their life according to your ethos or dispatch them in some way so they don't remain a problem. This is why a Utopia will never exist. And to be honest. I really wouldn't want to live somewhere that fits the description of a Utopia anyway. Who wants to live there? Everyone holding hands and singing happy songs."

There was a silence in the cell that didn't go unnoticed by Isaac.

"Are you still there?" Isaac asked Sato, aware that he was suddenly very quiet.

"I believe you and I are on a similar path Isaac" Sato said after a moment.

"What do you mean?"

"Unfortunately, I can't say much more but know that I am an ally to you, if and when I get my legs back I believe we can help each other."

Again the hum of the cell changed to the noise it made before someone was about to enter. The light began to illuminate the room and the door shimmered and disappeared. Outside stood Hal'ack. There was an armed guard on either side of him. He had a weasel grin on his face as he looked at Isaac.

"We have a big day today for us Isaac. We get to see what it takes to actually kill you. I hope you don't survive."

"How's you face?" Isaac asked bluntly.

"Quite well. The healing is complete and not a mark to be seen. Just like your existence won't leave a mark on the galaxy. Mine however. My existence will leave a giant exclamation point on the future of the galaxy, once your kind are extinct" Hal'ack said smiling at Isaac.

The two guards entered the cell and grabbed Isaac under each arm and raised him to his feet. He took a moment to steady himself as the effects of the last couple of weeks of tests and experiments had taken their toll on him. He was weak, tired and pretty much done. After he steadied himself he made a desperate lunge at Hal'ack. The guards were ready for him. One of them swung his baton and cracked Isaac across the back of the head. It wasn't a heavy hit, just enough to take him off his balance and drop him to one knee.

165

"You have no surprises left Isaac, you are finished" Hal'ack said, dismissing his effort.

Isaac got back to his feet and walked out the door flanked on either side by a guard. He realised that they were not going to give him any room to move and that he would have to just go along with what was happening. He walked down the long hall to the elevator, with Hal'ack walking behind him. They entered and Hal'ack followed them in. He turned and pressed the button to start the journey. Isaac stood there staring at the back of his head, longing to just plant his fist right through it and out the front of his face. He visualised it. The elation he would get from punishing him for all that he had done and all that he was planning to do. He could stop it all right here. All the death and suffering that was about to befall his home. He just had to figure out how he could make it a reality. As the lift descended, he was trying to formulate a plan. He was virtually scanning the room where the experiments had taken place in his head. What he could use to aid him? How could he take out the two guards in his weakened state? He would have to be quick, efficient and ruthless. He would have to take out trained professionals who we're absolutely expecting him to try it, with no knowledge of how to do it and absolutely no energy to mount a sustained attack. He looked again at the back of Hal'ack's head. Once more he ran through the vision of just punching him really, really hard. Then, spontaneously, the guard on his right did it for him.

He raised his baton and placed it at the base of Hal'ack's skull. A quick flash lit up the elevator and Hal'ack dropped down to the floor in a pile, unconscious. The guard then swung the baton across Isaac and slammed it into the visor on the helmet of his companion standing on

Isaacs left. As it connected, he lit it up again and the guard spasmed for a minute before falling to the ground in a pile similar to Hal'ack.

Isaac stood there frozen. It had all happened so fast he was unsure what had taken place.

"Damn, I'm getting good at this stuff" he said out loud.

He turned to look at the guard who had saved him as he was taking off the helmet. Car'esh was under the visor.

"Well, what are you waiting for, let's move."

"Move where?"

"Let's get out of here."

"Hey man, don't get me wrong. I've never been happier to see anybody, ever in my whole life. But we're in a lift, in a pretty secure facility on our way up to the most guarded part of it. Where are we going to go?" Isaac questioned.

"We need to get to the roof, then we will be gone" Car'esh explained.

He used the interface in the elevator to make it stop then change the direction they were heading in. Isaac stood there as the lift rose up towards the top, then suddenly had a realisation.

"Sato!"

Car'esh spun around to look at him. He had a look on his face that was new to Isaac. A looked of surprise. He was doing his best to try and disguise it, but it was clear as day.

"What did you say?"

"Sato, he was my cell mate. We have to go back for him."

"We don't have any time to go rescuing anyone. We need to get out of here now" Car'esh told him.

"He needs help Car'esh, I'm not leaving without him. It's on the way back up. It will add about two minutes to the whole thing. We need to go get him" Isaac demanded.

167

Car'esh turned his back on Isaac and looked out the window. He maintained this pose for a moment, then without saying anything he reached out to the panel and pressed a button.

"Thank you" Isaac said to him.

Car'esh didn't say anything, he just looked out the window all the way up, even though all that was visible was the shaft they were travelling through. When they got to the floor the doors slid open.

"Which way?" Car'esh asked as he walked out into the hall.

"Right, then all the way down. I'll know it when we get there" Isaac said as he walked past him to lead the way.

They stayed silent for the entire trek. Isaac could feel the tension from Car'esh. He wasn't sure what the problem was. It seemed like a reasonable request to go and save someone's life. Eventually they got to the door.

"Here," Isaac said pointing at his cell door, "this is it."

Car'esh walked up to the panel and pressed the screen a couple of times. They waited a couple of seconds before there was any response from the panel, then the screen turned green and the door shimmered and disappeared.

Isaac rushed in to Sato who was sitting in the in the same corner as always.

"Alright lad, time to go" Isaac said as he knelt down beside him. Sato looked over Isaacs shoulder.

"Oh" he said looking at Car'esh.

"I never thought it would actually be you" Isaac heard Car'esh say from behind him.

Isaac looked over his shoulder at Car'esh, who was staring intently at Sato.

"What's wrong?" Isaac asked.

"This man is a traitor and I won't be involved in saving him" Car'esh said.

"Same old Car'esh," Sato said, "desta as always. When Isaac said he was with a Car'esh I knew it would be you. Never thought you'd come for him though."

"Ok, so there's some history here, amazingly. Well that will have to do for later because we need to fucking move" Isaac demanded.

He reached down and grabbed Sato by the arm and tried to lift him, but the dead weight was too much and he couldn't get him off the ground.

"Get up or I'll leave you here" Car'esh shouted.

"I can't. Remember my implant. Well they turned it off" Sato replied.

"I am not carrying him" Car'esh said to Isaac.

"Just help me lift him, I'll carry him" Isaac insisted.

Car'esh begrudgingly bent over and helped Isaac lift Sato onto his shoulders into the fireman's carry position. The weight was overwhelming at first and Isaac nearly fell over but managed to gain his balance just before he did. Still weak from all he had been through in the time he had been imprisoned, he was finding it hard enough to carry his own body weight, never mind the weight of another full grown adult. Car'esh walked off back down the corridor toward the lift and Isaac followed slowly behind him with Sato draped across his shoulders.

They finally arrived and once they were all inside Car'esh pressed the button. The doors closed and the carriage began to ascend. The uneasiness was very evident and Isaac couldn't help but try to break it.

"So, you two know each other huh?"

"Yes!" Car'esh and Sato exclaimed simultaneously.

"Sounds like a story to me" Isaac offered trying to lighten the mood.

"Not for now" Car'esh said cutting him off.

The tense silence returned to the lift as they continued to climb. It was broken by the sudden sound of an alarm going off, followed by the lift coming to a screeching halt. Isaac looked at Car'esh who was looking back at him.

"Lockdown" Car'esh said turning to look at the panel on the wall.

"Are we fucked?" Isaac asked.

"Not yet. But it won't be long before we are" he said as he started to press buttons on the screen. Each time he was met with a noise from the panel like a buzz that screamed access denied. That didn't sound good to Isaac.

"So what do we do?" Isaac asked.

"Taretta, can you hear me?" Car'esh said talking to the ship through his com.

"Taretta is still with you? What about everyone else? Are Niers and Moga still taking your shit too?" Sato scoffed.

"I will leave you hear to die if you speak again" Car'esh said to Sato.

"Ok so obviously there's a major history here, but can we forget about it for the moment and concentrate on getting out of here alive maybe" Isaac said angrily.

Car'esh turned away from them.

"Taretta, are you there?" he said again.

"The lockdown has scrambled communications. Turn me to the screen and I'll direct you" Sato told them.

Isaac rotated and faced him to the panel on the wall. Isaac was now looking the other way so he couldn't see what was happening, he could only hear Car'esh and Sato arguing with each other.

"Ok highlight that subroutine, the second one from the top. No, the second from the top. The top Car'esh." he heard Sato say.

"Now what?" Car'esh asked.

"Ok now open the master command program and drop that subroutine into it. Good now go back to the main screen. Yes now press the override" Sato continued.

"And again?" Car'esh asked.

"Yes but, as soon as you hit that, they are going to know we're here so we better not have far to go from the lift because they will be on top of us in a minute, maybe less" Sato warned them.

"We just need to get to the roof and we will be gone" Car'esh assured him.

"Cool because I don't know how much longer I can carry you" Isaac added.

The lift started to move again. Isaac turned to face the door. The weight of carrying Sato was starting to become unbearable. His shoulders were starting to go numb and his calves and quads were starting to burn. He wasn't sure if he was going to make it. Then the lift slowed and came to a stop.

"Be ready" Car'esh said.

"I'm ready to run. That's about it" Isaac replied.

The door slid open and the wind hit Isaac in the face. This was the first time he'd felt real air on his face for quite some time. It was warm and fresh and felt good.

Car'esh stepped out cautiously and looked around. There was no one there.

"Alright, get to the end of the roof" Car'esh told them.

"How are we getting out of here. Are they going to use that transport beam thing?" Isaac asked.

"What transport beam thing?" Car'esh asked back.

"The one you used to bring me on the ship at the start of all this."

"That's more of a tractor beam. There's no such thing as a transport beam. We used it to steady you, not beam you on board the ship."

"Well can we use it anyway?"

"No, we can't use that. It malfunctioned when we used it on you. That's the reason you hit the wall so fast."

"You absolute fucker" Isaac shouted at him.

They walked down towards the end of the roof they were on. Car'esh led and Isaac followed behind, still struggling with the extra weight of Sato. When they reached the edge, Isaac looked over the side and down. Just as he did this a small ship came shooting up and stopped abruptly in front of him. After a second the back of the ship opened and he could see Niers standing at the door.

"Welcome aboard" Niers said smiling.

"Let's go" Car'esh ordered.

Niers turned and walked toward the cockpit and took his seat in the pilot's chair. Isaac stepped off the roof and onto the ship followed by Car'esh. The door closed and Niers began their ascent off the planet.

21

Isaac laid Sato down against the wall of the ship sitting upright. It was a small ship. About the size of two SUV's side by side, with enough room for Isaac to just stand up straight without hitting his head off the roof. The interior mainly consisted of a large open space in the back, about eight feet across, with two rows of four seats, bolted to the wall on either side, facing each other. There were two chairs at the front facing outward, with all the controls and instruments facing them. Isaac walked up to the front where Car'esh and Niers were sitting. Niers was piloting the craft and Car'esh was sitting in the co-pilots seat.

"Is that who I think it is?" Isaac heard Niers say.

"Yes" Car'esh replied.

"I don't understand."

"Neither do I."

There was a sudden jolt that rocked the ship and caused Isaac to fall back. He jumped up again and returned to the cock pit.

"What was that?" he asked.

"Cannon fire. Ground to air defence system. They know where we are" Niers replied.

"Can we out manoeuvre it?" Car'esh asked.

"I'm interfering with their scans. They have a general idea of our location but they can't pinpoint us precisely. As long as they don't actually see us or get a lucky shot we should be fine" Niers assured them.

Another shot rocked their ship but this one seemed a little further away so it didn't have the same impact as the first. Niers pulled the steering console towards him and the ship began to ascend a little steeper towards the atmosphere.

Isaac looked out the window to the right but all he could see outside was the clouds they were passing through. Once they broke through, the sky was clear above them. It was blue. Just the same as earth. Maybe a couple of shades darker but very similar. Isaac looked off into the distance and he saw something glint in the sunshine. He strained his eyes to see a little better and realised it was a ship coming towards them.

"Uh, we have a problem at three o'clock" he said.

Niers turned around and looked at him.

"We have a what?"

"Bad guy. Bad guy on the right!" Isaac shouted, pointing to where the ship was.

Niers looked right and spotted the craft coming towards them.

"Desta, they have a line of sight on us" he shouted.

"So now…" Isaac started to speak but was cut off by the explosion that rocked them. It threw him backwards all the way down the length of the ship into the rear door, slamming him off it. He hit the ground hard, knocking him senseless momentarily. He took a knee to regain his composure and then stood up and walked back to the front of the ship.

"Are you ok?" he asked Sato as he walked past him, who was now lying on his back looking straight up at the ceiling.

"Wonderful" Sato replied.

"What are our options?" Car'esh asked Niers as Isaac got back to his position behind them.

"Can we shoot that guy down?" Isaac asked.

"This is a transport ship. There are no weapons. Also from the little sensor readings I can get, there are two more ships surrounding us. In a moment, they will have triangulated our position and will have a direct line on us" Niers explained to Isaac.

"So what then? We're just done, are we?"

"No, I always come prepared. I just need a little more distance, then boom" Niers shouted the boom as he slammed his hand down on the console. There was an expectant silence between them all as they waited. Isaac wasn't sure what they were waiting on.

"Boom what?" he asked.

A sudden and brilliant flash of light engulfed them. It lasted for about ten seconds or so then it dissipated.

"Always prepared" Niers said.

"What was that?" Isaac asked.

"We were studying the planet before we came to rescue you and noticed that the clouds were highly charged with a very particular static atmospheric energy. It's probably why they picked this place to set up. It messes with most Assembly signals. We just dropped an electron pulse into the clouds and ignited it. The ships that were following us are most likely falling to the ground uncontrollably right now and if we're lucky we scrambled their com array on the ground for a couple of minutes which should give us enough time to escape the planet and get out of here" Niers told him.

"How long until we get to Altanto?" Car'esh asked.

"Maybe eleven hours. Twelve at the most" Niers replied.

"Eleven hours? I thought it took weeks to get anywhere?" Isaac asked.

Niers and Car'esh looked at each other, then Car'esh looked at Isaac.

"Ok, we have been lying to you Isaac. A lot. I promise though that when we get to Altanto I will be completely honest with you about everything. No more lies. I will tell you my entire knowledge on the situation" Car'esh said to him.

"Yeah, that's what you said about Tuchan" Isaac replied as he walked off and went to the back of the ship.

He sat down across from Sato who was still lying on his back looking at him. They didn't say anything. Isaac sat there in his own head. He thought about everything that had happened to him since he had left Earth. All he had been through. Every bit of it was Car'esh and his crews fault. They had snatched him up, brought him halfway across the galaxy and then delivered him to a psychopath who had been experimenting on him for weeks. Initially he had assured himself that he was safe with them but now he wasn't sure. How could he trust them when all they had done was lie and betray him? He felt truly alone. Lost and out of his depth.

"You can trust them" Isaac heard Sato's voice say, as if he could tell what he was thinking.

"How can I? All they've done is fuck me over" Isaac said, raising his head to look over at him.

"I know them."

"Yeah, that's another thing. How exactly?"

176

"It's a long story. I will tell you when we get to where we are going, but just take comfort in the fact that you are amongst friends now" Sato assured him.

"Easy for you to say. You're not the one they handed over to a mad man."

"True, but I doubt they would have done so had they known the way that situation would unfold."

"We'll see" Isaac replied looking away.

"Well if nothing else, trust me. I'll keep you safe to the best of my abilities."

"Uh huh. Not exactly the confidence boost that you might think it is my man. I don't want to be a dick, but you aren't helping anybody."

"Did they say exactly where we are going?"

"Some planet called Altanto" Isaac answered.

"Interesting" Sato replied as his eyes seemed to widen.

"What is it?"

"Altanto is a unique place. It's an extra solar planet."

"What does that mean?"

"It means it's not in orbit around any star. It was expelled from a solar system many millions of years ago. Most likely a larger planet pushed it out into the void of space and now it just travels through the black. It was discovered by accident a few hundred years ago and a few enterprising criminals set up an outpost on it that has grown significantly to be a hub for every scumbag and crook that the space has ever known. It's impossible to find as it's a dark object that's constantly moving against a dark background, so the only way to get there is to buy its previous coordinates for any period over the last seven days and then you pinpoint its position based on that. It's actually a really great place once you can get past the majority of dirt bags that inhabit it."

"So why are we going there?" Isaac asked.

"Well that is a good question. The answer to that can only come from Car'esh, but if I had to guess I would say that whatever is going on involves people in high positions in the government and the military and Car'esh is going off the travelled path to get to the bottom of it. That's interesting, as Car'esh never goes off orders. Ever."

Isaac looked forward to the cockpit and out the window of the ship. They were in space now heading out towards the stars.

"We're going to switch to the interstellar drive now" Niers told them as he pressed a few buttons on his console.

There was a sound like a charge building up in the ship, before they jumped forward with a jolt. The outside had changed. The darkness of space was still there but the stars were now flying past them at an incredible speed. Isaac sat there for a minute just looking at the universe rush by. He could feel his eyes getting heavy and he knew his body was weak, but he fought the urge to sleep as best he could.

"Rest Isaac. We have a long enough journey to go. You definitely need it" Sato said.

"I don't want to sleep. I don't know that when I wake up, I won't have been sold into slavery or be missing a kidney or something" Isaac replied, half serious.

"Well if nothing else, trust me. After what you did for me today, I swear I will look after you for as long as we are together" Sato replied.

"As much as I appreciate the sentiment, as I've already said, you can't move. How could you possibly do anything to help me if something were to happen?" Isaac asked.

"Ok, that is a fair point. Try and get some rest anyway. You definitely need it" Sato conceded, before closing his eyes to try and get some sleep himself.

Isaac lay down flat looking up at the ceiling of the ship. It was plain steel and was completely smooth, no design or grooves on it at all, like a blank canvass. He began to let some thoughts run through his head but before long, his brain had shut off and he slipped into a deep slumber.

22

Isaac woke up staring at the same ceiling that he had fallen asleep looking at. He took some time to just lay there to get his bearings. He was still on the cargo ship that Car'esh and Niers had used to rescue him. He looked over at Sato who had been looking forward out the window but had turned his eyes to Isaac once he saw him moving.

"Hello again," Sato said, "did you have a restful sleep?"

"Yes actually" Isaac replied, surprised at how renewed he felt.

"Good, you were out for quite some time" Sato informed him.

"How did you get up? You were lying down when I fell asleep."

"Car'esh lifted me."

"Oh. Is he coming around to you now?"

"Unlikely. I was asleep when he did it. I was in his way, so he moved me. I'm pretty sure he enjoyed waking me up though."

"Are we nearly there?"

"I believe we will be making our approach to Altanto in the next hour or so. Once Niers has confirmed coordinates and lines the ship up correctly."

"Lines the ship up correctly?" Isaac asked, wondering what he meant.

Niers interjected from the cockpit.

"The planet is in constant forward motion. We have to make sure we are ahead of its trajectory and we are on the correct line to enter the atmosphere. This all takes pinpoint calculations, as you can't see the planet with your eyes, because it is a black ball moving against a black background with no visible light source emanating from it. Everything has to be done by sensor readings and complex calculations. Otherwise you could miss completely, or worse, slam into the atmosphere at the wrong angle while going full speed"

"That's bad obviously?" Isaac asked.

"We would explode" Car'esh informed him.

"Ok, well then don't mind me. You just make sure you've got everything worked out" Isaac told him.

He sat back and rested up against the wall of the ship looking out the front at the empty blackness of space that seemed to surround them. It wasn't what he expected to see. When Isaac use to watch shows about space, they use to show the universe as full of nebulas that were bursting with shades of greens and blues. Regions that seemed to shimmer with a symphony of different colours, some he didn't even know the name for. Everything he could see was just black, with pinholes of light from the stars in the distance.

He lost himself in thoughts about home again. He was so deep into his own head, it took several attempts from Sato before he managed to get his attention.

"What are you thinking about?" was the question he had been asking.

"Just thinking about home."

"Anything in particular?"

"Honestly, something has been bothering me for a while now. I can't remember Fatboy Slims real name."

"Fatboy Slim?" Sato asked.

"He's a DJ and music producer from Earth. He uses the stage name Fatboy Slim but for the life of me I can't remember his actual name. I've been thinking about it since the first few days in the facility. It's driving me crazy. It's one of those things where you know you know it but your brain just can't seem to find the information in there. Normally I'd just Google it, but that's obviously not possible right now. It's seriously been niggling at me for a while."

"Google it?"

"Fuck man. I keep forgetting I'm talking to an alien. Yeah, it's like a search engine on the internet. You type your question in and it gives you the answer in less than a second."

"Ah yes. I understand. Why do you need to know his real name? If he was your friend, why would he not tell you his actual name?"

"I don't need to know. But I was thinking about it and now that I can't remember, for whatever reason, I just can't get it out of my head. It's nothing really. Just a little annoyance. Like an itch that's hard to scratch. That's all"

"Isaac, when I get to our destination and I get my limbs working again, I will get you home. I promise, you will see your fat friend again" Sato told him.

The sincerity Isaac felt in his voice prevented him

from correcting Sato's assertion that Fatboy Slim was in anyway his friend. Then he started to chuckle at the inference. It made him laugh. He hadn't laughed for what seemed like an eternity. It felt good. He began to howl laughing, uncontrollably. Then Sato began to laugh too. Isaac wasn't sure if they were laughing at the same thing or if he was just mimicking him. Although people do say laughter is infectious. Maybe that applied across the spectrum of life, once a common bond can be found, it didn't matter a damn bit. It felt better than he could remember feeling for a long time. His stomach was starting to hurt from it.

"What's so funny?" Car'esh called back to them.

"Absolutely nothing at all" Isaac shouted back.

"Then why are you laughing?"

"Why the fuck not man?"

Niers pressed away at the console inputting the last of the information needed to make their descent. He took a moment to double check everything was right.

"Ok here we go" he said as he put his hands on either side of the steering console and began to adjust the angle of the ship to land on the planet. Isaac couldn't see anything in front of them except darkness. There were stars visible in all directions but it was mostly just darkness. Then the ship began to shake a little.

"Well we're in the atmosphere now. That's the first task done" Niers informed them.

The turbulence from the atmosphere began to rock the ship a little harder. Niers adjusted the angle of entry again and it smoothened out a little.

"What's the next step?" Isaac asked.

"I have to make sure that we don't hit the ground or fly into a mountain once we've cleared the atmosphere" Niers said.

Isaac just gave him a thumbs up and forced a smile. Niers began to change settings on the steering console again and checked the information on his screen.

"All looks good" Car'esh said.

No sooner had the words left his mouth when an alarm started to ring out loudly from every speaker in the ship.

"What's that?" Isaac asked panicking.

"Collision alarm" Car'esh said.

Isaac looked out the window again. The stars that were in front of him were being swallowed by a black mass that seemed to be rising from the ground.

"There's a mountain right in front of us" Car'esh shouted.

"I see it" Niers said calmly.

"Up Niers. Up. Up. Up" Car'esh shouted.

Niers gently pulled the steering column towards himself and the stars began to come back into view out of the darkness that seemed to have swallowed them. Then the alarm stopped and everything became calm again.

"How close was that? Honestly" Isaac asked.

"Closer than I'd like to admit" Niers answered.

Isaac looked out the window again. In the distance, he could see a small light that seemed to be rising up from the ground.

"What's that?" he asked, pointing to it.

"That's where we're going. It's called the Abattoir. It's a bio-habitat, built three hundred years ago by a coalition of criminal outfits. They worked together to create it and then as soon as it was finished a Garian named Welton Fack staged a coup against the other parties that were involved. He executed anyone that opposed him and absorbed the

184

remaining members of each faction into his own to create the largest criminal organisation in the galaxy" Car'esh explained.

"So who runs it now?" Isaac asked.

"His grandson, Denson Fack" Car'esh said, as his eyes narrowed and his teeth clenched.

Isaac noticed this but decided not to pry any further. He turned his attention back to the front window. The light he saw was getting bigger and once close enough, he realised that it was a large building reaching up into the sky. A skyscraper, maybe two kilometres high. As they approached Niers lowered their altitude until they were just about skipping across the ground. Isaac saw an entrance where two ships had flown out of and were heading off the planet. He could see the terrain because of the lights of the building but it appeared to just be rock.

"Cargo vessel six two five one on approach, transmit your clearance code" a voice came across the communicator.

"Stand by" Niers replied as he typed on the ships console.

"Clearance granted, proceed to docking bay 12, level three, slot four five one" the voice instructed.

"Received" Niers answered.

He continued on the same course and they entered the Abattoir docking bay. The entrance ran across the whole width of the building. As they made their way through the structure Isaac couldn't help but notice the similarities between the docking bay and a multi-story car park back on Earth. This was just on a much bigger scale. The building itself seemed to be enormous. If it was two thousand metres high it was at least one thousand metres square at the base. There were ships of all types docked all around him. Some were similar to the one they were in. Others were much bigger like Car'esh's ship. Some were just really small, brightly coloured two seaters, shaped almost like Ferrari's while others were a little statelier, like Bentleys or Rolls Royce's on Earth. Personal luxury vehicles for the people with enough wealth to afford them. Exactly like their terrestrial equivalents.

The ship came to a stop and it began to ascend straight up. They passed one floor and when they came to the next it stopped again. Then Niers rotated it about ninety degrees and they moved forward slowly, into a space that seemed to be made to fit their ship exactly. Once they were in Isaac could hear the engines power down and there was a soft bang on the outside of the ship.

"What was that?" he asked.

"Docking clamp" Sato told him.

"Ok, were here. Let's go Isaac, we need to meet up with the others" Car'esh said.

"What about Sato?" Isaac asked.

"What about him?" Car'esh replied.

"We can't just leave him here paralysed like that."

"Until I know exactly why he's here and what he's doing, he's not going anywhere."

"Alright what is it with you. How do you know each other and why do you hate each other so much?" Isaac demanded to know.

"It's ok Isaac. I'm quite literally not going anywhere. I'll be here when you get back. If Sha'ala and Taretta are up there, I'm safer down here anyway."

"You know I trust him more than I do you two" Isaac told Car'esh and Niers.

Niers seemed to be genuinely disappointed by this revelation from Isaac. "It's not that simple Isaac" he said.

"Then make it simple. Tell me what this history between you is."

"Later Isaac. We don't have time now" Car'esh pleaded.
Isaac looked at Sato.

"It's ok Isaac, go. We'll Talk later."

Isaac turned and walked out of the ship and Car'esh and
Niers followed him. Outside there was quite a lot going on
around him. The door of the ship led to a gangway which
led up to a platform. Isaac stopped and waited for Car'esh
to take the lead then he quickly followed in behind him.
People were busy, rushing around, coming and going to
and from their ships.

"So this is an illegal operation?" Isaac asked Niers.

"Well no. It's not recognised by the Assembly as an
official colony or anything like that, but the sheer size of
what this place has become means they have to
acknowledge it, even if they don't approve. It has an
economy that would rival any of the Assembly worlds. All
of it is dark money though. It's like an independent
outpost, but because the Assembly have no official
involvement the rule of law doesn't really find its way
here" Niers answered.

"Which the Assembly is more than happy to take
advantage of" Car'esh added.

"What does that mean?" Isaac asked.

"The Assembly has no say in what goes on here. They
can't interfere because this place has grown to a ridiculous
size. So, since they don't have any control and they can't
stop it from existing, they use it to conduct research that
they would be unable to conduct on any Assembly-
controlled world that would be against the law. So they are
breaking their own laws in a lawless place" Car'esh said.

"If you can't beat them, join them I suppose" Isaac said.

"Yes, that is quite an applicable way of putting it" Niers
agreed.

187

"If it's lawless why does it operate so smoothly?" Isaac asked, noticing how efficient everything was happening around him.

"It's not so much lawless as it is not governed by the Assembly laws. However it's in the interest of Denson Fack to make sure it stays running smoothly. Therefore anyone who steps out of line answers to him. No one wants to answer to him from what I can tell" Car'esh said.

They reached a large elevator and got inside. There were four other people in it with them but it was so big that Isaac, Niers and Car'esh were able to stand in a corner away from everyone else. As the elevator began to rise Isaac turned to face them.

"Alright I have to know before we go any further, what is going on with you all, why have you been lying to me about everything and why is Sato still paralysed in that ship?" he asked.

Car'esh and Niers looked at each other.

"Isaac," Car'esh began, "you have to understand. We believe we have been lied to as well by the people we work for. We are trying to piece as much as we can together ourselves. Right now, we haven't got time to explain anything because we are so exposed. We're walking around in public with an unregistered alien species and Assembly world or not that is going to attract all the wrong type of attention."

Isaac looked around as Car'esh said that and noticed that although they had been able to separate themselves from the other passengers in the large elevator by some distance, he was sticking out like a sore thumb, drawing a lot of eyes to them.

"Ok, that's a fair point, but I want answers Car'esh."

"We are on our way to a private location. A room we have rented under an alias. Once there I will tell you everything I know, and if you tell us everything you know, maybe, we can start to get an idea of what exactly is going on. Does this sound fair?" Car'esh asked.

Isaac took a moment to think.

"Yes. It does." He answered.

23

   It had been about ten minutes since Isaac had stepped off the elevator. He was following Niers who in turn was following Car'esh. The whole set up of this place was absolutely incredible. The centre of the structure seemed to be one giant elevator shaft. There was a constant flow of them shooting up and down. The levels of the Abattoir seemed to resemble promenades. Well the one he was on right now did anyway. There were bright flashing lights in all directions, video billboards drawing your attention to each establishment enticing you to enter and see what was inside. Isaac wasn't sure what that might be as none of them said anything specific. They just seemed to be invitations to come in and find out. There were barkers standing outside trying to draw would be customers in too.

   "This doesn't really look like a place for scientific research" Isaac pointed out to Niers.

   "Well that's just one of the services available here. We're in what you might call the entertainment district right now. Everything's for sale here" Niers informed him.

Isaac looked around again. It looked like Las Vegas on steroids. He wasn't really looking where he was going when a Garian barker jumped out in front of him.

"Come inside my friend. Whatever you desire is waiting for you" he said to Isaac in what he probably thought was the most alluring tone imaginable.

"Uh, no thanks, not today anyway" Isaac replied as he tried to push past him.

"My friend, I promise you will not be disappointed" the barker insisted, putting his hand on Isaac's shoulder to slow his advance.

Isaac noticed that the barker was looking at him a little more intently now, like he hadn't really noticed who he was talking to at first. He placed his hand on his forehead like he was shielding his eyes from the sun and looked down to the floor, trying to hide his appearance beneath it.

"Not today" Niers said from behind him, placing his hand on the barkers' shoulder, applying enough pressure to show him he was serious without hurting him.

"No problem, excuse me please" the barker said as he moved back into the crowd.

"We need to move. Get out of sight of the population. We're starting to draw attention again" Car'esh told them as he looked around.

Another ten steps and Isaac was propositioned once more. This time a Magalian woman grabbed him by the arm and pulled him towards her. He looked her up and down. She was wearing a very scant bikini. It barely covered her chest, leaving very little to wonder about what it was hiding. The bottoms were like a thong. Her skin was a light shade of green. She was a petite size, but her body was quite toned and muscular. Not ripped like a bodybuilder but the definition of her figure was very pronounced. Isaac was a bit taken aback by how beautiful she was.

"See anything you like?" she asked.

"Well, now that you mention it…"

Isaac felt a vice like grip tighten around his arm and pull him away from her.

"We've no time for pleasure. We need to move" Car'esh said, letting go of him.

They exited the main street and walked through a single door. It was fairly unremarkable and inconspicuous, meagre in terms of everything that they had been walking through thus far. There was a desk with a Magalian man behind it and a door off to the right. Car'esh walked up to the door and swiped what looked like a card over where the handle on a normal door would be. It unlocked and slid across. Behind it was another elevator. This one was small. Isaac, Niers and Car'esh barely all fitted in it together.

"Thank God you didn't bring Moga along" Isaac said jokingly.

The elevator stopped after a short ascent and the door slid open. There was a long blue corridor in front of them with doors lined on either side of it. They walked down the hall until they got to the third door on the right. Car'esh once again swiped his card over the door handle and it slid open. He walked in and Isaac followed behind him.

Once they were all inside the door slid closed behind them. Isaac turned and was faced immediately with a narrow flight of about fifteen stairs. Once he got to the top the space opened out a lot more. The room was fairly modest. There was a large table in the middle with two couches on either side, facing each other at a slight angle. Taretta was sitting on the right one. A stair case to the left seemed to ascend up to another level in the room. There was what looked like a window on the far wall, but the view was of a lush looking oasis outside it, which was at odds with what Isaac had seen on his way into the complex. Isaac deduced that it was a projection of some kind.

"Isaac, it's good to see you are alive. I feared the worst" Taretta said from her seat, not looking up at him. She had a portable console on the table in front of her, not dissimilar to a laptop, that she seemed to be working on.

The sound of footsteps coming down the stairs turned Isaacs attention to them. Sha'ala came bounding down them and walked straight towards Isaac, throwing her arms around him and embracing him tightly.

"Isaac, I'm so happy you are alright" she said squeezing him tighter.

Isaac felt that her concern and her relief to see him was genuine and he returned her hug with one of his own.

"I wouldn't say I'm totally alright to be fair" Isaac said as he separated from her embrace.

"What do you mean?" Sha'ala asked.

"I'll tell you later," he assured her, "where's Moga?"

"Sleeping" Taretta said from her seat, still with her eyes fixed on her console.

"Ok Isaac, will you sit down please" Car'esh asked him, gesturing to the sofa across from Taretta.

Isaac sat down and then Car'esh sat opposite him, beside his engineer.

"Ok, speak" Isaac said.

"Excuse me?" Car'esh asked, a little taken aback.

"Speak. Tell me exactly what's going on."

"Actually I was going to ask you…" Car'esh started.

"Nope," Isaac said cutting him off, "you are going to tell me everything now. No lies, no omissions, no secrets, everything. If I decide I believe you then I'll offer up everything that I now know to you."

Car'esh looked at Isaac for a moment puzzled. Then he turned to Niers and finally to Sha'ala.

"I believe we owe it to him" Niers said.

"At the very least" Sha'ala agreed.

Car'esh looked down at the floor away from them for a moment.

"Alright" he said.

"Everything" Isaac insisted.

Car'esh paused for a moment before he began to speak.

"We've been working incognito, for so long now I feel we've started to forget who we really are. Over two years ago one of the Assembly leaders began to speak about how we were on the verge of great discovery. Something big. It's not very often that people from the Assembly chambers get excited about anything, so this was interesting, to say the least. Then this member who was very vocal about this great discovery was killed in a separatist attack on an official visit to Aeroen. The talk of this great discovery died with him. There was no one speaking about any of it. A week after the incident we were put on assignment by commander Aba'dal. He told me I was to investigate the murder and look for any discrepancies between the official report and anything we found. Needless to say, there were a lot. So we continued our investigation in every direction it took us and it took us to a lot of different places, eventually leading us to a new planet, your Earth, which was where we encountered you. One of the ways we worked our investigation was we would pick up jobs through proxies. Depending on what we were asked to do, we would determine whether it was a lead or not. The suspicious and secretive jobs we took usually led back to

Aeroen. The Ilians. So we would look for as many of those as we could find. On the last one we took, we were sent to retrieve a package. That's all the information we were given besides the signal we needed to track it. That package turned out to be the person you knew as Ben. We didn't know what to make of you when you showed up instead. Whether you were involved or not. To be honest at that stage we didn't even know what we were investigating anymore. So we withheld the truth from you. We lied to you to see if you would slip up and give away any information you might be hiding. We wanted to see if you really were just a human who had gotten mixed up in something they knew nothing about or weather you were manipulating us. Niers was your biggest advocate. We argued about it on the way to Tuchan but by the time we had concluded you we're being honest we we're already scheduled to meet Aba'dal. Then we we're ambushed by Olan'ko. Our meeting with Aba'dal never got a chance to take place. I'm Sorry Isaac. We failed you" Car'esh said solemnly.

"So why did you come back for me?"

"I follow orders Isaac. That's all I've mostly done my whole life and MOA or not, when a general gives me an order I am bound by rank to follow it. After speaking to Olan'ko we realised that something was amiss. It just didn't feel right. We decided that we needed to bring you to the Assembly to let you tell them your story. Plus we owed you."

"You owed me what?"

"You saved Niers' life. We owed you for that."

Isaac took a moment. He had a hundred thoughts swirling around in his head. The most prominent being weather he believed him or not. He could feel the eyes of the room on him. Waiting with expectation as to what he would say.

"Ok," Isaac began, before taking a moment to structure his thoughts properly, "well, as you all know, I've been a prisoner for a while now. I couldn't say how long as I have lost all sense of time since I was in there."

"Three weeks" Niers interjected.

"Three weeks? Damn, it felt like a lot longer than that. Well anyway, while I was a guest of Olan'ko, I have been subject to all sorts of, atrocities, I believe is the appropriate term to use. From being dissected alive, like a fucking lab rat, to having my DNA broken down and built back up again in the most painful way. I took a few beatings too. One or two slaps and a couple of broken bones for being a bit of a troublesome detainee. Got a good few knocks in myself on one or two of them though. Fucked this one guys face up bad."

"Why would he do this?" Car'esh asked, his look a mixture of disbelief and revulsion.

"I'm getting to that. Stay with me now. And don't you dare doubt the reality or the sincerity of what I'm telling you" Isaac told him sternly.

"I'm sorry Isaac" he heard Car'esh say, the remorseful tone in his voice sounded very sincere.

Isaac glanced around at everyone in the room. He noticed that Sha'ala had tears in her eyes.

"Are you ok?" he asked her.

"I'm sorry, I just, we're responsible for all this Isaac. We led you to him and then left you there to suffer. We had no idea what he was going to do, but I swear if we had, it never would have happened" Sha'ala told him as her voiced quivered.

196

He turned to Niers who was staring down at his feet, almost as if he was unable to look Isaac in the eye. Taretta was now turned away from her computer, the first time she had since he entered the room, staring in the other direction at the projection of the oasis on the wall. Isaac could feel the disappointment in the room that was radiating from everyone. He could feel their remorse at letting him suffer the way they did.

"Well anyway," he continued, "It would seem that Olan'ko is a part of some ancient organisation, or religion or something. Something about a race of people called The Karlal."

Everyone around him began to look at each other, confused by his inference to the Karlal as a religion.

"The Karlal?" Car'esh asked.

"Yeah, that's what he called them anyway. He said they were around tens of thousands of years ago, then they disappeared."

"They were the first race that we have evidence of, that became interstellar. They had colonised some worlds in the galaxy. Then they disappeared. No one has found any evidence to say what happened or where they went" Taretta told him.

"But they are a historical interest. There's no real focus on them from the Assembly other than a curiosity" Car'esh told him.

"Not for this wacky group of Ilians apparently. These mad fuckers seem to be obsessed with them. According to Olan'ko he says that everything about what he does is aimed at finding out everything he can about them and he's not alone. There's a whole secretive group whose only purpose is their weird infatuation with living like these Karlal. Abiding by the blueprint they left behind or

197

something. Well, he said that they found their home world. That they want their home world, but their home world, is my home world."

This revelation was met with silence from the room. Isaac was disappointed by this. He thought there would be gasps and shock.

"It wouldn't be possible for them to simply take your home world. The Assembly would stop them" Car'esh said in rebuttal.

"That's the thing. Of course they know that. So they're trying to engineer a virus or a disease, some type of biological agent to wipe us out. I don't think they managed to do it yet because they were still working on me when you came to get me. Thank you for doing that by the way, in all the chaos I don't think I've actually said that. But I don't know how far along they are. The way he described it, they have to do it while making it look like we did it to ourselves. It also has to be non-lethal to the current species, like you guys" Isaac explained.

He halted his debrief for a moment to try and gauge the reaction from the room to what he was saying. Each one of them was staring at him but Isaac got the impression that they weren't convinced by his story. He thought how odd it was that they would have such a human expression, before realising that it must be a universal expression for genuine disbelief.

"How could they do that?" Sha'ala asked.

"This is unbelievable if true?" Car'esh said.

"Hey if you don't believe me go ask Sato. He was there too. I'm sure he'll back me up. Even though, well, he never actually heard any of this directly" Isaac told them disappointed that they were doubting him.

"It's not that we don't trust that you heard these things Isaac. It's that they are so far beyond belief that we are having trouble comprehending the reality of them" Car'esh told him.

"Wait, did you say Sato?" Taretta asked, surprised by the name.

"Shit, I forgot about him" Niers said.

"Taretta. You need to focus. Now is not the time…" Car'esh tried to finish.

"Sato is here? Sato Halsa? Is he tied up? Chained down? Where is he?" Sha'ala demanded.

"That's another thing you were supposed to tell me. How do you know him?" Isaac asked.

"I'm going to kill that bastard" Taretta shouted standing up off the sofa.

"I'll help" Sha'ala said standing up beside Taretta.

"We need to focus. His spinal implant has been deactivated" Car'esh demanded.

"How do you know him?" Isaac screamed.

Car'esh managed to get Sha'ala and Taretta to calm down and then turned back to Isaac.

"He was assigned to work with us a few years ago, just as we were beginning this very mission. Being under cover was new to us. We are a strike team. Infiltrate and execute. That's all we knew. We were directed to take him to a classified location and assist him in whatever way he needed. We're not entirely sure about all the details, but at some point his mission went wrong and he sold us out to use us as a decoy to cover his own escape. His talent is espionage. He is part of the reason why we didn't trust you at first" Car'esh told Isaac.

"I see. So why do you think he was in the same place as me?" Isaac asked.

Car'esh looked around the room at everyone, then back to Isaac.

"I don't know," Car'esh said, thinking, "but I believe we should definitely ask him."

"Are you sure he was incapacitated?" Niers asked.

"He never moved once all the time we were in the cell. Unless he is a master of contortion, there's no way he can move" Isaac told them.

"He is a master of manipulation," Car'esh said standing up, "so we better go and make sure."

Taretta, Niers and Sha'ala all started to move around the room gathering up everything they had brought with them while Isaac remained seated.

"What's going on exactly?" he asked.

"You three get Moga and go back to the ship. Isaac, you come with me and we'll see if Sato is telling the truth or not" Car'esh ordered.

The three of them continued to pack everything up.

"Let's go" Car'esh said to Isaac.

24

Isaac followed closely behind Car'esh as they made their way back through the parking level. He had barely left six inches of space between them since they departed the hotel room and made their way down through the Abattoir. They were walking up the gangway to the ship they had arrived in and as they approached, Car'esh put his hand on Isaacs chest to stop him before he opened it.

"Stay behind me. If he is gone, there's no telling what booby trap he's left behind" Car'esh told him.

"I genuinely think your over reacting" Isaac protested.

"Sato Halsa is not to be trusted" Car'esh insisted.

"Can we just get on with it please" Isaac said gesturing to the door.

"Ok, hold on."

Car'esh placed his hand on the release mechanism and prepared to enter the vehicle. Isaac couldn't help but feel a sense of tension building at the way Car'esh was playing the situation out. Finally, he pressed the door release and it slid up and opened, then Car'esh bounded into the compartment and drew a gun he had concealed under his top, pointing it in the direction of where Sato had been before they left.

Sato was still there, lying in the exact same position he had been when they went to the hotel.

"See, I told you" Isaac said as he walked past Car'esh and sat down across from Sato.

"Did I miss something?" Sato asked, looking at Car'esh who was still pointing the gun at him.

"No, Car'esh just doesn't trust you" Isaac said.

"With good reason" Car'esh added.

"That's true" Sato agreed.

"So I've been told" Isaac concluded.

"I thought you had forgotten about me."

"To be fair, we had for a moment" Isaac said honestly.

"Is there any chance that I will get my ability to move back anytime soon?"

"That depends, on whether or not you tell us everything about Olan'ko" Car'esh informed him.

"I would imagine I know everything you do about him" Sato replied.

"Ok well start Talking and we'll see if you do" Car'esh insisted.

"Well, he's a general for the Ilian infantry. He also seems to be running some sort of secret and illegal operation out of some clandestine Ilian instillation on an uninhabited world that we've all been to."

"Yeah I'm going to have to stop you there for a minute," Isaac interjected, "we mean tell us about the facility, what he's doing in it besides the wacky genetic experimentation we already know about."

"Oh, I don't know much about that place at all. Only what you told me while we were sharing a cell."

"Why were you there?" Car'esh asked.

"Car'esh, I know you don't trust or believe anything I say and you have every right not to. I promise you I was just in the wrong place at the wrong time. I was on an assignment on Kavalron for the Assembly. Reconnaissance only, no direct action."

"Kavalron?" Isaac asked.

"It's an industrial colony, a fuel refinery plant. It's the biggest one in the galaxy. It's run by a mining consortium based on Gar" Car'esh told him.

"Yes, and I was there following a lead that someone high up in the organisation that runs the refinery was selling fuel in large quantities off the books to some insurgent movement. I was in a bar watching my target when these mercenaries in matching armour came in and grabbed him. I'd never seen them before. I was just sitting there letting it happen as I was under strict no intervention order"

"Black armour with no identifiable markings?" Car'esh asked.

"That's them" Sato replied.

"The same people who attacked our ship. It's like Olan'ko has his own private army" Car'esh said to Isaac.

"Well they must have had inside information because as soon as they had snatched up my target they came over and grabbed me too. I went along with them planning on losing them once we got outside but before I got the chance, I was unconscious. Next thing I knew I was waking up in the cell and none of my limbs worked."

Car'esh looked at Isaac for a moment. Isaac wasn't sure why. He had nothing to add.

"What are you thinking?" Isaac asked.

"If they came to Kavalron, but they knew that Sato was there, then there's a good chance someone is feeding them classified information" Car'esh told him.

"Ok, so who? I mean the obvious answer to me would be Olan'ko is just tapped into some part of your Assembly information network. He's high up. Well informed." Isaac said.

"Olan'ko is a member of the Ilian army. He is highly ranked with them. But the Ilians have never really committed to the Assembly. They cooperate with us when it suits them but officially, they have never obliged to becoming part of the wider collective. He wouldn't be privy to any of what we're talking about." Sato told him.

Car'esh sat there pondering for a minute while Sato and Isaac waited for him to speak.

"Car'esh, would he be able to find out that you and your crew are on assignment, and then track your ship through the military transponder on it" Sato asked.

"No, we disabled it when we found out Isaac had been taken prisoner. We knew we couldn't trust too many people after that."

"What about that thing we took out of Ben. They used that before right?" Isaac asked.

"They tried to but we managed to block the signal. Anyway Olan'ko took that when we came across him on Tuchan."

A look of dreaded realisation spread across Car'esh' face.

"What is it?" Isaac asked.

Car'esh didn't reply. He just jumped up and ran out of the ship and back up the gangway without saying a word. Isaac jumped up and followed him leaving Sato behind again. He heard him shout something after them but he was already too far away to hear what it was. He followed as closely as he could to Car'esh but he was falling behind.

"Car'esh, where are you going?" Isaac shouted after him, but Car'esh didn't stop or answer. He just kept moving, picking up his pace with every step as he made his way through the parking garage.

By now Car'esh was a good fifteen feet or so ahead of Isaac as he turned a corner. Isaac pushed his way through the crowd to try and keep up but as soon as Isaac had followed him around the bend he stopped in his tracks.

He saw Car'esh struggling with two of Olan'ko's soldiers who were trying to restrain him. Car'esh knocked one of them down and was about to take out the other when he took a hit from a gun that lit up his entire body with electricity, causing him to spasm and fall to the floor unconscious. Isaac made a move to go and help him but stopped as soon as he saw four more of the mercenaries approach. They put restraints around his ankles and his wrists, which were behind his back. Isaac slid back up against the wall and hid behind a pillar that blocked the line of sight between him and the mercenaries. He waited a minute then peered out around the pillar again to see what was going on. The soldiers had lifted Car'esh up, one on each limb, and were carrying him off. Isaac wasn't sure what to do. He was rooted to the spot. He knew he wouldn't be able to take on a squad of highly trained soldiers, but he also wasn't going to just sit back and do nothing. He peered around the pillar one more time while deciding what action to take, but it was too late. The mercenaries had already made it to Car'esh's ship and had brought him aboard. Before he could move, the door closed and a moment later the Sao'ise was flying past him and heading toward the exit.

Isaac stood there terrified. He thought for a minute. They must have taken everyone. All of the crew had been sent to the ship except for him and Car'esh who had gone to speak to Sato. All he could do now was head back to him and hope that he could help him.

He made his way back through the levels of the parking garage. As he walked past people, he couldn't help but notice the looks he was getting. In all the commotion he had forgotten where he was and what was going on. People were starting to stare now. The ruckus that the soldiers had caused had drawn attention to the area, and now that attention was turning to him. He tried his best to slip through the crowd as nonchalantly as he could. Eventually after a few wrong turns and dead ends he found his way back to the ship that Sato was on. Isaac pushed the door release and stepped inside the ship. He sat down across from Sato and just stared at the floor.

"What happened?" Sato asked.

"I'm not entirely sure, I was a little behind him. I saw Olan'ko's soldiers stun Car'esh and take the ship. I can only assume that everyone else was there too."

"Ok, were now in the worst case scenario."

"What does that mean? I'll be honest I'm a little dismayed by the fact that after everything that had taken place thus far, we are only now reaching the worst case scenario."

"We have a rogue general conducting unauthorized experiments on non-citizen species, to achieve his goal of creating an extinction level event on their home world. The only people who know this and that can do anything about it are us and the team that he now has in his possession and we don't know who we can trust to send reinforcements to help me get them back."

"I see what you mean. Also, you aren't really in a position to do anything about it either" Isaac admitted.

"Well if you would just activate my biochip I could certainly give it a try" Sato told him.

"Sorry, but I don't know the first thing about how to help you."

"Well, you just have to get to the activation sensor up my anus and switch it on" Sato said, straight faced and unapologetically.

"Come again?" Isaac asked.

"I keep a control switch up my anus in case of a situation just like this. It's not easy to deactivate a biochip as they operate on unique frequencies. I always expect the worst though and plan for every situation."

"I don't suppose anus has a different meaning where you come from?" Isaac asked expectantly.

"It's the exit for waste from my digestive tract. It's where the surplus material from the food I eat exits my body. It's a hole at the base of my spine hidden between my buttocks" Sato reliably informed him.

"Of course it is. I know what an anus is, I was just hoping it was something different to you" Isaac replied, disheartened.

"I understand it's going to be uncomfortable for you, but it really is our only option."

Isaac took a moment to compose himself. Then he stood up and walked over to Sato.

"Right, what do I have to do?" he asked.

"First you'll need to roll me over onto my stomach, then take my trousers down. It's about a finger length up there so you won't need to go too deep to find it" Sato told him.

Isaac grabbed Sato by the arms and lay him face down on the floor. He reached around to the front and undid the latch that kept Sato's trousers closed.

"You may want to close the door, just in case" Sato said.

Isaac looked up and realised that he hadn't closed the ship on his return. He looked over to see something that vaguely resembled an oversized hairless Koala bear, standing on the gangway looking in. He got up and walked towards the door. The unnerving little thing was licking his lips, like a hungry soul, staring in the window of a nice restaurant.

"Sorry, private party."

As he pressed the button to close the door, he could swear the little guy let out a disappointed sigh, then went back and took up his position behind Sato.

"Wellians," Sato said, "little perverts the lot of them."

Isaac grabbed his trouser waist and began to pull them down, all the way to his ankles. Then he looked at his goal. It was pretty much identical to a human buttocks, apart from the colour of his cheeks. Isaac took a deep breath, then used his left thumb and index finger to separate the glutes so he could get a better look at his goal. Sure enough, the anus looked the same as a humans too. He steadied himself and then just shoved his finger up into Sato's arse. While he was rooting around, he could feel the excrement squelching up there. Isaac dry heaved as he searched for the button.

"Hold it together Isaac, it's there somewhere" Sato assured him.

After another moment Isaac felt his fingertip touch something solid amongst the softness. He pushed a second finger inside and used them both to get a grasp on the switch and pull it out. It fell to the ground on extraction and just stuck to the floor, covered in excrement. Isaac dry heaved again, before throwing up the entire contents of his stomach, which wasn't much to be fair. He collected himself and picked the device up off the ground. It just looked like a piece of plastic with a small circular button in the middle of it.

"So what, do I just press this now?" Isaac asked.

"Yes."

Isaac pressed down on the button. Nothing happened at first.

"Is it broken?"

"No, it just takes a moment to fully activate" Sato told him.

After a few tense minutes Isaac could see Sato start to wriggle his fingers. Then his arms began to move a little. Not long after he used his arms to pull himself up into a seated position.

"It's starting to take effect now. Just give it a little more time" Sato said.

"So, what's the plan?" Isaac asked.

"I'm not sure. I should probably report in to my superiors, but we don't know if I can trust them. Maybe we could report to Car'esh's people" Sato told him.

"Sorry Sato, there seems to be some confusion. I mean what's the plan for getting me home?"

Sato looked around at him, completely blindsided by Isaac's selfish request.

"You don't want to help them? You want to just abandon them to their fate?"

"Hey, I feel for them. I really do. But I'm done lad. I have a planet full of people I have to warn about the most ridiculous and absurdly unbelievable threat it's facing. I don't even know who to tell or how I'm going to do it. I think I've pushed my luck as far as it's going to go out here. I'm a fish out of water right now. I need to get back to the sea."

"I don't understand. So, you normally live in water?"

Isaac didn't answer at first. He just dropped his head into his hands and let out a sigh of frustration.

"Yes. I normally live in water. Or, it's a metaphor. I'm out of my depth, struggling to stay alive and I need to get back to my natural habitat to keep breathing. You said to me, you promised me that when you got the use of your limbs back you would do everything you could to get me home. Well now it's time to deliver."

Sato looked at the floor. He seemed a little deflated.

"I thought there was more to you than that" he whispered, loud enough for Isaac to hear.

"Sorry to disappoint. I suppose I'm not the man you thought I was" Isaac admitted to him, quietly ashamed by the brazen cowardice he was displaying.

"Ok. I will take you home before I go and find them myself. Where is it?"

"It's Earth. I told you that already."

"Yes but where is it? How do we get there?"

"You fly the ship I imagine. I doubt we'll make it in a canoe."

"Which direction do we fly in? What are the coordinates?" Sato specified, getting annoyed at Isaac's inability to comprehend the question he was asking.

"Well I don't know. I thought you would" Isaac answered, perplexed at how Sato didn't know how to get to his planet.

"You thought that I, someone who has never been to, or heard of your planet before, would know how to get there, just because I have the ability to fly the ship?" Sato said, shaking his head disapprovingly.

Isaac went a little red in the face, embarrassed by his now obviously ridiculous assumption.

"Well I mean, when you say it like that of course it sounds stupid."

"Sorry Isaac, but unless you can sit at those controls up there and point this ship in the direction you want us to go, you are not going home. Fortunately for you I know two people who have the coordinates to your planet and they just so happen to be in the same place. We just have to figure out where that might be."

Isaac closed his eyes and placed the bridge of his nose between his thumb and his index finger and began to massage the skin there, tempering his frustration. He knew he didn't want to go back to Olan'ko's facility, but he also knew he had no choice.

"Alright," he said looking back at Sato, "let's go and get them."

25

Isaac sat across from Sato as he moved around the ship, checking different systems as he did. It was odd to see him walking. Not too long ago, Sato was a quadriplegic. Now he could move freely and he was moving with purpose. They had been using their last couple of hours to recount their time spent sharing a cell together, trying to pinpoint details to maybe spark some inspiration for finding out where the facility might be. So far, they had come up with nothing. Sato sat back down in the pilot seat, while Isaac was in the co-pilot seat beside him.

"We were there, in this very ship. How do we not know how to go back?" Isaac asked, a little frustrated.

"I've already explained that. Due to the fact that we are on a planet that does not have a fixed orbit, we can't just retrace the previous route this ship took because our current location will be a completely different point of origin" Sato replied.

"All your fancy tech and you still haven't mastered a decent satnav" Isaac jeered.

"OK, this is proving a lot harder than I had anticipated. Without the resources of the Assembly, we are at a serious disadvantage. Let's try again. So what do we know about the place? It was a prison, yes?" Sato asked Isaac a little rhetorically, like he was just thinking out loud.

"Well yes and no. It was a mineral refinery, but they had converted it into a dual purpose type place, so they could have a space to work, away from the prying eyes of the council, is how I believe he put it" Isaac said answering the question he wasn't really asked.

This broke Sato's train of thought and he stopped and turned to look at Isaac.

"How do you know that?" he asked, surprised by the disclosure of this new information.

"Olan'ko told me, when we were in his weird overseers office. It was early on. Like in the first week I'm fairly sure. They took me out of the cell and I was brought up to this big round glass room and he started telling me about all they were planning to do. Did I not tell you about that?" Isaac asked, surprised that he hadn't brought it up before.

"No. No you didn't" Sato replied seeming to quell his desire to slap Isaac. "What else did he say?"

"I'm pretty sure he said it was the biggest one they had" Isaac added, thinking back as best he could.

"Pretty sure or very sure? Because I'm going to need you to be very sure if we're going to start down another line of inquiry" Sato pressed him.

"Very" Isaac responded.

"Ok, we can get this. It's just going to take a little digging" Sato assured him.

"Can we not just look up the biggest Ilian mineral refinery?" Isaac asked.

"No it doesn't really work like that with the Ilians. We could look up almost any other races facilities, but the Ilians are strange. They don't really offer up that type of information openly. We'll have to figure it out ourselves." Sato pressed the console in front of him and began to search for information on the what was essentially the interstellar version of the internet.

"What are you looking for" Isaac asked him.

"I'm going through the Assembly's archives. The Ilians wouldn't publish that information openly but they would still have to log all schematics with the Assembly records by law if they wanted to trade any of the material they process there on the open market. They may not actively participate with other civilisations but they still rely on commerce with them in order to function as a society."

He scrolled through some menu's before trying to open a folder. The screen flashed red.

"What's the problem?" Isaac enquired.

"The file is sealed on a secure server" Sato told him.

"So are we at another dead end?"

"No. It's secure but I have access codes. It's a government server and I work for the government."

Sato logged in and began to download the schematics for all Ilian mineral refineries. There were fifteen in total and he went through them, one by one, until he had mapped them all out by size.

"Alright. From what I can tell this is where we need to go" he said eventually, bringing Isaac back into the moment. He had been staring off into the distance, trying not to freak out about his next expedition while Sato had been working.

"How long will it take to get there?" Isaac asked him.

"Just under a day. But we have a few things to do to prepare before we go."

"So, what do we do?" Isaac asked.

"We need to stock up on supplies before we go charging in" Sato said with a determination to his voice.

"By supplies you mean what exactly?" Isaac cautiously enquired.

"Lots of weapons and explosives."

"Just so you know, I'm not a soldier of any description. I'm not someone who is going to charge into danger and save the day" Isaac told Sato, feeling really apprehensive now that this was fast becoming a reality.

"Yes, you are" Sato replied.

"I'm not in any way trained to rush into a gun fight, let alone in bleedin space" Isaac snapped back.

"Isaac, I saw you charge head first into a fight already, more than once. I've seen you stand up to Olan'ko's mercenaries without a drop of fear in your eyes. You have it in you. You just don't recognize it. And the idea is to sneak in and quietly retrieve them unnoticed. Not charge in and take the whole facility head on. Now if your telling me you're not up to it, that's fine. I'll take you to the nearest Assembly world and leave you there until I get back, or not, depending on how the rescue goes" Sato reassured him.

Isaac paused a moment to try and get a grasp of the task he had in front of him. What an insane decision he had to make. The thought of not storming into a battle with just him and Sato, against who knows how many soldiers Olan'ko has appealed to him. Then the other side of that was if Sato didn't make it, he would be stranded on an alien planet with no means of getting home.

"Alright," Isaac said, "let's do it."

215

"Good" Sato replied, standing up.

"So where are we going now?"

"There's a arms dealer on the two hundred and twenty third level of this place. We're going to see him."

"So I'm on my way to an illegal arms deal now. This shit's getting out of hand man. We're moving into a whole new level of crazy I have to admit" Isaac said as he got up and followed Sato out the door.

26

Isaac stood leaning against a wall. He had been there for about five minutes, waiting. Sato had left him to go and get them access to whatever was taking place in the venue he was loitering outside of. He hadn't been too forthcoming with the details. Isaac was doing his best to stay out of sight of people and to try and hide his face as best he could under the newly obtained and surprisingly stylish hat he was wearing. Most of the people walking past him weren't at all interested in him though. They seemed to be too excited about entering the floor of the Abattoir behind him. There were a lot of people going in. Isaac felt a hand being placed on his shoulder and he turned to see Sato standing beside him.

"Come on. We're in."

He followed Sato towards the entrance. It was fairly plain, a big departure from the other floor he had been on. This was just one big entrance with a fairly reserved sign above it. A massive divergence from the neon jungle he had been on first.

"Hold out your wrist" Sato told him.

Isaac did as instructed and Sato wrapped a plastic bracelet around it and fastened it in place.

"What's that?" Isaac asked, examining the band.

"It's your ticket to get inside."

"So where exactly are we going?"

"This is the arena. It's a place where people go to gamble, drink and let off some steam. It's full of the wrong sort of people. We're trying to find someone who can get us into the weapons dealer. She likes to frequent this particular establishment for this event."

"And what is the event?"

"Rhalk fighting."

"What's that then?"

"You'll see. Here take this" Sato said, handing Isaac a little device that looked like a small smart phone.

"What is it?"

"It's a credit log. It's how you pay for things. There are a thousand credits loaded onto it. When we get inside, I want you to go to the bookmaker and place a bet on the main event. Then go get yourself a drink and hang around the pit. I'll find you when I'm ready."

"Ok, any suggestions on what I should drink?"

"I'm partial to some sonato myself."

They stepped inside the door to the arena and followed the crowd as they filed in through the ticket gate. Isaac stayed close to Sato as they approached the people checking the tickets. They seemed to all be Caninans. Although none of them seemed to be quite the size of Moga. Intimidating none the less. Just as Isaac and Sato got to the one who was checking tickets in front of them a commotion broke out just to their left. It wasn't clear what was happening but it was resolved fairly quickly as one of the Caninan security guards picked up the Talanite who seemed to be causing the problem with ease and dropped him straight down on his head. Isaac wasn't sure if the Talanite was dead or unconscious, but he wasn't waiting to find out. He flashed his wrist at the waiting behemoth standing in front of him who duly checked its validity with a scanner before gesturing for Isaac to proceed.

"Some people just don't listen" he heard Sato say.

They once again joined the crown filing into the venue. Walking down the hall, Isaac could hear a swelling of noise in the distance, that seemed to be a mixture of different sounds. They turned right and came back on themselves, before walking through an archway and out into the open space. The arena was the perfect name for what they had just entered. It gradually dropped down about fifty steps to the main area. The first thing Isaac noticed was the smell. It hit him like a punch in the nose. It was raw. There was definitely faeces in it, a little blood and also really bad body odour. Then there was another sweet scent sitting behind all of that, which seemed like a feeble attempt to cover all the bad stenches that were present.

They walked down some steps towards a railing surrounded by people, all looking down into a large pit, about one hundred feet in diameter, shouting and salivating, erupting with blood lust at the two creatures currently locked in battle below them. Isaac took a moment to observe the carnage. The drop down was about fifteen feet. The creatures were alien. Long thin bodies, with similar limbs. Quadrupeds, with long slim snouts and razor sharp teeth protruding from their blood soaked lips. Large black soulless eyes. They had long, hanging ears, although one seemed to be missing half off its left side. The wound seemed to be bleeding so it must have just happened. The top half of its ear was sitting on the brown dirt that made up the floor. Isaac was pretty disturbed by the whole thing.

"You can watch the fights later. Go and blend in" he heard Sato say.

He gladly walked away from the pit and followed Sato a little further into the venue.

"Up there behind those caged off windows. Those are the touts. Go place a bet, then get a drink and wait by the bar. I won't be long."

Isaac walked up the steps towards the betting booths. As he did, he realised he hadn't got a clue about who or what he was betting on. He slowed down a little to try and look at the boards above the betting hub. They weren't very clear or written in any way that he could really understand. The best he could tell, there were two events left, the last one being the main event. There seemed to be a colour coding scheme applied to the contenders. The main event had a green dot beside the name on the left and a yellow dot beside the name on the right but what those names were, Isaac had no clue.

"Fuck it" he said as he walked up to the counter, a steely determination in his eye, wading through the sea of tickets of lost bets that had been discarded on the floor after the previous fights had finished.

The clerk behind the counter looked at him as he approached. A Magalian, with a bored uninterested look on her face.

"Five hundred on the yellow guy" Isaac said as he got to the counter.

The Magalian clerk typed something into the little screen she had on the counter in front of her. Then looked up at Isaac. He looked back at her not too sure what was going on.

"Money" she said, in an annoyed grunt.

Isaac fumbled around in his pocket until he found the credit log that Sato had given him. He took it out and went to hand it to her. She looked back at him like he had two heads.

"Put it on the sensor" she said, gesturing to the counter in front of him.

Isaac looked down and noticed a small square on the counter, with a red light on it. He held the credit log against it for a second. The light turned green and a little ticket came sliding out of it. Isaac picked it up and turned and walked away, stuffing the ticket down deep into his pocket. He looked around the arena to try and spot the bar to get a drink. As he did a loud cheer rose up from the patrons who were surrounding the pit. It sounded like the fight was over. An announcement rang out over a loud speaker to inform the crowd that the next event would be in ten minutes. People filed away from there observation position and started to break off in different directions. Some were heading toward him. Some were heading in other directions. He surveyed the crowd until he spotted a few people stop at counter on the far side of the building enjoying some drinks and headed over towards them.

After a brief wait, he got to the counter and ordered himself a sonato. It came in a glass that was about the size and shape of a tennis ball, that had a small round opening at the top to drink from. The drink was an off yellow colour. Not too inviting to the eye, as it had a distinct hue of urine off it. The smell wasn't too tempting either. It was very reminiscent of dead fish. Isaac put the glass to his lips and took a quick sip. The taste matched the smell exactly. He spat the liquid out and made a face like he had just sucked on a lemon wedge. Two people beside him laughed as he did this. He turned to them, annoyed by their ridicule.

"What's so funny?"

"You" the one on the left said.

"What's funny about me?" Isaac asked.

"You don't sip that stuff. You drink it in one go. The taste doesn't allow for savouring" the second person informed him as they both burst out into laughter again.

Isaac looked back at his glass. He braced himself and poured the entire contents of it into his mouth and swallowed it in one go. The drink burned on the way down his throat. Like a whiskey burn, only with twice the intensity. He coughed and spluttered for a couple of seconds, to the great amusement of his two onlookers, then the burning went away and he settled down. The drink took effect immediately. It felt similar to the first time he got drunk. Not the same as being drunk, but a similar sensation. A warm content feeling stirred inside him. He could feel his anxiety fade a little. He became a little more relaxed in his surroundings and grew a little more confident in his footing. He looked over at the two people who had been laughing at him and gave them a pleasant smile. Then he walked back to the bar an ordered another, before taking a stroll around the rest of the arena. There was a mixture of all different races occupying the occasion. Isaac figured there was a large amount of illicit deals being sealed and perverse plans being hatched all around him. He didn't care though. The sonato was looking after his anxiety for the minute.

He drank the second glass he had been carrying around in one quick gulp, handling the initial impact of the drink much better the second time, then placed the empty container on a counter behind him, just as Sato returned.

222

"How many of those have you had?"

"That's my second. I like it."

"Ok well two is plenty. Come on. I've found who were looking for."

Isaac followed Sato back down to the railing surrounding the pit. There were more people filling up the spaces at the front, trying to get the best vantage point to see the coming attraction. Sato slid into a narrow space between two Magalians, one male and one female, resting his arms on the barrier. Isaac followed him over and stood watching them.

"Mir'hah, long time no see" Sato said to the lady on his left.

The first thing Isaac noticed about he was her striking beauty. She was an alien, but the symmetry of her face was undeniable. Beauty is beauty, regardless of what planet you were born on. This was a stunning woman. She turned all the way around and put her back up against the railing, her body facing Isaac, but her head turned toward Sato. She was wearing a dress. It was black, low cut at the front and it clung to her perfectly contoured body like it had been woven around her, rather than put onto her.

"Sato. What the fuck do you want?" was her reply.

"Business, always business. I need to see him."

"He's big time now Sato, he doesn't deal with common criminals."

She turned to look at Isaac now. Isaac noticed that she had a scar on the other side of her face. It ran from her left eyebrow, back towards her ear, then turned again, finishing just below her bottom lip. It only added to her beauty.

"Who's your friend?" Mir'hah asked, gesturing to Isaac.

"Hi, my is Isaac. Sorry, I mean my am Isaac. I am, am, I am Isaac. It's my name" he said, putting his hand out to shake hers. She just looked down at it, then back up, completely bewildered.

"He's an associate, I'm actually doing this for him. I have a list. I'm fairly certain it's big time enough for him."

Sato took a small hand held out of his pocket and handed it to Mir'hah. She scanned the list briefly before handing it back to him.

"That's a lot of money. You sure you can afford all that?" she asked, the words to Isaacs ears, a sultry and seductive tone. Isaac couldn't help but stare at her. He was enamoured. He followed the lines in her skin all the way around her face. Taking in each little wrinkle and blemish. He lowered his gaze study of her features further down her body. Her dress was so tight he could see little indentations on her stomach beneath it. The dress wrapped around her thighs perfectly. It cut off at the knee. For a brief moment in Isaac's head, they were the only two souls in existence. Isaac was unaware but his head tilted sideways the lower down he looked to the point here he was now in the process of ogling her. A fact Mir'hah was very aware of.

"Is he ok?", she asked, looking at Isaac a little concerned.

"Oh yes, he just had two sonatos for the first time. I doubt he's even aware of himself."

Sato and Mir'hah shared a smile at Isaacs expense over this, then she returned to her all business façade.

"Five thousand. Facilitation fee. You get me that and I'll have you in there before the end of the day."

Sato took out a credit log and handed it to Mir'hah.

"By the end of the day."

She took the log and slipped it into the hand of a Garian that was standing on the other side of her.

"Go and place that on the mutt to win" she said before turning back to Sato. The Garian walked away headed in

224

the direction of the tout. "My, you have changed. When was the last time you could hand over five thousand, just like that?"

"I told you. I'm big time now too."

She nodded and turned her back on Isaac, facing the pit again. Sato grabbed Isaac by the arm and gestured him to leave and they both walked away as Isaac took a few final glances over his shoulder back at Mir'hah. As they headed past the pit Isaac put his hand on Sato's shoulder and forced him to stop.

"Come on. We don't have time."

"But I have a bet on. I want to watch."

"Show me."

Isaac rummaged around in his pocket for a minute until he found the slip he had taken from the tout and handed it to Sato.

"You bet five hundred credits on a one thousand to one underdog."

"Well it's not like I had any tips or inside information. I don't even know what it is I bet on."

"Ok, it's about to start. We might as well watch you lose your money."

They found a spot where they could both fit standing at the rail and leaned in to get a better view.

"So what is this exactly" Isaac asked, his head still woozy from the drink.

"It's Rhalk fighting. Two Rhalks enter. One leaves."

"Sounds barbaric."

"It is. I despise it."

A loud horn sounded and the crowd erupted into a chorus of cheers as the lights in the arena dimmed a little and the pit lit up. There were two large steel doors on either side. Isaac and Sato seemed to have managed to find themselves

225

right in the middle. The one on the left opened and a quadrupedal creature emerged from it. It had tan coloured fur and it was immense. Isaac was a good fifty feet away from it but even still, the animal looked enormous. It stood about ten or twelve feet high. Maybe six feet wide at the shoulders on the front. Its front legs had the circumference of a couple of small trees and its back legs weren't far off the same size. It had muscles protruding from its muscles. Its sternum ran from its neck down to close to its knees before curving around, back towards its rump. It had a short snout, with two large fangs protruding on either side of its mouth and it had horns that extended about a foot past its shoulders on either side and then turned straight up into a point. The top of its head had a large round surface to it, like it had evolved to have a helmet of bone under its skin. The beast let out an almighty roar that shook Isaacs ear drums to their very limit.

"He's your guy" Sato told him.

"That's my guy. Then what the fuck are you worried about" Isaac said, jovially slapping him on the back.

The second gate opened and another Rhalk emerged. This one looked the same as the first but with two very noticeable differences. It had a brindle colour pattern to its fur, a combination of grey and black and it was about three feet taller and about two feet wider than the other. Isaacs heart sank.

"Oh, I see."

The two monsters locked eyes on each other and they both reared up and charged. They made it about two steps before a chain that was attached around their necks pulled them back. Then a voice came booming out all around the venue.

"People feast your eyes on the main event of the evening. The underdog, coming from Ilaak Sarg promotions, a relative newcomer to the scene. This animal has a record of ten fights, three of which have ended in a one shot kill. Make some noise for Alpha Mutt."

The crowd gave a reserved cheer. Not the introduction that Isaac had been hoping for. Nor was it a name that inspired any confidence.

"Now the favourite. This monster comes from Bet'ron entertainment. It appears before you today with a record of thirty nine fights, all thirty nine coming by way of one shot kill. Patrons, go wild for the unmatched, the unbridled, the untamed, Spirit Bitch."

The crowd erupted in a volley of noise that seemed to startle both beasts and they reared up on their hind legs, snorting and snarling at each other. Isaac leaned in to Sato.

"What's with the weird names?"

"What's weird about them?" Sato replied.

A horn sounded three times then the chains attached to each animal fell to the ground and a fourth horn signalled the start of the fight. The animals both began to circle to the right, moving around the pit but keeping the same distance between them and their eyes locked on each other. Eventually Isaac's bet was standing right below him and his opponent was on the opposite side of the circle. The beast stomped its foot on the ground and began to paw at the dirt beneath it, getting ready to make its move. Then they suddenly charged. Isaac could feel the vibrations from each of the beasts' steps reverberate through the floor beneath him as the animals bounded straight towards each other. Just as they reached the centre of the pit they both lowered their heads. The collision was wicked. It sounded like a ferocious clap of thunder rang out around the arena as both animals' helmet skulls collided. Neither of them took a step back, they just reared up and began to throw their front legs at the other, in an attempt to land a strike, like two pugilists in a Markus of Queensbury rules street fight, before landing back on all fours. Then they both attacked with their horns. Each one swiping at the other as best they could, trying to stab or slice its opponent. A fencing duel, the swords extensions of their bodies.

"Holy shit, this is intense" Isaac said to Sato.

"Yes, but it won't be long now I imagine. These fights rarely last. The animals don't have much stamina" Sato replied, not looking away from the action.

Then Spirit Bitch landed a blow, a sneaky headbutt that stunned Alpha Mutt a little, before slicing across his front right leg with his horn, lacerating his quadricep, then taking a few steps back. Alpha Mutt also stumbled backwards to the edge of the pit, again just below them, as some blood flowed out of his freshly opened wound, before trying to regain his footing. Spirit Bitch steadied himself and readied for his final charge.

"Well, that's how it goes I suppose. This one is over anyway" Sato said to Isaac.

They both stood up off the rail in anticipation of the inevitable finish to the fight that was merely seconds away. Then a commotion rose up to their right. A fight seemed to break out between two patrons. Neither Isaac nor Sato could see exactly what was going on.

Spirit Bitch charged, lowering his head as he did. Then the fight between the spectators got out of hand. It turned into a brawl. There were several people involved now. One of them was sent tumbling over the rail into the pit below. It looked like a Talanite as he fell to the ground and landed with a thud ten feet from the fighting Rhalk. This drew the attention of both animals, who turned to see what had entered their domain. Spirit Bitch kept running, looking to its left as it did. Alpha Mutt also turned towards the new entrant into the combat zone, just as Spirit Bitch arrived into his space, impaling himself on his opponent's horn. The bone entered his chest, then Alpha Mutt drew back, ripping it out of him, along with what looked like several of his vital organs. Spirit Bitch stumbled around, before falling over on his side as gallons of blood spilled out of him onto the dirt below. The Talanite now regained his consciousness and stood up, a little confused and unsteady on his feet, before being instantly eviscerated by the charging Alpha Mutt. A stunned hush fell over the crowd, broken suddenly by Isaac.

"Yeeeeees, you fucking dancer."

27

Isaac stood at the back of the giant platform as it sped up through the Abattoir. He had discarded his hat in favour of the hood of his recently acquired jacket to try and mask his appearance but also, to shield his eyes from the light as much as he could. The effects of sonato don't last for very long as he was finding out and the hangover is intense. Sato assured him it would pass soon. Not that Isaac was too bothered by it. He was buoyant from his newly acquired half a million credits he had just won. So far nobody had given him a second glance. Everyone around him was just minding their own business and going about their own day. Sato had stood at the front of the elevator. He decided it was a good idea to separate a little, pretend they didn't know each other just in case there was an incident along the way. He had told Isaac there were currently one and a half million people occupying the five hundred and fifty levels on the Abattoir. That was an approximation since there was no real register or customs on entry for people as they came and went. So the chances of them actually being seen was quite low, but better to be safe than sorry.

The lift stopped at several floors on the way and people got on and off. Magalian's, Garian's, Talanite's, one or two Ilian's, and two other species that Isaac hadn't seen before now. One was short, about four and a half feet tall and appeared to be covered in fur beneath the clothes it had on, with small beady eyes and an elongated nose. The other was tall, about seven feet, but thin and frail looking. It had very pale skin and it had a mask on that looked like some sort of breathing apparatus, covering its nose, mouth and chin, which made it hard for Isaac to get a real good look at its features. This was the last person to accompany Isaac and Sato on the lift. He got off on level one hundred and eighty nine.

Even though they were alone, Isaac and Sato didn't say anything to each other. They just stayed on opposite sides of the elevator looking in different directions. Sato had told Isaac not to acknowledge him once they had gotten on, as anyone could be listening. Isaac was a bit sceptical of the whole thing, but he didn't argue. Only one of them was an expert in interstellar espionage and it wasn't him. That wasn't really a concern Isaac ever thought he'd have in his life.

The elevator arrived at level two hundred and twenty three. Sato exited first, with Isaac hot on his heels. This floor once again was very different to the others that Isaac had been on since arriving at the Abattoir. All the other floors were both full of people and places to go. The connection and exuberance that they had made the Abattoir feel like a vibrant city as you walked around. Depending on where you where, you would forget that you were inside a giant structure and would get lost in the illusion that you could be in any major urban hub anywhere in the galaxy. This floor was a pale grey colour, all the way around.

231

There was only one door on the whole floor, about twenty feet in front of them. This floor definitely broke that illusion. A thought immediately occurred to Isaac. All the other floors had passageways to walk around almost like streets, that took you in different directions and into different enterprises. On this floor there was about twenty feet of walkway before you met a wall in every direction. Just how damn big was this arms dealer's operation.

"Can we speak now?" Isaac asked.

"Yes of course." Sato responded turning to face him.

"How likely are we to pull this off?"

"Pull what off, getting what we need in here, or the whole thing in general?"

"The whole thing in general."

"I mean honestly, I'm giving us about fifty-fifty."

"Oh really", Isaac said a little surprised, "you're that optimistic?"

"It's only the two of us coming so if we do it right they won't know anything about us, and once we get to the location, if it's where we need to be, as long as our infiltration goes well our odds dramatically increase."

Isaac wasn't sure if he was more or less confident after Sato's pep talk but he was still willing to go along, so at least that was something. Sato turned and walked towards the door and Isaac followed him. They remained silent again for the short walk to it. Once there Sato pressed a screen on the right of the entrance and they waited for a response. A smiling female Garians face flashed up on the display.

"Hello, may I help you?" she asked politely.

"Sato Halsa, here to see Yangar."

The Garian woman looked down from the screen for a second, then back up to them.

"Of course sir, welcome" she smiled and then disappeared from the video.

The door slid open and they both walked inside. There was a long corridor, about the same width as the entrance door, that travelled straight to a desk about fifty meters or so away. As they walked towards the desk, Isaac couldn't help but notice the two laser cannons that were on rails on either side of the corridor, following them as they walked, aimed perilously at their heads.

"Should we be worried about those?" Isaac asked, gesturing to them.

"Not overly, security in a place like this is impenetrable. That's how they operate so successfully."

"I'm starting to sweat. I think it's a combination of the booze and the absolute terror I'm feeling right now."

"Just follow my lead, move when I move and all will be well" Sato assured him as they arrived at the desk.

"Hello Mr. Halsa, and welcome. Please wait one moment for your escort to arrive."

"Of course" Sato replied.

They stood there for a moment in silence waiting. Isaac was uneasy, which didn't go unnoticed by the Garian receptionist.

"Is everything alright? Can I get you anything?" she asked Isaac.

Isaac turned to look at her before trying to reply, but his words wouldn't work properly due to a combination of cotton mouth and his current cognitive impairments and all he managed was an indistinguishable grunting noise. She looked back at him a little confused before Sato stepped in.

"He's fine, just a little Tuchan flu. Bed rest is the only thing he needs but unfortunately we have a schedule to keep."

She looked back at Isaac again with a little more intention this time.

"Wow, you are so pale, are you sure I can't get you drink or something?" she asked.

"Fine" was all that Isaac could manage.

Just as he said that a hidden door to their right opened up, seemingly out of nowhere as far as Isaac could tell and a gentleman wearing what looked like a nice tailored three piece suit came out of it and walked towards them. He was Talanite, maybe six foot, but with a slim build. He had an air of confidence about him in the way he moved. Razor sharp features, even for a Talanite.

"Gentlemen, my name is Enack, I'm an associate of Yangar. If you would like to follow me I'll take you to see him so we can conduct our business."

"Of course" Sato replied, as Enack walked through the door and they followed him.

Once through, they were met with a wall about ten feet in front of them. The door behind them closed and they were now sealed in some kind of containment room. Enack walked past them and placed his hand on the wall. A small thin blue light traced the shape of a door out on the wall as it moved around, then the wall shimmered and disappeared, similar to the way Isaacs and Sato's cell use to do.

"Fingerprints?" Isaac asked.

"DNA" Sato answered.

They walked through the opening which led into a large warehouse space. They followed behind Enack as he made his way through the operation. There were conveyer belts of merchandise moving along in all directions as far as Isaac could see. There were small and large ships, all black with no distinguishable marking on them being loaded with crates and boxes. They looked like delivery trucks from

Earth, but these ones could fly between worlds. Isaac looked on in awe. It was like Amazon for weapons.

"Holy fuck" was all he could manage to say.

"Yes, it's quite the operation. We are the largest supplier of privately owned weapons in the galaxy. Hence all the security you've had to endure thus far" Enack responded.

"I don't understand, I thought the Assembly ran everything. Who would be buying all this?" Isaac asked Sato quietly.

"You've read the Assembly history and watched their news. It's biased. It's not corrupt, yet, for the most part, but it still has an unreliability problem. There are seventy six planets under the Assembly's rule, remember. Less than half of these are major colonies. The larger colonies and home worlds house a significant portion of the population, so they have the loudest voice and wield the biggest political influence, but you're still talking about billions of people outside of those worlds. Many of them are either resource colonies or smaller or fledgling settlements. There's plenty of lawlessness and corruption to be taken advantage of, for the right kind of entrepreneurial mind set."

"Christ man, how is it that politics can fucking suck on the far side of the galaxy?"

"It's the nature of it. A Crisian can only dance once in the light."

"Fuck knows what the hell that means man, but I'm sure it is profound and inspiring."

Isaac walked on, still so amazed by all that was going on around him, he didn't realise Sato and Enack had stopped and he continued on into a wall. Or what he thought was a wall at first, until it moved. He was now staring at the biggest individual he had ever laid eyes on. The Caninan must have been about eight and a half feet tall and about three feet wide at the shoulders. Isaac took four steps back and he still had to look up to see this things face. He thought Moga was big. The Caninan just grunted.

"Yangar" Sato said, in a friendly familiar way.

"Sato, I got your list. Very interesting" Yangar replied, his voice so deep, Isaac swore he could feel it vibrating in his chest.

"Were you able to round it all up for me?" Sato asked.

"Yes, not easy though, may cost extra" Yangar told him.

"Money is not an issue Yangar, I have told you this already" Sato assured him.

Yangar took a big whiff in through his nose. It was so deep Isaac felt the air whoosh past him into Yangar's nostrils.

"Your friend smells funny. What is?" Yangar asked in that unmistakable Caninan way.

"A new species from a planet called Earth. I have the pleasure of looking after him for the time being. Not relevant to our business though. Are we ready to go?" Sato asked impatiently.

"But it has everything to do with our business" Enack interjected.

"Oh?" Sato replied.

"Who do you think supplies Olan'ko with all that he needs to run whatever it is he's doing? It's obvious when you think about it. It could only be us. And you have brought the exact thing he is looking for right to us" Enack sneered as he took a pistol from the back of his waist band and pointed it in Sato's direction.

Calmly, several other people who had been patiently waiting close by for their ambush to be initiated drew their weapons too and surrounded them, all pointing pistols at

236

Sato and Isaac. Isaac looked at Sato, but Sato was looking directly at Enack, his expression unchanged.

"Of course you do. It's so obvious when you think about it" Sato said.

Enack looked a little surprised by this response. Yangar just looked expressionless.

"Are you saying you are aware of our dealings with Olan'ko?" Enack asked.

"No not aware, just suspicious. Now I have confirmation. I was never really looking for everything on the list I sent you. I just needed to get you interested enough to do business with me so you would let me in the building. It's not like we could break into a place like this. Your security is incredible. We'd be dead at the front door."

"Oh really. And what was the point of walking into our trap then?" Enack asked with an unmasked distain.

"Well that's the thing. Let's be honest. Your trap was obvious. Mine, not so much."

A dazzling flash of light rendered Isaac blind. All he could hear was ringing in his ears. He was unsure of what had just happened. He was calling out to Sato, but he couldn't hear his own voice. He could just feel the words vibrating in his throat as he said them. Panic set in. What had Sato just done? Isaac waited for a shot from one of the guns that had been pointing at him to take him down. But thankfully it never came. Then he felt someone's arms wrap around his waist and hoist him up in the air. Someone was carrying him.

28

Isaac could begin to see outlines of shapes around him. His vision was slowly returning. His ears were another issue. He could still hear a loud ringing in them but that was just about all he could hear. He could only assume he was with Sato and he was safe but that was yet to be determined. Eventually he could see movement in front of him. The silhouette of a figure. He was also starting to hear his name being called but it sounded way off in the distance.

"What? Who's there? Sato is that you?" Isaac asked loudly.

He heard a muted voice in response but still couldn't determine who it was or what they were saying.

"No, it's no good. I can't hear a fucking thing. I can kind of see though" Isaac offered in response to whoever was talking to him.

The figure moved closer until they were right in front of Isaacs nose. Mercifully, it was Sato standing there. His lips were moving but there were no words coming from them that Isaac could distinguish. That was initially a relief to Isaac but now his anger at being rendered blind and deaf had returned.

"…a moment…patience." Isaac heard Sato say through the ringing in his ears finally.

"Is this shit going to wear off?" Isaac shouted just as his hearing seemed to return to normal.

"See, all is well" Isaac heard Sato say as clear as could be.

"How did you do that?" he asked.

"I have a device to counteract the effects the flash bomb had on your ears. Your hearing should be working fine now"

"What about my eyes?"

"They will return in their own time. I can't do anything about those unfortunately."

"So, what the fuck?" Isaac asked, annoyed.

"What the fuck what?" Sato replied.

"What just happened? One minute we're in the middle of an arms deal, the next, I don't know because I was rendered fucking useless" Isaac demanded angrily.

"My sincerest apologies Isaac, but we are in a very time sensitive situation, I need to be able to assess and improvise based on how the information presents itself in real time. I am used to working alone and being able to be reactive. I had an idea that we were walking into a trap, but I couldn't be certain. I had no time to advise you of the different scenarios that could possibly unfold in that situation."

Isaac took a moment to consider this. It was actually a very reasonable explanation for what had taken place. It kind of made it hard to be mad at Sato, which was very annoying, because he really wanted to be mad right now.

"Ok, I'll accept it. Though I'm not happy about it" Isaac admitted.

"Understood" Sato replied.

Isaac rubbed his itchy eyes and noticed that his vision was staring to improve more. He could make out details around him clearer. The first thing he noticed was that they were in a ship, a small one similar to the one they had been rescued from Olan'ko's secret facility in. The interior was a little different though. They were also in transit having clearly departed Altanto.

"So, we're in a ship I see, travelling somewhere. Do you feel like sharing now?" Isaac asked sarcastically.

"Yes of course. As I said, I had an idea that Yangar and Enack were behind Olan'ko's weapons. The only way to be sure was to put you in front of them and see how they reacted. They didn't disappoint"

"Ok, so I was bait?" Isaac asked annoyed.

"A little, but I was there every step of the way so you were in no danger. Or rather you were only ever in the same danger that I had put myself in. Either way it worked out" Sato reassured him, not very convincingly.

"Ok, so what was the point of the whole thing then?"

"Well since we now know that they are supplying him, we now have a way into the facility undetected."

"How, this ship?"

"Yes. Yangar and Enack will have ships coming and going from the facility all the time. They will have access and clearance codes programmed into their navigation systems to ensure smooth and seamless entry and departure with minimal disruption to the operation. We merely need to fly up to the front door and walk in, so to speak."

"Ok, but what if Yangar and Enack contact Olan'ko and tells him we're on the way?"

"Well I have made sure that nobody will be speaking to either of them, for at least a couple of days. It will give us plenty of time to get in, rescue everyone, shut down the operation and get out."

"How? Isaac asked.

"I sealed them all in a shipping container and sent it to the Assembly. With all the red tape that deliveries have to go through once they arrive there, it will be a while before they are speaking to anyone" Sato professed, a little smugly.

"Right, well, I suppose I can't really complain since you seem to know what you're doing. Is there any chance you could include me in the planning going forward, so I at least know what's coming next time?" Isaac asked.

"Of course, I will need your assistance for the next part anyway" Sato assured him.

"Great. We're making progress. So, what is the plan for when we get there?"

"I can't tell you that" Sato replied.

"What? Seriously, we just had this conversation like, two seconds ago. It's better when I know. Remember?"

"No, I said I would include you in the planning going forward. I can't tell you what comes after this because I won't know until we get there and I determine the best course of action to take. I will then include you in the planning when we make it that far" Sato told him as he smiled.

"Fuck sake man. What the hell are you smiling about? It's creepy."

"I've always wanted a protégé" Sato replied.

"I'm not that. No way."

"We'll see" Sato said smiling again.

They sat there silently. Isaac was pondering what he was about to be involved in. He was screwed. No matter what, no matter the outcome, his life would never be the same

241

again. Considering the past few months he just had, that was really saying something. He had no idea what in the hell might be going through Sato's head.

"Can you at least tell me what we're about to do? Like a general idea. Maybe just the bullet points so I have some semblance of what might be required of me" Isaac pleaded

"We are going to land at Olan'ko' facility. Once there, we will proceed inside. You're to stay close to me. I mean right on me. Once we gain access to a console, we will be able to locate Car'esh and the rest of his crew. When we do that you will go and free them while I make arrangements for our escape."

Isaac sat slack jawed at this new information.

"We're going to split up? You want me to sneak around some alien facility like I'm James fucking Bond?"

"Is James Bond good at sneaking?" Sato asked, genuinely curious.

"Yeah, in fantasy land" Isaac shouted at him.

"We'll then yes, exactly like James Bond."

"I don't believe this."

"Sorry Isaac. I was under the impression that you wanted to help" Sato said.

"I am. It's just a lot to take right now, you know." Isaac said, quite flustered.

"I'm sorry. I have been doing things like this for a long time now. Almost forty years. It just comes as second nature to me. I never considered your position" Sato told him earnestly.

Isaac looked at him with surprise etched on his face.

"You've been doing this for almost forty years? How old are you?"

"Sixty two" Sato replied.

"Wow, your looking good for an old man." Isaac told him.

"I'm not old. I'm only starting the second phase of the life cycle" Sato replied, a little insulted by the inference.

He turned his concentration back to the helm of the ship. Isaac looked out at darkness of space that they were travelling through. He got lost in his head for a minute thinking about all that lay ahead. All that could go wrong and what it could mean. He could be killed. He could be captured, a fate worse than death if his last stay at the facility was anything to go by, or they could be successful, which offered up its own set of problems, but was definitely the preferred outcome of the situation.

"Have you ever snuck around anywhere before?" Sato asked, pulling Isaac out of his thoughts.

"Sorry?" Isaac replied.

"When you were a child, did you ever sneak into a place you weren't supposed to be, just to do it, or to see or do something you shouldn't have?" Sato elaborated.

Isaac tried to take a moment to think about this, but Sato spoke again and broke his concentration.

"When I was enrolled in the Assembly's educational institution, I was educated at an ingiral. It's a place where you live while you receive your education."

"Do all Garian children go to these places?"

"No. I was identified early as a strong candidate for military service."

"How come?"

"I was born on a farm. Every year we would have a problem around harvest time with wing rat infestations. My father and I would have to take care of them. We would spend a week taking them out. I would shoot fifty a day at least. Never miss. Fifty shots. Fifty dead wing rats.

243

My parents eventually took me to the enrolment office to have me assessed for service. I was admitted on my first evaluation."

"Isn't that a little cruel. Sending a child to the military?"

"No. My parents could only dream of an education like that for me and they definitely couldn't afford to get me one themselves. It was the only option really. And it wasn't like they were sending me to fight a war as a child. I was simply learning until I graduated and was then old enough to be deployed."

"Yeah I suppose that's fair enough. We have something like that too by the way, they're called boarding schools."

Sato acknowledged Isaacs information with a nod before continuing.

"Some nights my friend and I would sneak out of our rooms and make our way across the property, avoiding the teachers who would be on patrol or out enjoying their evening. We would make our way through the library and climb onto the roof."

"Why? To look at the stars or something?" Isaac asked.

"No. You could see into the changing room of the girls ingiral from that roof" Sato said, laughing.

"That's called being a pervert my friend. You'd get arrested and put on the sex offenders register for that where I'm from."

"Did you ever do anything like that?" Sato asked.

"Nope. I ain't a pervert like you and your weird friends" Isaac assured him.

"Not specifically like that. But anything similar" Sato clarified.

Again, Isaac took a moment to think. He thought all the way back as far as he could remember and started to work his way forward. Then he recalled something that fit the bill but it was so embarrassing that he was reluctant to share it.

"Well there is one thing that comes to mind" he began.

"Tell me" Sato encouraged him.

"When I was a kid, I snuck out of my house one Christmas Eve" Isaac began.

"What is Christmas?" Sato asked, interrupting.

"It's a holiday on Earth when you get together with family and friends and exchange gifts and spend time together, eating, laughing and just generally having a good time."

"Sounds nice" Sato replied.

"Yeah it is. I was in bed, but I was being really annoying to my mother because I was so excited. I wouldn't go asleep. So she told me she had painted a giant x on the roof of our house to tell Santa Clause that he wasn't to stop there and to leave me no presents" Isaac continued, pausing as he fondly thought back on the memory.

"Who is Santa Clause?" Sato interrupted again.

"He's the man who goes around on Christmas Eve delivering presents to all the good girls and boys" Isaac explained, a little too simply.

Sato took a moment to consider this.

"You have a magic man who travels your whole world in one night to deliver presents to all the children who dwell there?" Sato asked genuinely confused.

"What? No, it's a story we tell kids. You know, to try and add a little magic to their lives once a year. Anyway, you're missing the point. I snuck out of my room, past my parents and out the door. I was trying to find the black x to remove it."

"Did you?" Sato asked.

"No. There was no x. Now that I think more about it, I fell off the roof of my house and nearly broke my neck, so

245

it wasn't that successful. I don't think your little mental exercise has been triumph here to be honest" Isaac professed.

"Your story makes no sense" Sato told him, a little agitated.

"What was the point of you getting me to think about that anyway" Isaac asked, frustrated.

"Oh yes. I wanted to get you to think about a time when you had to be stealthy. To be unseen because there would be consequences if you were. Because that is all you're doing tomorrow. The only difference is the consequences could be fatal. Although from the sound of it, your last attempt at something like this could have been fatal too, so that difference is nullified" Sato explained.

"Yeah. Ok I see what you're doing. I'll focus on that" Isaac agreed.

"You should try and get some sleep. Go and lie down. We've still got a good few hours to travel" Sato said.

"Yeah I suppose you're right" Isaac agreed.

He stood up and made his way to the back, looking for a spot to get comfortable in. He pilled some exosuits that were lying around and made a makeshift pillow with them, before lying down and closing his eyes.

"I would like to revisit this Santa Clause person later" Sato called back to him.

"Sure. When we get through this I'll tell you all about him" Isaac assured him.

He closed his eyes and tried to get some sleep.

29

Isaac woke up with a start. He hadn't been asleep that long. He had been lying down for hours but was having trouble shutting off. Impending doom would definitely have that effect on you. He shifted his position a couple of times trying to get comfortable again but wasn't having much success. He lay there looking at the ceiling of the ship. It was black. There were no distinguishing features on it either. It was just a smooth black surface.

Isaac sat up and looked around. Sato was sitting at the front of the ship, where he was when Isaac had fallen asleep. He got up and walked to him and as he sat in the co-pilots chair, he noticed they were stopped. Outside the window he saw a massive planet, just in front of them. They were so close to it that he could only see a portion of the world. It was various tints of blue and yellow in colour, different shades weaved together, giving the distinct impression that they were stacked one on top of the other, layered to perfection. There were some patches of wispy gas clouds floating across the blue scenery that had captivated him. Some swirled around each other, then crashed into others to create larger formations all across the sky. Isaac spotted a small moon stationed off to the right of their position. It was oval shaped.

"Where are we?" he asked, entranced by the view.

"P30571. It's another planet in the same solar system as Olan'ko's facility."

"It's incredible."

"I had to stop because I picked up a signal for a scanner just behind that moon. Had I passed it without knowing it was there we would have announced our arrival to whoever is keeping an eye on it."

"Good thing you were paying attention so."

"Yes, indeed it is. Are you ready to go?"

"Yeah. I mean as I'll ever be I suppose."

"Ok. Let's head in."

Sato began to move the ship away. As they passed above the planet, Isaac caught sight of something spectacular. An aurora was igniting in the sky at the pole. It was a red ring of light, like a halo, sparkling and flaring, against the blue and yellow contrast that the planet itself presented behind it. He was mesmerised by the display and watched it intently, completely lost in its majesty, until they had passed by it entirely and it disappeared from view. For a moment he was an eight year old again, looking at the spectacular images of dreamt up far away worlds, presented by television shows and documentaries about what space might look like. Except here he was, looking at the wonder with his own two eyes. It was surreal.

Isaac looked down at the navigation console and saw that they were moving through the solar system quite quickly. He got up and moved to the back of the ship to have a word with himself, in his head, to try and fully psyche himself up. There were two screens on one of the walls and he noticed that one of them had a picture of Sato on it. The

248

picture then changed. It was another still image. Isaac recognised that it was an image from inside the Abattoir. He sat up straight and began paying more attention to it. Then the screen changed again and there was an image that seemed to be taken from a security camera. It was a picture of him. Not a great picture. He had his hood up so his face wasn't really on show, but he recognised himself.

"What's this?" he called out to Sato.

Sato looked over his shoulder to see what Isaac was talking about.

"It's a comm-net terminal. That is a news bulletin you are watching."

"I know it's a comm-net terminal. I mean why are we on it?" Isaac asked.

Sato tapped some commands into the controls, then stood up and walked over to stand beside him. They both looked at the screen for a moment as Isaac's picture was spread around the galaxy on what was the most available news program to all the citizens of the Galactic Assembly. Sato put his fingers on the screen and slid them upward, increasing the volume so they could hear what was being said.

"Again, they are armed and considered extremely dangerous. If you encounter either of these men do not approach them. Contact your local security office and let them handle it. Once more, the person accompanying Sato Halsa is a species we have not encountered before and therefore could be carrying any number of pathogens that have yet to be identified. As much as the capture of these two men is high on the Assembly's agenda, the safety of the public is the Assembly's number one priority" a voice said over the picture of Isaac.

"Fuck" Sato shouted.

"Most definitely" Isaac answered.

"This doesn't make any sense. There is no way that Enack and Yangar could have gotten out of that crate I locked them in that quickly. I mean they wouldn't have even arrived where I sent them yet" Sato said as he took a moment to think.

"So what does this mean?"

"There must be someone working hard for Olan'ko inside the Assembly. There is someone high up, much higher than I thought, either working with or working for Olan'ko."

"For the plan. What does it mean for our current plan?" Isaac clarified.

"Not a lot. Unless they figure out exactly what it is we're planning on doing in a very short amount of time, nothing has changed. I doubt they will have figured it out this quickly. This looks to me like whoever is doing Olan'ko's bidding is just casting a wide net to try and snag us in it. They must be so desperate to find you that they've enlisted the help of the Assembly without fully showing their intention" Sato reassured him.

"Right, but what if they have figured it out?" Isaac asked, concerned.

A low beeping noise started to chime out from the control console at the front of the ship.

"Well, too late now. We're here" Sato told him as he walked to the front of the ship and sat down on at the controls.

"So, just stick to the plan?" Isaac asked as he sat down beside him.

"Just stick to the plan. If I have to improvise, I have to improvise" Sato informed him as he took manual control of the steering.

He pressed a few buttons in front of him then placed his hand on the steering console and pulled it back towards him. The ship made a noise like it was powering down. The space in front of them changed. It shimmered a little, then suddenly there was a planet in front of them.

"Someday someone is going to have to explain to me how all this space flight stuff works" Isaac said, looking on in wonderment.

"What do you mean?"

"Well one minute we're flying through space, then you press buttons, the space I'm looking at changes and all of a sudden there's a planet in front of us, just there."

"Sub space. We travel between stars in sub space. The interstellar drive uses an element to distort normal space, bending it, to allow us to travel in sub space. Once we get where we're going, we exit sub space and fly in normal space" Sato explained.

"I see" Isaac said, not actually seeing.

Sato was adjusting the controls some to fly the ship when a voice started talking to them through the comms, or what Isaac assumed was the comms.

"Transport one seven five two. This is flight control. Please proceed to docking bay five one for offload and inspection" the voice instructed them.

"Copy flight control. Docking bay five one" Sato replied.

"Is that it?" Isaac asked.

"That is our access point. I believe we may have trouble with the inspection part though. I wasn't expecting that."

"So, time to improvise then?"

"We'll see how we will proceed once we get to the docking bay" Sato said.

"Damn it. That never works out for me" Isaac shouted, slamming his fist down on the console in front of him.

"Go put one of the exosuits on. At least you will be dressed appropriately."

Isaac stood up and moved to the back of the ship where he had piled the suits up to sleep on. He picked up the first one and started to put it on. It was the same type of suit that he had worn when he and Car'esh's crew had landed on the planet to fix the ship after their first encounter with Olan'ko's army. He put his feet in first, then pulled the rest of the suit up. He slid his arms in, then once he was ready, he pressed the button on his collar and the suit firmed up and shaped itself to fit him.

"Ok, now come here and fly for a minute while I get ready" Sato said to him.

"Fly the ship?" Isaac asked with concern, as he walked toward the front again.

Sato stood up and gestured to Isaac to sit in the pilot's chair. Isaac obliged him, reluctantly.

"You know I have no idea how to do this yeah?" he protested.

"You don't really have to do much. Just aim it the way we need to go. I'll be ready by the time we need to land" Sato reassured him.

"How do I know where we need to go?" Isaac asked.

Sato leaned down and pressed a button on the controls. The heads up display on the window in front of them changed and two red lines appeared, similar to the white lines on a road you would use to keep your car in lane back on Earth.

"Just stay inside the lines. We will arrive shortly."

Sato stood up and moved towards the back of the ship. The planet looked a little different than the last time they had been here. For one it was dusk, so the light level was lower. Also there were more clouds in the sky. Isaac paid attention to the lines. They seemed to be rising up, so he pulled the controls toward him and the ship raised its nose a little, to match the line of ascent on his screen. It was directing him over the peak of a mountain in front. Once clear of the mountain, the line began to descend and Isaac pushed the console in, lowering the nose to follow the lines down again. Once it had levelled off, the lines seemed to bend around to the left gradually. Isaac once again directed the console the way the lines were going and the ship moved to stay on the same path.

"I'm getting the hang of this" he happily proclaimed.

"Good. Now take this and put it on your hip" Sato said as he came back to the front of the ship to stand beside Isaac.

Isaac looked at him and realised that Sato was handing him a gun of some sort. A black pistol like weapon. It was smaller than Isaac thought it would be. Very light to hold. It looked like it had a similar composition to plastic and seemed to be one solid piece. There was no sign of any parts or ways to disassemble it. The handle was rectangle in shape, the barrel was flat on the bottom where it met the trigger and the handle, with an oval domed shape on the top.

"What do I need that for?"

"Protection."

The gravity of the situation hit Isaac like a truck all of a sudden. He had been trying to mentally prepare for what was coming. Trying to psyche himself up to be ready when it all kicked off, but now it was real and he didn't feel remotely ready.

"I've never fired a gun before" Isaac admitted, with a little shame in his voice.

"Well hopefully when this is over you still won't have. But you need to be armed, just in case."

253

Isaac stood up and placed the weapon on his hip. A magnetic clamp on the side of his suit grabbed onto the pistol and it attached itself to him.

"How does it work?" Isaac asked.

"See that little red button on the side?"

Isaac looked at the gun and saw the button he was talking about.

"Yes."

"Press it."

Isaac did as instructed. The button turned green.

"Ok now what?" Isaac wondered.

"Now it's ready to fire. Press it again to return it to safe mode."

Isaac did and the button turned red again.

"How do I reload it?" Isaac asked.

"Reload what?"

"The bullets."

"What are bullets?"

"They're little small pieces of metal that, where I come from at least, usually fly out of a gun towards whatever you are aiming at. Well whatever this thing fires then. How do I reload the ammunition?" Isaac asked, a little nervous.

"It fires condensed energy blasts. Just pull the trigger to fire. There are no bullets to reload" Sato informed him.

"So there's no ammo to worry about running out of then?"

"There is a power source that depletes after every shot, but if you get to the stage where you have completely run out of that, reloading, as you say, will be the least of our worries. The gun is a last resort. I don't want you rushing in anywhere shooting up the place like a mad man. That's my job if it comes to it."

Sato walked back down to the end of the ship again, this time he approached what looked like a container that was

254

sitting on a shelf. It was rectangular in shape, about four feet by two feet by two feet. He began entering some sort of command into a keypad that was fixed to the side of it. The container split in two, the top half raising up from the bottom to reveal an empty glass cylinder inside it that ran along the length of the box.

"What's that?" Isaac asked as he sat back down at the controls of the ship and reassumed his duties as the pilot.

"This is what's called a mobile arsenal. It's used to supply soldiers with weapons on a battlefield."

"How does it work?"

"Each one has the schematics and enough raw materials in it to manufacture one hundred assault rifles, twenty explosive grenades and twenty mines. Basically you drop one of these in a location and you have enough hardware to supply a platoon. This is what Enack and Yangar we're selling to Olan'ko, off the books."

"What do we need it for?"

"I need some of the explosives."

Sato stepped back as the machine fired into life. Inside the glass tube lit up with a red hue and a small component began to move around, placing more and more material on top of each other to form an unfamiliar object. The process repeated itself five times until there were five separate disc shaped objects sitting on top of each other inside it. When it finished Sato opened a hatch and retrieved them.

"Oh, so it's like a 3D printer of doom" Isaac said.

"You have a machine like this on Earth?" Sato asked.

"Something like it. They're not sophisticated enough to print and entire functioning weapon or explosive, but it's only a matter of time I imagine."

Sato placed the explosive disks in a backpack and rested it on the floor beside the rear exit of the ship. Then he made

255

his way back to the controls. Isaac moved from the pilot's chair, standing beside the co-pilot seat and Sato resumed command of the ship.

"Ok. I've got this" Isaac said, completely unconfident in himself.

"Excellent. Right here we go."

Sato moved the flight controls forward to start to descend.

Isaac looked out the window and realised that they were coming up fast on the landing pad. He sat down in his chair as Sato brought the ship in for a landing. They came to a stop about ten feet above the ground. before they slowly descended down onto the designated spot. There was a slight thud as they hit the pad. Sato jumped to his feet immediately.

"We need to move." He said as he walked past Isaac to the back door and opened it.

Isaac didn't question him, he just followed closely behind like Sato had instructed him earlier. They hurried out the back of the ship. Sato was moving fast and Isaac was doing his best to keep up. The platform they had landed on was a large round area. It had a diameter of about thirty feet. The ship was in the middle and there was a double door not too far away. There weren't any other ships around, like they had been sent to this isolated part of the compound deliberately. They walked towards the entrance but about halfway there a light above the door started to flash.

"They're coming. Quick, follow me" Sato said as he ran to the left towards the edge of the platform.

Isaac followed and stopped at the edge to look over. There was a drop of at least a couple of hundred feet to the ground below.

"Jump" Sato shouted.

"No fucking way!" Isaac replied.

"Jump" Sato shouted again, this time pushing Isaac over the side.

Isaac tumbled over into a free fall towards the ground. He could feel the wind rush past him and as he began to reach terminal velocity, his eyes began to sting from the gale that was blasting him in the face. The ground was fast approaching but then his descent began to slow before he came to a sudden stop in mid-air. He appeared to be floating. He looked to his right and after a brief wait Sato arrived, coming to a halt just beside him, also appearing to be inexplicably floating.

"What was that?" Isaac shouted, over the noise that seemed to be coming from the facility they we're trying to infiltrate.

"A grappling line. I attached it to your belt before we went over. I've come to the conclusion that if I act first and apologise later, you seem to be fairly forgiving. We need to get to the ground quick and find a way in. They'll be looking for us now" Sato explained.

"How? We're about fifteen feet up in the air."

"How durable are your people?" Sato asked him.

"What do you mean durable?" Isaac asked, concerned at what the answer to his question was going to be.

Sato appeared to have some sort of blade in his hand. Isaac wasn't sure where it had come from. It was like he had produced it out of thin air. He swung it about a foot over Isaacs head and Isaac began to descend again. The surface of the planet rushed towards him and he hit it on his side with a thud that knocked the wind out of him completely. As he struggled to get some air into his body, Sato landed beside him on his feet, like a gymnast that had just executed a perfect dismount.

"Show off" Isaac wheezed as he slowly got to his feet with some help.

"This way" Sato pointed, as he moved off.

Isaac took a moment to collect himself then chased after him, limping slightly as he did, still a little sore from his less than stellar landing.

30

Sato was moving through the terrain quickly and Isaac was struggling to keep up. He was finding the extra weight of the exosuit to be more cumbersome than he originally thought it would be. The ground they were having to cover didn't make life any easier either. It was jagged rocks for the most part, uneven and hazardous. Also, where they were heading seemed to be constantly uphill. Isaac was following Sato who was following directions from a device he had on his arm. It was like a watch, but it was projecting a 3D hologram, with two little dots on it, separate from each other. Isaac had deduced that one of the dots was them and the other must be where they were going. Sato stopped and took a closer look at the readout on his arm.

"It's just over this ridge"

"What is?" Isaac asked.

"The entrance. Well, an entrance. I'm not entirely sure what it is but I'm assuming it's a way in. It's the only reading I can get for miles, so it has to be something" Sato confessed.

"Cool. I genuinely thought you would be a little more professional then assuming but fuck it. We've gotten this far."

Sato started off again with Isaac in tow. They climbed another fifteen feet or so until the came to the top of a ridge. There was a steep drop off on the other side of roughly fifty feet or so that led to a flat clearing at the bottom. It was so flat compared to the rest of the ground they had covered that Isaac assumed it must have been artificially created for some purpose. On the far side of the clearing there was a metal square, ten feet wide, that had been fitted into the solid rock. A siren started to ring out, coming from the direction of the facility.

"What's that?" Isaac asked.

"I don't know. We'll soon find out though I imagine" Sato replied.

The metal began to rise upward and created an opening into the mountain. There was a hissing noise that began to build, coming from the hole. Suddenly a wave of what looked like steam came pouring out of it and spread across the clearing. It continued for a couple of minutes before subsiding and then stopping completely. Once it had finished the metal door lowered and closed tight again. Isaac immediately realised where the flat clearing had come from.

"So it's some sort of exhaust or something" he said.

"So it would seem" Sato replied.

"Can we get in through it?"

"I'm not sure. There are a lot of variables here. How long does the cycle of whatever is happening take? How long does it take to get through the vent and where does it lead? Is there a way out once we get there? It's a huge risk but there are no other readings of anything else for miles. So we need to make a decision."

"Let's go" Isaac replied without hesitation.

"See, you are brave" Sato said, smiling.

He stood up and began to move towards the vent opening and Isaac followed behind him again. It took them a few minutes to make their way down to the clearing. The drop off was steep and there was very little to hold on to on the way down, but they made it in one piece. Once there, they hurried across the flat ground and got to the large metal rectangle that had opened to let the cloud of gas out. Sato moved around to the side to stay clear of the blast of steam that would inevitably come and Isaac followed. They stood there in silence for a few minutes while they waited for the process to begin.

"So once inside we stick to the original plan then?" Isaac asked, almost to just break the silence between them.

"Yes. Nothing has changed really. Our way in may be different but the objective remains the same" Sato replied.

They stood there in silence again for a few more minutes. Isaac couldn't think of anything else to ask so decided that the best thing to do was keep quiet and wait. The minutes rolled by as nothing happened. Then a low rumble began to permeate the rock that they were leaning against. It started to build a little bit at a time.

"Ok, here we go" Sato finally said.

The sound of the gears that worked the door kicked in and they could hear it begin to rise.

"If the timing is consistent then we have twenty minutes once were inside the door to make it to wherever it goes before we get hit by the exhaust and most likely get melted" Sato informed him.

"Well I haven't been melted yet so that'll be another first" Isaac quipped.

"Sarcasm in the face of impending death. You are beginning to impress me Isaac."

Isaac mustered a half-hearted smile in response. The door to the vent slammed to a halt after raising up to open fully. A hiss started to build up until the steam exploded out of the vent all across the flat landscape, then rose up and evaporated into the sky. Sato moved inside the door and Isaac followed him in. Once inside Isaac looked around to see what they had to do. The first thing he noticed was that the vent went up, not down like he was expecting. So, they would have to climb, not descend. He wasn't sure how they were going to achieve that. Especially since they didn't seem to have anything that resembled climbing equipment with them. The space they were in was about ten feet across, the same size as the entrance they had just walked in and about five feet deep. The walls were covered in some sort of tile. They were a charcoal colour and they covered the entirety of the inside of the cavern. There was three of them in a row across and they stretched up so high that Isaac couldn't see the top. It just went black after about a hundred feet or so. The sound of the gears of the door kicking in brought Isaac out of his deep examination of his surroundings and back to the task at hand. The door seemed to move quickly and before either of them could do anything it slammed closed locking them inside. The cavern was in complete darkness and Isaac couldn't see anything around him.

"So what now?" Isaac asked Sato in the darkness.

A light switched on and shone right in his face. It was coming from Sato's suit.

"Now we start to climb" Sato informed him.

"How do we climb a flat smooth surface?" Isaac asked.

"Well, that actually remains to be seen if I'm being honest. I thought the vent would go down, so I wasn't expecting this."

Isaac stood there in silence. He didn't reply because he didn't have anything to add to the discussion. He felt it would be best if he just shut up and let Sato concentrate.

"Clocks ticking" he finally said.

"Yes, well, I feel we've hit a dead end here. We may have to just wait it out until the door opens again and head out to find a different access point" Sato told him.

"Ok sounds like a plan" Isaac replied.

He moved over to the wall to look at the tiles that were lining them. He ran his hand up and down on one. It seemed incredibly smooth. The constant effect of the steam on them would have probably cased that to happen. All of a sudden, the tile popped out about six inches from the wall. It caught Isaac by surprise, causing him to lose his balance. He grabbed both sides of the tile and hung on to prevent himself from falling over. The tile flew up in the air with Isaac still holding on to both sides. He was lifted about ten feet or so before it came to a sudden stop. He nearly lost his grip but just managed to hang on to it. He looked down at the ground to see what was happening. Sato was standing right below him bathed in a light that was emanating from the newly found hole in the wall. He had his hands raised in the sign of surrender and he started to walk backwards. A rifle slowly moved out from the entrance that had suddenly appeared and the guard that was holding it came into view. Then another one followed the first one out. Isaac held on for dear life. He was struggling with the strain of trying to hold his entire body weight up at an awkward angle.

"See, I told you those motion sensors were the right call. No one will ever try to break in through this vent you said. Good thing I always expect the worst" one guard said to another.

"Yeah. You're a damn genius" the other guard replied.

"So, you must be who the boss is expecting. We were told to keep an eye out for intruders. Who else is here with you? How many? Where are they?" the first guard barked.

Sato said nothing. He just stood there with his arms extending upward. The guard raised his rifle a little higher and pointed it at Sato's nose from about a foot away, with serious intentions in his disposition.

"Where are the rest of you?" he shouted again.

"On your knees" the second guard ordered also elevating his rifle too.

Isaac tried to adjust his hands to reach for his gun but holding himself up was becoming an issue. The muscles in his forearms were starting to burn from the stress of supporting his entire body weight. He looked down again and noticed he was directly above one of the guards. At least he had the element of surprise. He aimed himself the best he could then just let go of the panel.

Isaac dropped about four feet onto the guard's head knocking him to the ground. He saw Sato react immediately, grabbing the other guard's gun, who had been distracted by the sudden chaos behind him. The guard Isaac had landed on pushed him off and made a reach for his weapon. Isaac scrambled to his knees and knocked it out of his reach. The guard turned and grabbed him by the arm and tried to wrestle him to the ground. Isaac did his best to keep his balance so as not to lose any leverage he had, so he could stay upright. They fought mainly with their hands, each trying to gain control of the others, to get a dominant position. Isaac's opposition managed to get a hold of his wrist, and used it to turn Isaacs weight against him, causing him to go slightly off balance. The guard then used Isaacs momentum against him and managed to climb on top of him. Now fully mounted, he tried to reign down blows, but Isaac was able to deflect them, or at least take the sting out of them by using his forearms to block. The guard persisted for a minute but realised he wasn't being very effective, so he switched tactics.

He put his head on Isaacs chest to get inside the guard he was using to protect himself. Once he managed to do this, he put his hands on Isaacs shoulders and forced himself up, separating Isaacs arms, leaving him totally exposed. Isaac knew he was in a fight for his life. He grabbed both of the guards' wrists again to try and get some control of the fight back. The guard used all the strength he had to get his hands onto Isaacs face. Then he stuck his thumbs up and placed them right over Isaacs eyes. Isaac could feel the pressure of the thumbs on his eye balls as they started their descent into his eye sockets. Then there was a blast sound that rang out around him. The pressure from the thumbs abated and the guards' hands slid to the side of Isaacs head onto the ground.

Isaacs vision was blurry for a split second before it came into focus. He looked up at the guard who was still sitting on him. He was looking down at Isaac. His chest had been blown wide open, his suit had been ripped apart and his blood began to flow out of the massive hole, right in the middle of his sternum. He began to fall forward but Isaac pushed him to the side as he did, causing him to land face down on the ground beside him, then he wriggled his way out from beneath him. He just stared at the guard's lifeless body briefly, then the commotion beside him brought him back to the ongoing pressing circumstance. Sato was still fighting with the other one of Olan'ko' henchmen. He had managed to get a moment to save Isaac from death, firing a shot at his assailant, or maybe it had happened by accident, but it had cost him. Now he was in trouble as the guard he was struggling with had a better grip of the gun they were fighting over and was turning it to aim at Sato. Isaac stood up, took his gun from his hip and raised it, aiming it at the second guard. This caused him to hesitate and gave Sato the opening he needed. Sato slid his arm around the guard's neck and began to squeeze. Once he had the leverage he needed he twisted as hard as he could. There was a snap and the guards body went limp. Sato dropped him and he fell to the ground, landing face down, motionless. Isaac stood there. Looking back and forth at the two guard's lifeless bodies. He thought he would feel guilty. He was waiting for some emotion to flood his senses. But nothing happened. He felt nothing. It just was what it was. He looked over at Sato who was looking back at him.

"You've got some blood on you" Sato said to him.

"Where?" Isaac asked looking down.

"Well, it's kind of everywhere."

Isaac could see his chest had a mass of crimson stains on him.

"Lovely."

"You have a penchant for this Isaac. You just reacted. No thought, no hesitation" Sato told him.

"So it would seem." Isaac replied, absolutely stunned that he felt no remorse or guilt, having just been complicit in killing two people.

"Well, come on." Sato said moving through the newly discovered entrance to the facility.

"What about them?" Isaac asked gesturing towards the guards remains they had left on the ground.

"The steam from the vent will take care of the bodies and even if it doesn't, we should be long gone before anyone discovers them here" Sato told him.

Isaac shrugged his shoulders and once again followed Sato into the unknown.

31

They moved through the bowels of the facility with ease.
There was no real security to speak of where they were.
Why would there be Isaac thought. Although they knew
security was looking for them now, it was unlikely they
would be aware of their exact location. They were in an
area of narrow passageways, being guided along by low
level amber lighting that made it hard to see ahead of them.
The poor illumination was causing Isaacs anxiety to go up a
few notches. He was on his toes, ready to turn and run at a
moment's notice. Every shadow a potential threat. Every
dark corner a possible ambush. They had about ten feet of
visibility.

The ground they were walking on was a grated platform,
that was about three feet wide. There were no handrails to
stop you from falling over the side, but the drop was only a
couple of feet so there was no real need for them. The
passageway was round and not very big. Both Isaac and
Sato had to hunch down to make their way through it.
Pipes and cables ran along the walls on either side of them.
Ahead Sato gestured for Isaac to stop moving, so he did.
They listened to their surroundings for a minute, but there

was nothing except the mechanical noises of an industrial complex to be heard. Sato reached over and ran his hand along the wall beside them. After a minute he found what he was looking for. He placed his hands shoulder width apart and pressed the wall in and a panel slid up, revealing a small opening into a shaft.

"Ok, this is it" Sato said to Isaac, as he stuck his head in the opening, to check that the path ahead was clear.

"This is what?" Isaac asked.

"This is where we separate. You get into this shaft and follow it until you come across a terminal. Once you do insert this into the port it fits into and it will tell you where Car'esh and the others are."

He reached into his suit and pulled out something and handed it to Isaac. Isaac inspected it. It looked like it was plastic. About the length and width of a pencil but it was square.

"What is it?"

"It's a data stick. I've programmed it to bypass security and find their location. All you need to do is plug it into a port and it will do the rest for you."

"Well I've been thinking. Maybe we should stick together. Strength in numbers and all that" Isaac said, the concerns he was now harbouring, considering this was the do or die moment he had been dreading since they left the ship written all over his face.

"Isaac, I have faith in you. You have already shown that you are well capable of taking care of yourself. Once you find the others, you'll be fine" Sato said, trying to assure him.

"What about you?"

"I'm going to find a way out of here, then I'm going to set up a disturbance to cover our escape."

269

"Where will I meet you once I've found the others."

Sato reached out and rubbed his finger down the base of Isaacs skull, just behind his right ear. Then he reached down and grabbed Isaacs hand, bringing it up to feel the spot he had just touched.

"When you are ready press here on this strip to tell me where you are."

Isaac could feel a small piece of what felt like rubber that Sato had stuck on him.

"What is it, a tracker or something?"

"No. I'm assuming that when they brought you on board the Sao'ise, they implanted a translator chip in your head. Otherwise we wouldn't have been able to have all those wonderful conversations we've shared. That strip I just put on you will transform it into a two-way radio that we can communicate through once activated. I mean press right here and speak. Tell me where you are, and I'll come and meet you" Sato clarified.

"Why don't we just use it to stay in contact while we're separated?" Isaac wondered.

"Then you will start to give off a signal, and it will become a tracker they can use to locate you."

"Fair point."

Isaac had all he needed to know. He climbed into the shaft and stood up.

"Good luck Isaac."

Sato sealed the access panel behind him and Isaac was alone. He turned the light in his suit on. The shaft was not much bigger than he was. It was quite claustrophobic. There was a ladder that went up inside the tunnel but he couldn't see how far it travelled as there was very little light which meant he could only make out a few feet ahead of him. That was it. Isaac took a moment to steady himself. What was he doing? He wasn't a spy or a secret agent. He wasn't a soldier. He wasn't even a boy scout. He had no training to do what he was doing. He had survived on blind luck so far. Surely that was about to run out. His heart beat began to quicken. He could feel himself breathing heavier and heavier as the seconds ticked past. His hands began to tremor uncontrollably and he realised he was on the verge of a full blown panic attack. He tried to steady himself and began to take deep breaths in through his nose and exhaled out his mouth, thinking calming thoughts to try and centre himself. He did this for about a minute or so until he had regained control of his nerves. His heart beat began to slow down and the tremors in his hands began to subside. Isaac placed his hands on the ladder. His legs felt so heavy, for a moment he thought he had lead in his boots. He reckoned that it was the adrenaline dump from the panic attack that had momentarily sapped him of a lot of his energy. He gathered all the strength he could to raise his foot and place it on the bottom rung of the ladder. Then he forced himself to start the climb.

After about four or five steps he was sweating. His legs felt like jelly and he was having a hard time concentrating. The stress of the situation was really taking a toll on him. Isaac was a little disappointed in himself. He thought he would be better in a situation like this. Granted only five minutes ago he had been giving himself the, I'm not a soldier speech in his head, but he really needed to pull himself together. Not that he ever thought he would actually be in a situation like the one he was in, but he did think that he would manage a stressful situation better.

He stopped for a minute to try and regain his composure again. Deep breaths in through his nose and out through his mouth.

"One step at a time" he said out loud.

Once he had regained control of his faculties again, he returned to his climb. With each step he took he seemed to regain a little more discipline of his breathing. The shaft seemed to go on forever. Then he had a realisation. He had no idea how to get out of the shaft. So far, he hadn't seen anything that looked like an exit point. The walls around him all seemed solid. There were no buttons to press to open any panels or doors. There were some symbols written on the walls periodically, but he didn't understand them. His translator didn't seem to work on things that had been physically written down. Isaac wasn't sure how long he had been climbing, but it felt like an eternity. There was no end to the shaft in sight though. It just seemed to keep going. He stopped again to get his bearings. Then he heard something. There was a voice coming from the other side of the wall. He couldn't make out what it was saying, but it was close. There was a couple of inches of steel between him and it. His heart beat began to speed up again. But this time it wasn't fear. It was excitement. The reality of what was going on was hitting him hard, and it was exhilarating.

He waited for a moment for the voice to pass, then he returned to his ascent again. After another few minutes of climbing, he reached the top. The shaft now split off in two different directions, one left and one right. Isaac took a minute to try and deduce which way he should go. He tried to picture in his head where he might be in the facility, but this was absolutely pointless. All he had seen was a tiny unmanned entrance, a poorly lit service area and a narrow maintenance shaft. He had no idea where they had entered in relation to where he had been before, nor did he know what direction he had travelled in.

"Eeny, meeny, miny, mo" he said, trying to make up his mind, before just deciding to go right. On the up side, at least he wasn't climbing anymore. Now he was crawling along on his hands and knees, barely, as the shaft was just about big enough for him to manoeuvre. Isaac thought about Sato for a moment, wondering how he was getting on. At least Sato had experience in what they were doing, so Isaac felt he would be fine. He continued on for what he estimated to be another hundred yards or so before stopping to try to orientate himself again. Isaac sat down resting his back up against the wall. Judging by the amount of time he had been climbing and crawling around the shaft, he figured he must have gone up several stories and crawled halfway across whatever area he was in. Now all he had to do was find his way out.

There were soft banging sounds coming from above his head. Footsteps. He was beneath a floor. He looked up and noticed that there was a handle sticking out of the panel just above him. Finally, he had found a way out. Now all he had to do was gauge if the coast was clear, so he could exit. He sat and listened. The banging of the footsteps seemed to fade off into the distance. Isaac waited another minute or so to see if any more came along, but none seemed to materialise.

He reached up and gripped the handle, trying to twist it. Nothing happened. It appeared to be stuck. He tried again with more effort, but it wouldn't budge. He let go and slumped back down against the wall again. Was it a handle, or was he trying to turn a random piece of steel? He grabbed it again, this time pulling it towards him. The

273

handle slid out and the shaft opened upwards, revealing a hatch, two feet square right above his head. He quickly stood up and peered out of the opening. There were what looked like shipping containers in front of him and a wall behind him. He stood up and climbed out of the shaft. The area he was in seemed to be well lit. Isaac realised very quickly he was out in the open, totally exposed. Anyone could come wandering past and spot him. He stepped out of the hole in the ground and hurried to the corner of one of the containers, peering around it but trying to keep himself hidden, he could see he was in a large open area of the facility. There were rows and rows of the containers that seemed to form pathways around this giant zone. This was a good thing for him as there was a lot of cover for him to conceal himself. He checked again that the coast was clear and then moved out from the container he was behind towards one of the pathways. He skulked along, checking that he was alone periodically. Every time he got to an intersection, he would stop to look around the corner before moving forward.

After several minutes of doing this, he realised he wasn't getting anywhere. Either that or the place just went on forever. It was a maze of different directions and dead ends. He would take a turn, realise there was no way forward and would have to backtrack, until eventually he turned a corner that lead into an open space. Across the clearing he saw one of the workers from the facility. He was scanning the containers with a little handheld device, oblivious to Isaacs presence. Isaac decided that enough was enough and this was his best shot at finding a way to his people. The worker turned his back to scan a container behind him and Isaac made his move. He charged out into the clearing and ran towards him. Every step he was sure that they were going to turn around and see him coming but they just kept doing what they were doing. He was about ten feet away from them before he realised that he had no plan beyond charging at them. Once there he didn't really know what he was going to do. It was too late now though, he was committed. The plan never came, so Isaac just improvised. He kept running at full tilt all the way up to the worker and not once did they turn around. They were too engrossed in whatever their task at hand was. Isaac barged right into him, slamming the top of his head into the container he was scanning. The worker hit it with a thud, then slumped to the ground. Once again Isaac wasn't sure if he had knocked him out or killed him. Hopefully the former, as he needed to probe him for information. Grabbing him by the legs, he began to drag him up the aisle. At the top he came to an intersection. He looked to the right and saw a dead end. Then he looked to the left. At the end of the aisle there was a workstation that had a console on it.

"Finally" Isaac said.

He took the worker by the ankles again, dragging him towards it before finally making it to the station and then letting go of his captive's legs. He searched the area for some form of restraint to secure his prisoner, finding what looked like sticky tape after a quick rummage through the surrounding clutter. Isaac wrapped it around the persons arms until he felt it was secure, then he repeated the process around his ankles. Finally, he stuck some over the workers lips to make sure he couldn't call out for help once he regained consciousness. If he regained consciousness. Isaac still wasn't sure if he had knocked him out or fractured his skull. Once he was satisfied that the bindings were tight enough, he sat at the work station and began to search for the port that Sato had assured him would be on any terminal he could find. After a quick look he located it and took the data stick out of his suit and slid it in. There was a flash of information that ran up the screen followed by what looked like folders opening, one after the other. Eventually the flow of information stopped and an icon appeared on the screen. Isaac pressed on it and another stream of information started to load. This went on for several minutes before all the folders closed. There was a new message on the screen now. Not able to actually understand what it said, Isaac just sat, waiting, until another icon appeared. Again, he clicked on it and streams of data flooded the screen, way too fast to make any sense out of. What he could make out just looked like jumbled nonsense. Computer code most likely.

He waited patiently for it to do its thing, then the captive he had secured began to stir. First, he moved a little, then tried to move his arms. Eventually he opened his eyes and looked straight at Isaac. He began to thrash around but couldn't do anything. Isaac was relieved as he wasn't sure the tape he had used as restraints would be durable enough. So far so good. The worker stopped moving and tried to call out, but all he could manage was a muffled cry, not loud enough to attract any attention as far as Isaac could tell.

"Hello there" Isaac said, before turning his attention back to the screen.

The flow of data had stopped and there was a new icon flashing. Isaac pressed on it and a video feed opened up. It was broadcasting from inside the facility. The image on the screen was out of indecipherable, pixelate, so badly it was just a bunch of shapes on the screen. Then it stuttered into focus. It was Niers. He was in a lab, similar to the one

Isaac had been held captive in. He was strung up, held in place by a restraint on each limb in a position that resembled a crucifixion. . He had been lacerated from the top of his chest down to his pelvis and from one side of his rib cage to the other, peeled like a banana, the skin and tissue folded back and pinned to his shoulders and his hips with metal spikes, to keep it separated. He could see his organs, some of which were hanging loose. Niers was limp, lifeless.

"I'm too late."

He looked away as he could feel his emotions swelling up inside him. His eyes began to well with tears. His whole body began to quake with anger. He restrained himself as best he could. All he wanted to do was scream out, but he couldn't. If anyone heard him, he would be done for.

Isaac sat there, silently. Then he reached up to his ear to press the button on the thing Sato had put on him to make contact and give him the news. Before he managed to, movement on the screen caught his attention again. There was someone else in the room with Niers. Whoever they were, they were dressed the same as Hal'ack was when he was torturing Isaac. They walked up to the restraints that were holding Niers in place and checked them. Then they stepped to the side and began to press buttons on a keyboard that was attached to the contraption detaining him, before stepping away. Then they turned and raised some sort of device. Niers began to thrash around uncontrollably Whoever was in the room with him seemed to be electrocuting him. They stopped and Niers moved. He seemed to look up at them and say something. A flood of relief washed over Isaac. He was alive but for how much longer. The scene he was observing was like a grim snuff movie. Niers was most likely hanging to life by a thread. Isaac pulled his gun off his hip and rested against the temple of the captured Garian worker.

"I'm going to ask you a question, then I'm going to uncover your mouth. If you make any noise, other than the words that will answer my question, I'm going to air out your fucking brain. Do you understand me?"

His captive seemed to look Isaac up and down. Isaac followed his eyes to see what he was inspecting and realised he was eyeing the blood that he was covered in.

"That's right. That's the blood of everyone who has tried to stop me so far. It didn't work out for those people. How do you think you are doing right now?"

He believed that the anger in his voice was convincing as the worker looked at him, eyes open wide, and nodded. Isaac turned the screen to face him.

"Where is this and how do I get there?"

32

Isaac was on the move again. Thanks to Eidian, the Garian worker he had captured, who it turned out was more than willing to pass on all the information he had in exchange for not being executed. Isaac was never willing to go that far. Cold blooded murder wasn't going to be his style. Eidian didn't need to know that though. He had explained to Isaac that he just needed a job. He wasn't committed to the cause. In fact, he wasn't even fully aware of what the cause was. All of the civilian staff manning the facility were there for that reason. Only the soldiers and those close to Olan'ko, like Hal'ack were devotees. He swore he had no idea of the experimentation and torture that was taking place. The reason Isaac believed him was due to the genuine look of disgust he had when he turned the monitor to face Eidian and he saw Niers. He told Isaac they would constantly refer to what they were doing but they spoke in code that the people working there didn't fully understand. He also revealed that most of the facility was vacant. There was only about five hundred or so people there and only fifty were civilian. Isaac was surprised due to the sheer size of the place but as Eidian described the operation around them, it became clear there was a lot of automation, so a skeleton crew was all that was really needed. He had also given Isaac directions for the best way to get around without being seen. Once Isaac had gotten all he felt was relevant out of Eidian, he sealed him in a container that was scheduled to ship off in a few minutes on a long journey. He just followed the example that Sato had set when dealing with Enack and Yangar. Then he got annoyed when he realised what Sato had said about him being his protégé was starting to come true.

Eidian had directed Isaac to a lift. Once there he was to take the lift down to sub level two. It was an unmanned area that would only be patrolled every hour or so. Once he made his way across that section he would find a stairwell. He was to use this to go up to level thirteen. That's the general area where Niers was being held. He wasn't really familiar with it as he was rarely in there and never without an escort. It was mostly restricted. Eidian had also given Isaac the suit he was wearing which had a chip inside it that would allow him to access the relevant zones unrestricted.

Isaac had changed his clothes and was moving again. He smiled at the idea of a huge facility, being run for despicable purposes, manned by contractors because he couldn't help but think about the scene in the movie Clerks about the Death Star. He had arrived at the lift. The new suit he had also came with a helmet, which would be useful for moving around the more populated area he was now traversing. He slid the helmet on and walked around the corner to the lift. He pressed the button and waited. The doors slid open and thankfully there was nobody on board. He stepped inside and the doors slid closed behind him. Isaac looked at the display inside the lift and searched until he found the button for sub level two. He pressed it and then leaned back against the wall in a relaxed fashion, feeling accomplished that he had made it this far alive. He was on level twenty when the lift started to descend. At around level twelve it began to slow down, before stopping completely at level ten.

"Shit" Isaac said as he stood up straight before the doors opened.

Hal'ack was waiting at the entrance to the lift. He had his head down looking at a tablet in his hand. He stepped into the lift and turned his back to Isaac without paying him any notice.

"Ground floor" Hal'ack said out loud.

Isaac stood there staring at the back of Hal'ack's head. He slid his hand down to his pistol and gripped the handle tight. He thought about just doing it. Just taking the pistol and putting an end to Hal'ack then and there. Revenge for what had been done to him and Niers, while also preventing him from doing it to anybody else in the future. Then the rational side of his mind spoke up. He realised he had no idea who or what would be waiting on the far side of the doors once he reached the ground floor. He would have a hard time explaining to anyone who might be there why Hal'ack was lying face down with a hole in the back of his head, with him the only other occupant of the lift. He released his grip on the pistol. Hal'ack looked up from his tablet and around at Isaac, who just remained looking straight ahead. Isaac began to sweat. He was rumbled. Hal'ack was onto him. He must have recognised him through the visor, or maybe he had a scent that he was giving off that Hal'ack could pick up on. Isaac was going to have to act. At least this way he could shoot him in the face and not have to worry about the moral quagmire of executing someone from behind like a coward might create for his conscience. His hand twitched ever so slightly as he was preparing to make another move for his side arm.

"Ground floor!" Hal'ack said again, this time with a hint of acrimony in his voice.

Isaac then realised Hal'ack had been talking to him when he said it the first time. He had just assumed the lift had an automated function and Hal'ack was speaking to it. Isaac reached over and pressed the button for the ground floor.

"Sorry sir" he said, as he stood back at attention behind him.

Hal'ack just eyed him up and down for a moment, before turning his attention back to his tablet. The lift started to descend slowly again. Isaac could feel the tension in the air. He hoped Hal'ack couldn't. Each floor that passed felt like a ten minute journey. Isaac went stiff and just stared straight ahead. Eventually the lift stopped and the doors slid open. Hal'ack stepped off and walked away still looking at his tablet, not paying any more attention to Isaac. The doors slid closed again and Isaac breathed for the first time since the lift began its descent into Isaacs personal hell. He relaxed, letting his shoulders sink a little, leaning back up against the wall.

"Fuck me, that was close" he said out loud.

The lift started to move again, and with only two floors to go, the journey didn't take long. The doors slid open at sub level two and Isaac stepped off. He looked around to try and orientate himself. It was exactly as Eidian had described. It was a functional floor in the facility, meaning it was all machines, pipes and steam. The area seemed to go on for quite a bit, but it was exactly what Isaac needed. A way to get across the facility without being seen. As long as he moved slowly and kept down, he could get to where he needed to be without incident. He crouched down and crept along as best he could, keeping himself hidden from view. There was nobody there to hide from, so he just looked kind of ridiculous. He was following some stainless steel pipes, because they seemed to be going in a straight line in the same direction that he needed to go.

After several hundred meters of walking in a crouched position, Isaac realised he hadn't come across anybody and his legs and back were starting to ache. He decided the coast was clear and he stood up, putting his hands on his hips and pushing his chest out, stretching his back and making an audible groan as he did so.

"Who are you?" he heard a voice say to his left.

He turned around to see who was there, coming face to face with a Talanite standing about five feet away from him. The row of pipes Isaac had been following, which was a little over waist height separated them.

"Uh, maintenance" Isaac said unconvincingly.

"No, I'm maintenance" the Talanite replied.

Isaac just stared at him through his visor, The Talanite just staring back.

"Oh yeah, what division?" Isaac said trying his luck.

"Division?" the Talanite replied.

"You heard me" Isaac said with as much conviction as he could manage.

Isaac panicked. He didn't know what to do. He knew the Talanite wasn't buying his ruse. He grabbed his pistol and raised it pointing it at him.

"Alright don't move" Isaac said.

"Control this is…" we're the Talanite's final words.

Isaac fired. The blast sound was much like the one he had heard earlier that killed the guard trying to push his eyeballs in. It just seemed to rip the suit the Talanite was wearing open, along with the skin on his chest too. As he fell to the ground, Isaac jumped onto the pipes and climbed over them to where the Talanite had landed. He stood watching as he gasped for air, the blood flowing out of his wound. He could see some of his vital organs beneath his skin. A Rib was sticking out, pointing the wrong way, having been snapped from the force of the weapon. After a couple of seconds, he stopped breathing entirely and just lay there, lifeless. Isaac searched around him but didn't find any weapon. He hoped there would be one, but all he could find was a toolbox. Even though he had thought that cold blooded murder wasn't going to be his style, it turned out it was going to be inevitable. He had just shot and killed an unarmed worker. Probably a maintenance person or an engineer. He began to panic, dropping his pistol on the ground beside the body. What had he done? From what Eidian had told him, this Talanite was just a guy doing his job. He wasn't an enemy. He didn't have any malevolent plans of galactic conquest or planetary genocide. He was probably just changing a lightbulb. Isaac stood there just staring into the dead eyes of his victim. They were looking off into the distance, with his face a picture of confusion and disbelief.

"Why did you do that? Why didn't you just keep your mouth shut?" Isaac shouted at the dead body on the floor.

He took a moment to collect himself. He was shaking from a mixture of adrenaline and fear. Then he came back to his senses quickly. They would be coming. He needed to move now and deal with the guilt later. He started off again in the direction the pipes were leading him. After another few hundred meters he found the door he was looking for. It was a small non-descript door. He walked up to it and put his hand on a panel on the left side and pushed. The door opened, and Isaac stepped through it into the stairwell on the other side.

He took his mask off and began to breathe heavy again. He couldn't get the image of the Talanite taking his final breath out of his mind. The life visibly leaving them. His limp figure sprawled on the floor. It was strange because, amazingly, he wasn't the first person he had killed since he left Earth. So why was he having so much trouble with it. Ok so he was unarmed and just doing his job. But he chose to take the job on the evil villain's base. He had made the decision to put himself in that situation. Isaac tried telling himself he shouldn't feel guilty about it. It wasn't his fault. It didn't work. He still felt like shit, but again, he reminded himself that he needed to keep moving. If someone answered the call and didn't get a reply, they would be hot on his heels. He looked through the stairs above him. They seemed to go eternally up. However he only needed to conquer thirteen flights. He took a deep breath to ready himself, then started the climb.

33

Isaac stopped for the second time to take a breather. He had made it up seven flights of stairs so far. The going was starting to get tough. Each flight consisted of three blocks of stairs, each block having fourteen steps in them. He knew this because he started counting about three flights ago to try and distract himself and abate the growing desire that was rising within him to just sit down and rest. Only five more floors to go. Then he heard a noise below him. He peered over the side of the stairs down, all the way to the floor beneath. He heard the noise again. Then he saw movement at the bottom. Someone had come in the same door as him and were starting to make their way up. He reached for his pistol to have it at the ready, but it wasn't there. He swiftly realised he had dropped it beside the body of the dead worker and walked off without picking it up. So now there was a body and a murder weapon. If he ended up in court over this, he'd be convicted due to pure stupidity. The sound below him was getting louder which meant whoever had come into the stairwell was getting closer. Isaac started to move again, trying to be as silent as he could be. He was actually doing a pretty good job to be fair. He guessed that whoever was below him was about five flights down, so as long as he moved at the same pace they did, he would make it to thirteen just fine.

He had just two flights to go and he would be in the clear. Isaac bounded up the stairs as quick as he could until he got to the thirteenth floor. The door was the same as the one he had entered through, so he just put his hand on the panel and pushed. It opened on the first try and he stepped out of the stairwell and into a corridor. It looked familiar. It was identical to the one he had been dragged down while he was a guest at the facility before. Now all he had to do was figure out which way to go. Instead of hanging around to try and make a decision he just turned left without breaking stride, mainly because this was the closest way to a corner and he needed to be gone before whoever had been following him came out of the door he just had. He walked past several people. All of them were either Ilian soldiers in their armour, or Ilian scientists, all wearing the same clothes that Hal'ack had been wearing. He must be close to Niers. He just had to find him. As he walked down the corridor, he noticed that most of the rooms were closed. Then he came across one that was open. He walked up to it and looked inside. The room was empty, but there was another door at the back of it. Isaac walked inside and opened the door. Behind it was Niers, still strung up. His wounds seemed to be on the mend, the gruesome scene he had witnessed on the video feed was now sealed up, some scarring the only evidence he had been just recently dissected, so that was a good start. Isaac walked up to him and put his hand on Niers' shoulder.

"Hey" he said in a calm tone.

Niers recoiled back from him as far as he could.

"Don't touch me" he shouted.

287

"Wow, easy man, it's me" Isaac said as he took off his helmet.

Niers thrashed around like a fish out of water flopping on a deck for a while longer, before coming to his senses at the sight of Isaac standing in front of him.

"Isaac?" Niers asked in disbelief.

"Yeah kid. I'm here to get you out. Can I move you? How do I get you down?" he asked.

"Over there. There's a release button on the wall" Niers said, gesturing to the other side of the room.

Isaac walked over and pressed it. The restraints released him immediately and Niers fell to the ground and landed on his side.

"Shit, sorry. Are you ok?" Isaac asked as he ran back over to Niers and helped him to sit up.

Niers rubbed the side he had landed on as Isaac crouched down beside him. Niers looked up at him, then grabbed him and gave him a great big kiss on the lips.

"Please tell me that's just a way of showing gratitude on your world" Isaac said as he wiped his lips with the back of his hand.

"It's a way of showing deep personal desire for someone" Niers explained.

"I see" was all he said.

"That was a Joke Isaac, I'm just surprised to see you and elated that you are here" Niers said.

Isaac smiled, half a smile of happiness to see Niers and half a smile of relief.

"Where is everyone else?" Isaac asked.

"I don't know. I'm not even sure how long I've been in this room. They could be anywhere."

"Shit. Well we'll just have to get looking I suppose."

Isaac stood up and helped Niers to his feet.

"Isaac, don't get me wrong, I'm ecstatic that you are here, but how did you manage it?" Niers asked.

"I had help from Sato. Well actually he did all the leg work, I just followed him" Isaac told him.

"Sato. That man is full of surprises" Niers said, a little bemused.

"We better get moving. They know I'm here now, so they'll probably come looking in the obvious places that I'm likely to go" Isaac said moving toward the door.

"Look at you Isaac. Taking it to the bad guys head on" Niers said, laughing as he followed him.

"Let's not get carried away. I've already messed up twice" Isaac replied.

"How?" Niers asked.

"Well, I shot and killed an innocent man on my way through the facility. He was just a guy doing his job. I told him not to move, but he didn't listen. Then I dropped my gun beside him and forgot to pick it up when I left, so now I'm unarmed" Isaac told him.

"Isaac, listen to me. There are no innocent people here. They may not be military, or fully committed to whatever the agenda Olan'ko has talked them into, but they chose to work here. They made the decision to do what they do" Niers told Isaac solemnly.

"Not all of them. Some are just looking for work" Isaac said, looking back at him.

"They know that something is not right. That's on them."

"Ok" Isaac replied, thankful that Niers was trying to ease his guilt.

"Dropping your weapon is inexcusable though" Niers added.

"I know. I'm really pissed at myself for that one."

He stuck his head out of the door and had a quick look in both directions. The coast seemed to be clear. He moved back inside the office and turned to Niers, putting his helmet back on.

"Ok, here's the plan. I'm going to lead you out and we're going to quickly find somewhere that we can use to look for others. Simple" Isaac said.

"Ok. Where's Sato though?" Niers asked.

"He's busy planning our exit. I'll contact him once we're ready" Isaac told him.

"I don't like the sound of that. Sato has a tendency to be over exuberant" Niers replied.

"Well no time to worry about it now. Let's go."

Isaac stood up and got behind Niers. Niers stepped out into the hallway and turned left, heading toward the end of the corridor about twenty or so feet away. When they turned there was another long corridor for them to walk down.

"Why did we go this way?" Isaac asked.

"I don't know. Instinct I suppose" Niers replied.

They walked along for another few meters until they came across another open door that led into an empty office.

"Quick. In here" Niers said as he ducked inside.

Isaac followed Niers as he walked across the office to an open console. He sat down and began to type as Isaac kept watch at the door for anyone coming.

"Hurry man. There has to be someone coming soon" Isaac implored him.

"Nearly there" Isaac heard Niers say over his shoulder.

Isaac stood cautiously keeping watch out the door. He was tense, expecting to see someone come around the corner any minute. But no one materialised.

"Got it" he heard Niers shout.

Isaac turned around to look.

"So, where are they" He asked.

"One floor up."

"Ok let's go."

They got up and moved out of the office, heading down the corridor. Halfway down on the right hand side was a lift. They got to it and pressed the button. After an anxious minute of waiting it finally arrived. The doors opened and they both boarded it. The journey one floor up didn't take long. The doors opened and Isaac and Niers stepped off. The surroundings looked very familiar to Isaac. He had been here before. This was the same prison he had been held captive in. Again, Niers took the lead and Isaac followed him.

"So where are we going? Do you know what cells they are in?" Isaac asked.

"I believe that Car'esh is down here on the left and Taretta and Sha'ala are over the other side. I'm not sure where Moga is. Hopefully when we get to Car'esh he'll have more answers" Niers replied.

They moved down past the cells until they got to the one that Car'esh was supposed to be in.

"I don't like this" Isaac said.

"What?" Niers asked.

"Where is everybody? I know that it's a small crew that runs the place, but we haven't seen one person in forever. It's almost like they're avoiding us. Letting us get to where we want to go" Isaac told him.

"Why would they do that?" Niers asked.

"I don't know. It just doesn't feel right" Isaac confessed.

Niers pressed the release for the prison cell. The opaque window began to clear. Isaac remembered the process from his earlier experience.

"Relax, we're nearly there" Niers told him.

The door disappeared and the cell was open. They both looked in, then both recoiled united in their repulsion of the distressing scene they were met with.

"Jesus Christ" Isaac exclaimed.

Niers fell to his knees and placed his head in his hands.

It was Moga. He was impaled on some sort of poles. There were two driven through his arms and into the wall behind him, and two driven through his feet, into the ground below. He was slouched over, being held upright by the implements that had been pierced through him. He was motionless. Most of his clothes had been removed, apart from the trousers he was wearing. There were slash marks on his chest and stomach where he had been tortured with some sort of sharp cutting implement. There were pools of blood on the floor where it had run out of his wounds and congealed beneath his feet. There were also splash marks on the wall behind him caused by the poles that had been driven through his arms. His face had what looked like heavy bruising on it. Most likely the consequence of a severe beating. So bad in fact, his left eye looked to be swollen shut. Niers moved into the cell and placed his hands on either side of Mogas face as he wept for his friend. Moga roared into life, rearing his head back, letting out a howl of defiance. He tried to move, to grab Niers, but his hands were useless and his arms were going nowhere.

"My friend it's me. Be calm" Niers said, trying to ease Moga's fury. Moga didn't heed Niers, he was only semi-conscious, confused and enraged.

Niers summoned all the strength he had and forced Moga to hold his head still so he could look him in the eye.

Eventually he succeeded and the Caninan calmed, before he slumped over again.

"Help" the only word they heard him say, a weak and feeble effort in its delivery.

Then the sound of the cell doors powering down all around them filled the silence. Isaac looked on as all of the cells opened at the same time. One after the other, Olan'ko's militia piled out of them and surrounded him and Niers. Isaac stood up and put his hand on Niers' shoulder. Niers didn't move. He was frozen.

"Step out of the cell and surrender" one of the soldiers demanded of Niers but he didn't respond. He was too busy tending to his friend.

The soldier grabbed Niers by the head and pulled him out to the corridor.

"Hey" Isaac shouted as he reached for him, but he received a blow to the back of the head that knocked him to the ground. He felt hands grab him and pull him back to his feet.

"Move" someone behind him ordered and pushed him in the direction he was to go.

Isaac looked around to see Niers. He was on his feet moving, looking down at the ground. Isaac could tell he was momentarily broken.

34

They had stopped moving several minutes ago and Isaac had just been standing still staring at the floor. The image of Moga, nailed to the cell wall, like an animal that had been captured, wouldn't leave him. It was the look in his eyes that was the most haunting. The look of defeat, a look Isaac probably never expected to see from such a proud and ferocious warrior. Isaac couldn't get the picture out if his mind no matter how hard he tried. Now he didn't care about the Talanite he had killed on his way to Niers. If he could he would kill all of them. He couldn't even imagine what Niers must be feeling. He hadn't said anything to him for a while. He felt it would be best to leave him to process it on his own for the time being. Isaac looked around and realised they were in Olan'ko's room. The one he had been in before, that looked out over the facility. It was just him and Niers standing in the middle of the room across from each other. He looked behind him to see where the couch was, then he walked backwards to it and sat down. They weren't going anywhere, and he was weary from everything he had gone through in the last few days. It just sort of hit him suddenly. Since he hadn't had a chance to stop for quite some time now, he didn't realise how tired he was, until he sat down. Once he did he felt like he may never get up again. He was almost tempted to lie down and have a snooze.

"I'm going to kill them Isaac" Niers said.

He looked up at him but Niers was still just staring down at the floor.

"Huh?"

"I'm going to kill them" he repeated.

"Kill who?" Isaac questioned.

"All of them. Everyone I come across in this place, or anywhere else I encounter them out in the galaxy. I'm going to execute every fucking last one of them" Niers said as he raised his head to look Isaac in the eye.

Isaac could tell he was serious in his intent. There was a look in his eyes he had not seen until now. A look of cold, callous, righteous determination. When Niers had told him earlier that he had killed people, Isaac had trouble seeing it in him. He just couldn't imagine Niers hurting anyone. Now he believed him. If he could he would help do it right now with him.

"Well let's focus on getting out of here first, then we can plan on revenge. Don't worry about that" Isaac replied.

Isaac couldn't help but think how it was funny how your whole perception of something could change so drastically, so fast. Before he entered the facility, he wasn't going to get involved in the business of death. Now he was considering mass murder on a large group of people.

"Why would they do that?" Niers asked, more in general wonderment than a direct question to Isaac.

"I honestly don't know. I mean I can imagine they wanted to do something horrific just for their own sick, twisted beliefs. But why the pantomime. Why leave him in the cell like that? That's what I don't get" Isaac pondered.

"I'm going to kill them" Niers repeated, as his voice broke and the emotion he had been trying to hide came through.

The door to the room opened and they both looked around at the same time to see who was there. Olan'ko entered, flanked by four of his guards. Niers let out a roar of both pent up emotion and unbridled hatred at them as they made their way towards him. Isaac watched as Niers, most likely acting on instinct charged them. It didn't really matter that he was unarmed and most likely weak from his ordeal. If he had any weapon it would have still yielded the same result, which was a baton across Niers' head that put him onto the floor, on his back looking up at the ceiling. The guard followed up with a boot to his side that caused Niers to fold up in the foetal position.

"Alright, that's enough ya fucking ball bags" Isaac shouted at them.

Olan'ko looked up at him, his sneer of disgust he had been wearing while looking down at Niers turned to a smug smile of satisfaction as his eyes met Isaacs. He held up his hand in a gesture to the guards to stop the assault.

"So Isaac, here we are again" Olan'ko began, as he walked over and stood in front of him looking down. Isaac could feel this was an attempt to intimidate him, the figure looming over him. He didn't care though. He had nothing left to lose. He just stayed his gaze, looking down at the floor. Not willing to give him the satisfaction of even looking him in the eyes.

"Why?" Isaac asked.

"Why what?" Olan'ko responded.

"Why the charade, having me skulk around this place for no reason other than some twisted fucking joke?" Isaac demanded.

"Oh, we had no idea it was you. I thought some special operations team had infiltrated this facility. I was pleasantly surprised when I saw you standing outside the cell we had placed Moga in. Impressed in fact. I thought you would be long gone. Halfway home by now."

"I wanted to be, believe me. But I couldn't."

"Why? Did you feel the need to repay a debt to these people? A sense of duty to them? A deluded notion. You've made a foolish decision coming back here."

"No I actually couldn't. As in I was unable to. I didn't know how to get home. I had to come get this lot to show me how to get there."

Olan'ko looked at him and let out a chuckle that seemed to take even him by surprise.

"I see. Well, I didn't see the point of playing games, chasing around whoever had encroached on my facility. I felt it would be easier to allow them to get where they were going and apprehend them there. The cells being the obvious target. You have quite a natural talent for infiltration it would seem" Olan'ko informed him.

Isaac took no pleasure from the backhanded compliment. Although that was two people so far who knew what they were talking about, that had told him about his impressive penchant for espionage.

"You don't know the half of it" Isaac simply replied.

"Where is he?" Olan'ko asked.

"Where is who?"

"Sato Halsa. The one you freed from here when you left. I know he's with you. There's no way you managed to get

297

here by yourself and he is the only one who would have the skill and the resources to get you inside."

"I've no idea what you're talking about" Isaac said, trying his best to lie.

"Not to worry. We'll find him soon. That I guarantee."

"Why did you do that to Moga? Why impale him with those things?" Isaac asked again, trying to change the subject from Sato.

"He's a beast Isaac. A simple minded animal. If you want an animal to do your bidding, you must first break its spirit. Then you can mould it in whatever way you please. It was supposed to be a test of character. To demonstrate commitment to what needs to be done to ensure that our goals are met. There is no stopping the Ilians Isaac. You will either serve us or be destroyed. The citizens of all worlds will learn this soon enough. Moga failed that test. Now he must live with the consequences. Or not live with them, as it were" Olan'ko told him, with a distinct note of satisfaction in his voice.

"So, everyone will have to face this test?"

"Eventually. When we're ready to bring our goals to light for all to see. Except your kind of course. They won't need to worry about it."

"I genuinely don't get this. So not all are Ilians allied to this cause, but you claim to speak for your people. Are you sure not all of your people are gutless cowards who hide behind a lie to pursue some evil galactic conquest?" Isaac asked.

"No, not all. Only the ones who can truly call themselves Ilian. Those of us who have pure body and mind."

"Seriously man. What the fuck does that even mean? In fairness I know what you're getting at. There are plenty of racist fuck holes on my planet too, but I would have thought that you would have progressed beyond that type of small minded thinking."

Olan'ko walked over to the sofa and sat down. He looked up at Isaac for a moment, contemplating where he would begin.

"What do you know of my people Isaac?"

"Not a lot to be fair. I haven't had the chance to get caught up on the minutia of details for every world of all the civilisations out here. History books haven't been high on my agenda, ya know. What with all the death defying I've had to participate in recently."

"Do you know what The Decimation was?" Olan'ko asked as he sat back in his seat.

"Nope."

"Ok, well, have you ever wondered why most Ilians have a Magalian, Garian or Talanite name?"

"I Genuinely didn't know they did."

"Have you taught him nothing?" Olan'ko asked Niers.

"I'm going to kill you" Niers replied through his clenched teeth.

"Yes of course you are. Well, here's the abridged version. Many thousands of years ago, my people were found by the Magalians. They came to our planet on a voyage of discovery and found remnants of an advanced civilisation. They though it was extinct, until they found what remained of my people, hiding in caves, living like savages, spread out on an island in the middle of our biggest ocean. There was only about five thousand of us left. The survivors of what had taken place. They didn't know what that was. Neither did we. We were a species with no memory of who we were or what had happened to us. An entire species of people with collective amnesia. Advanced in some respects and primitive in others. The majority of

299

those left behind were young children. There were less than one thousand adults. We were dying. So I suppose the Magalians saved us. They took us to their world and offered us a second chance at civilisation. We took it. After we began to grow as a population again, some set out to explore other cultures. Most of us integrated into the society we were settled in. They lived lives as Magalians, Talanites or Garians. But there were a few of the adults who stayed loyal to the Ilian way of life. They did all they could to preserve the shreds we had of what memories there were of our people. Some of them, my ancestors. They taught us what it meant to be Ilian, a real Ilian. A secret history if you will, passed down orally through generations. Then when the time was right, those who knew the truth led the expedition back home to resettle our world. To reclaim our heritage. There, they showed us what our true purpose as a people is."

He stopped to give Isaac a moment to take in all he had said.

"And what is that exactly?"

"To rule Isaac. To be the guiding light that is needed in dark times. To show all the people of the galaxy how life should be. To continue the legacy left by the Karlal."

"Right. So I suppose the moral of the story is that your true purpose as a people is to be a bunch of hoofwanking bunglecunts."

Isaac said this to try and get Olan'ko to react in anger. He just sneered at him though.

"I suppose that's an insult that is intended to get me angry. That won't happen. I have won. Do you know what it's like to carry the weight of expectation of hundreds of generations of your predecessors on your shoulders, then be the one who finally sees their vision come to fruition? To have the goal they set out to achieve all that time ago, be in touching distance for you?"

"No, I sure don't. But I can imagine that if you've been passing this history down through generations without writing anything down your original message could have gotten easily changed. A misplaced word and sentence could drastically distort a message over that kind of time."

"The message is sound. You will never have the desire to see a vision like that fulfilled. You will never understand the true meaning of whatever it takes."

"Well I'm gonna have to disagree with you on that one. If you'd seen some of the shit I've had to do recently I think you'd take a different view. I bet you've never had to stick your finger up another blokes arse to find something you needed."

Olan'ko frowned at him. He held an expression that suggested he was trying to say something but couldn't find the appropriate words required.

"Where are the rest of my crew?" Niers shouted from across the room, removing him from his bewildered contemplation.

"Bring him in" Olan'ko ordered.

Isaac turned to look at the door. It slid open and Car'esh came walking through. His hands were bound but beyond that he looked unharmed. He was flanked by Aba'dal, Car'esh's superior. Isaac had only seen him once before, when Car'esh had the conversation with him over the comm terminal on the Sao'ise. He was wearing one of the exosuits that the guards and soldiers Olan'ko employed wore.

"Car'esh?" Isaac said.

He looked at Niers, who was being lifted back to his feet by the guards standing over him. Car'esh was marched past Niers then stopped a few feet away.

"What's going on?" Niers asked confused.

"You wanted to know about the test. While your filthy Caninan friend was too stubborn, or stupid to pass, your commander was able to join us without issue. He was more than happy to, honestly. He was even gracious enough to drive the stakes through that filthy animal for us" Olan'ko explained.

Isaac looked over at Niers, who had his eyes locked on Aba'dal. He looked so lost and confused that his face was just a mess of all the different reactions he was having at once.

"Car'esh? What's going on?" Niers asked him.

"It seems that we are betrayed Niers. I realised on Altanto there was only one person in a position to do what was being done but by the time I got to you, it was already too late" Car'esh responded to Niers, looking disdainfully toward Aba'dal as he spoke.

"Fools. You should have just followed your orders. Then you wouldn't even be here." Aba'dal said to them.

"What are you Talking about?" Car'esh asked him.

"Why do you think I put you on this mission? Because I could control you so easily without you being aware of it.

We sent the squad to retrieve the storage device from the Magalian we had stationed on Earth. You thwarted them even before we had time to fully activate the tracking beacon inside his implant. Then you disabled your own ships signal. So we sent that phony information to Ran'gis about the communications involving you and the human, knowing he would contact you, then that in turn would eventually send you to me. You are so predictable and were so easy to manipulate. Or at least you were until you unexpectedly you went against orders. You should have just left this human to his fate and this would all be over. Olan'ko would have had his prisoner, you would be no wiser and we would all have continued to live on happily. I never thought you would be foolish enough to come back to get him" Aba'dal told them, shaking his head.

"Where is the agent you originally picked up?" Olan'ko asked, interrupting.

"I killed him. I turned his head into mush. Completely by accident of course" Isaac replied.

Olan'ko was a bit taken aback by this revelation.

"You betrayed us? You betrayed your sworn loyalty to the Assembly? For What? Money?" Niers shouted at Aba'dal, stunned.

"Money?" Aba'dal replied, visually insulted by the suggestion.

"Why then? What other possible reason could you have for this? How much do you expect to get paid?" Car'esh demanded to know.

"You idiotic runt. I have spent so much time trying to teach you, but here you are having learnt nothing. I used to think it was my fault. Then I realised you were just not capable of seeing the truth." Aba'dal barked at him.

"What truth?" Car'esh asked.

"Niers you speak of a sworn loyalty to the Assembly. Is that really who we are loyal to, or are we loyal to the pay cheque they provide us? We do their bidding because they pay us to. We go where they say and do what they command and for what? Supposedly the betterment of all our peoples. Yet it's at their discretion, their whim. I've seen it too many times. Orders sending soldiers away from where they need to be and sending them to protect interests, assets or locations. The politicians talk and when they are finished they send the soldiers to die. All for their benefit. This is not the oath I took. I was to serve the people, not the infrastructure. When I met the general all those years ago, we bonded over a similar set of moral values. As we got to know each other he shared with me his vision of what our societies could be under one rule. I believe in that vision. It's a cause that I can truly be loyal to. There is no pay cheque that can match the value of that."

Aba'dal let his revelation to Car'esh and Niers linger in silence. Everyone in the room was quietly letting the weight of his words press them to look deep inside and see if any of what he said rang true in their minds. Then Isaac piped up.

"I have to hand it to you, you make some solid points about corruption in government. But just so we're clear, you were dissatisfied with what you saw as an abuse of power in the upper ranks of your elected officials and when some bloke came along and offered you genocide and a move towards a fascist dictatorship you thought, yeah, this is the answer to the problems I'm seeing, let's have a bit of that?" Isaac asked, deliberately stepping on Aba'dal's moment.

Aba'dal's eyes, although big already, grew a little wider as he turned to face Isaac with a contemptuous look.

"Don't speak to me mutt" was all he got in return from him though.

"No, no. Of course not. I'm just saying. Maybe they're one problem and you're a completely different type of problem."

"That's enough. Let's reunite them all please, shall we. I believe the rest are here" Olan'ko said interjecting between the two of them.

Taretta was marched into the room, followed closely behind by Sha'ala. They walked into the middle and stopped beside Niers.

"What do you want from us?" Car'esh asked Olan'ko.

"I want you to follow me. I want you to take my lead and be a part of the new order we plan to establish. I want you to see the opportunity we have in front of us and grab it with both hands" he replied.

"You want the impossible" Niers snapped back at him.

Olan'ko stood up and walked towards them leaving Isaac standing alone on the other side of the room. He placed his index finger under Taretta's chin and used it to raise her head up so that their eyes met.

"Hello my dear. Are you ready to die for what you believe in?" Olan'ko asked her.

"Aba'dal, stop this" Niers shouted.

Taretta stood there staring back at him, trying to project a look of defiance, doing her best to mask her fear that was on display.

"Oh, I see your look of rebelliousness. You wear it so well. You are determined to not submit to me. To fight to your last breath for what you believe in. I applaud it. I know how it can drive you. It's what got me to where I am today. Defiance is a wonderful motivator. That belief that what you're doing is righteous. That you won't be denied, because you stand in defiance of evil for the betterment of others."

He walked over to one of his guards and removed his side arm from his hip, then strode back to Taretta. "Right now, you believe that this virtuous disposition will be enough to carry you through this situation you find yourself in. Let me show you why you're wrong."

He raised the pistol and fired. Isaac couldn't tell where the shot had been aimed. He looked around. Niers was still there. Taretta and Sha'ala were standing in the opposite direction of the pistol blast. Then Car'esh fell to his knees just inside Isaac's peripheral vision. Isaac wasn't sure what he was looking at when he turned to see what had happened. A large section of his face wasn't there anymore. There was an enormous wound where it had been. His right eye was still in place. It seemed to look over at Isaac as he fell. His left eye was nowhere to be seen. Neither was his nose or his lips. His tongue however was still intact. It rolled out of where his mouth had been, resting on his chin. The shot didn't seem to pass through his head entirely. It just dug out a crater in it. The canals of his nasal passage began to ooze blood. Some remnants of the flesh that had been his face hung down around the edges of the hole that his features had occupied up until now. There was a slight gurgling sound emanating from him as he choked on the blood streaming down his throat. Isaac heard the word no echo around the room, but he wasn't sure who it was that had shouted it.

35

"What the fuck is wrong with you?" Isaac demanded from Olan'ko.

"What?" was the only answer he got from him, shrugging his shoulders, displaying a blatant indifference for what he had just done.

Taretta and Sha'ala, stood there stiff, both in shock. Niers too most likely.

"This is madness" Isaac shouted at him.

"No Isaac. That was essential. Madness would be me believing that Car'esh would actually align to my goals. That he would fully commit to what I need to do. I'm no fool. I would never take his word for anything. In fact, I believe all of you are useless to me."

"Alright stop this. Whatever you want, just take it from me. Leave them alone" Isaac said as he stood in defiance of his enemy.

Olan'ko turned to look at him.

"Leave them alone? They are the only ones outside of my people who know any of this. Aba'dal has done a tremendous job of keeping us out of the eyes and ears of the Assembly leaders. They are the only credible threat to all I have worked for. I also don't need anything from you Isaac, beyond your genes and your inevitable demise. You and your filthy species" he said as he walked towards him.

"Filthy?" Isaac asked, feeling a genuine hit to his pride at the intimation that his entire species are filthy.

"Yes, you are filthy. You live in your own squalor. Pumping excrement into your own habitat. Poisoning the very ecosystem you rely on to sustain you. You're an infestation to the world you live on. Barbaric in the way you have evolved. You don't deserve a planet to live on. Never mind the world of the greatest race ever to exist. I've read the reports we gathered from your world. You're despicable" Olan'ko told him, their noses now millimetres from each other.

"Barbaric is a bit rich coming from someone intent on the extermination of an entire population. Here's another problem with that. I'm just not on board with people who think like you do. Idiots who bang on about life being a disease or an infection. It's the mindset of a simpleton. Someone who has no accountability for themselves. I'm on the side of people. I want people to succeed" Isaac replied, in no way intimidated by Olan'ko anymore.

"The Assembly will stop you" Taretta shouted at him through her anger.

"The Assembly? They will do nothing except what they always do. Debate and discuss and then act according to what is in their best interests. They only have one purpose, to accumulate as much wealth as they can to sustain the masses to the point that they will stop asking for more, because they are content, so the assembly can take the majority for themselves. But they will never be content. The nature of all the people who live under the Assembly is to keep wanting more. Because that is what they have been taught. Excess and greed. They spend their time squabbling over trivial matters. Too blind to see the bigger picture. They are asleep at the controls. We intend to change that. They rely on a strategy of combining forces to deal with any threat that appears. A coalition of different tactics and policies trying to mesh with each other at a moment's notice. There hasn't been a reason for them to mobilise on any grand scale for millennia. They will be disjointed and easily defeated by a well prepared and disciplined militia that they will never see coming until it's too late. Like the one we Ilians have been building in secret. The Galactic Assembly is a fragile alliance at best. They will be easily dispatched when we need them to be."

Isaac began to laugh which caught the attention of everyone in the room. Olan'ko turned to look at him along with everyone else.

"You find that amusing?" he asked

"No. I just think you're putting a lot of faith in your men. I find that funny."

"Why?"

"Well, I'm not exactly combat proficient. No training of any kind and I've managed to take care of a few of them. I wonder what will happen when they come up against an actual organised force."

"We will be victorious."

"Well, best of luck with that Himmler. I've read about this before in history books on my world. It's not going to end well for you."

"The Karlal have shown us the path. We will follow it. So will all the people of the galaxy."

"If they were so fucking superior and enlightened, where are they now" Isaac jeered.

Olan'ko moved back and turned again to the rest of the crew of the Sao'ise, ignoring Isaac.

"Now, who is going to die next?" he asked.

"Well here's the thing," Isaac began, "I know I'm the outsider here. You folks have been doing this shit a lot longer than I have. You have causes and beliefs. I've never had a cause. I never really gave enough of a fuck about anything to get involved. I've always been a bit of a useless wanker. Recently though I've met these people who have shown me that there are things out there worth giving a damn about. Things that are greater than me, cliché as that may sound. Things that, and I mean this with all sincerity, I would be willing to die for. I'm not saying this because I think it makes me in some way special. People do that shit all the time. It's just a new way of seeing things for me."

Olan'ko looked at him, puzzled by his sudden declaration of nobility.

"You will die. That I can promise you. You will die and in doing so you will help me eradicate your filthy populace" he told him.

"There you go with that word filthy again. I'm going to hit you with a filthy slap now in a second. Christ man. You're ready to wipe out life on a planetary scale to try and achieve some absurd notion of a utopia so you can honour the memory of a dead race from a fairy tale. You're cracked in the head lad. You can't build a utopia on a foundation of genocide. That's insanity. I was never really the revolutionary type, ya know. I never thought about other people's lives or the value of them. But then I listened to you tell me about how your psychotic plan is to snuff them all out for your own personal interests. To exterminate my people. Innocent people. Sure, some of

310

them are arse holes but they don't all deserve to die because of a few dick heads. You don't see or care about the carnage that you want to leave behind. It's all just numbers on a graph to you. But I can see it. I can visualise the nightmarish images of the dead bodies of children, who through no fault of their own, would miss out on their future because of a psychopath's fantasy. And let's be honest. What a future it could be now that I know about all that's waiting for them out here. So no, my cause, my only purpose in life from now on is to end you and everything that you stand for. I mean, come on man. If fighting back against your demented plans is not enough to motivate someone into taking action, then nothing would be. Now, I'm ready to get the fuck out of here."

There was a moment of silence as everyone in the room looked at him. Then Olan'ko began to laugh. He was soon joined in a chorus by all of the minions that occupied the room. His laughter turned maniacal, as everyone else upped their volume too. All except Niers, Taretta and Sha'ala. Then the laughter stopped and Olan'ko turned to him. Still with a smile on his lips.

"By all means Isaac, escape if you can. I actually look forward to your heroic attempt" he sneered.

"Huh? Oh no, I wasn't talking to you ya cock faced barnacle. Norman Cooke! That's his name. It just came to me. What do you mean who? Fatboy Slim. The DJ from home who's name I couldn't remember. No, he's not my friend, he's a musician. I don't actually know him. Christ man I'll fucking explain later. What's a reactor core? Well how big of an explosion? What do you mean you don't know?"

The words left his mouth and seemed to hang in the air for a second. He looked around the room as every eye was fixed on him, absolutely hypnotized by his incoherent ramblings. There was no time to warn anyone that he had a plan. Well not that he had a plan. That there was a plan in place to escape. He didn't know what the plan was himself, he just knew he had set it in motion. At least he hoped he had. After Sha'ala and Taretta had entered the room, Isaac had pressed the strip Sato had placed at the base of his skull when they first arrived. The one that turned his translator into a communicator. Sato had been talking in his ear for the last few minutes asking him to stall and keep Olan'ko monologuing so he could get everything he needed to, set in motion. Since Isaac wasn't sure how to do that, he just decided to give his own little off the cuff, heartfelt speech. Sato had just told Isaac that he was ready, whatever that meant.

There was a low rumbling noise that started to permeate the area almost immediately. Then Isaac started to feel the sound in the room all around him as the walls began to vibrate. The vibrations quickly became shaking. Like an earthquake had just began to rumble. Everyone in the room looked around them as the intensity of the shaking gradually increased.

"What have you done?" Olan'ko asked, the look of pure joy he had been flaunting, now changed to one Isaac hadn't seen before. Uncertainty.

Before Isaac had a chance to respond, a series of explosions could be heard from outside the window. Olan'ko rushed towards it and looked out. Not too far away there was a giant chimney that bore a perfect resemblance to the type you would see in a nuclear power facility, sticking out from the top of a mountain. The explosions were coming from that general direction. A series of flames came shooting out of the top of it, each one brought a tremor that would have registered high on the Richter Scale. Then it erupted. A massive blaze rocketed out of the top of the chimney that seemed to reach the clouds in the sky. The chimney itself began to crack up the sides. Olan'ko turned to Isaac.

"What have you done?" he screamed.

The mountain that the chimney was on started to crumble. Giant boulders began to break away and tumble down to the ground beneath. The chimney itself tipped over slightly before it evaporated in a brilliant flash of light, along with the top of the mountain it had been sitting on. Isaac could see the force of the explosion that had just taken place speed its way across the landscape towards them, obliterating everything in its path.

"Get down" he shouted, looking towards Niers and the others before throwing himself to the floor behind the sofa, the only cover he could see anywhere in the room.

The brunt of the explosion hit the windows, shattering them, propelling splinters of glass across the room. Part of the roof flew off and several of Olan'ko's soldier were flung backwards through the air into the walls, having been transformed into pin cushions by the broken windows. The sound of the wind rushing overhead was deafening. It ripped over them for several seconds and then stopped suddenly. Isaac remained curled up having made himself as small as he could momentarily after the force of the blast had passed, before getting back to his feet. He looked around at the annihilation that surrounded him. There was a ringing in his ears. A cloud of smoke and dust filled the air, the smell of scorched earth burnt his nostrils. There were bodies strewn everywhere. The one remaining wall that wasn't made of glass at the entrance to the room had been pebble dashed with blood. He couldn't make out who

313

was who. Then he saw movement. First he saw Niers, then Sha'ala stood up beside him. Both seemed to have heeded his warning and found protection from the flying debris.

"Where's Taretta?" Sha'ala asked.

They looked around until eventually Niers spotted her. She was draped across two bodies toward the entrance. They all rushed over to her and Niers knelt down beside her, putting his hand on her shoulder. There were two large shards of glass embedded in her. One in her abdomen, the other in her right shoulder. She was motionless, facing towards the sky. One of her legs seemed to be twisted in an unnatural position from the knee down.

"Taretta?" Isaac heard Niers say, his voice quivering.

There was no response. Isaac could hear muffled sobs coming from Sha'ala. Then suddenly Taretta drew in a deep breath and jerked back to life. Isaac could see she was in trouble and not entirely there. Niers turned to him.

"What now" he asked.

Isaac wanted to answer but the reality was he didn't have a clue. There was an awkward silence as Isaac tried to think of something to say, while Sha'ala and Niers looked at him expectantly.

"Well, what the hell are you waiting for. Let's get the fuck out of here" a voice came calling from behind them.

Isaac turned to see Sato standing in the back of an open shuttle, hovering just outside the room. He turned to tell the others to move, but they were way ahead of him. Niers had one of Taretta's arms and Sha'ala had the other. They were carrying her towards the ship. Isaac got up and walked behind them, surveying the room as he did, looking for any evidence of Olan'ko or Aba'dal, in the bodies that littered the room. He couldn't identify either of them as he stepped into the shuttle.

"Is she alive?" he heard Sato say.

"Barely. I can treat her wounds temporarily with a med kit, but we need to get her to a proper facility right away" Sha'ala replied.

"Where are the other two?" Isaac heard Sato ask.

"Just go" was the reply from Niers.

Isaac looked out the back of the craft at the devastated structure they just fled as they began to soar toward the sky. There were explosions firing in many different directions as they made their way up into the clouds. Half of the facility had been mangled, reduced to rubble, littered with random infernos burning. The door began to close and Isaac turned and walked into the craft.

36

Isaac stood at the back of the ship looking on as Niers was desperately searching for a med kit, anything they could use to try and tend to Taretta's wounds. She was lying on the floor, still unconscious. Eventually he found one and brought it to Sha'ala. Sha'ala took the kit from Niers and had a look through it.

"There's not a lot I can do with these scraps," she lamented, "but I'll do all I can."

She knelt down beside her and began to asses her injuries. Niers followed her to his knees and positioned himself above Taretta's head, ready to assist in any way he could. Isaac realised he was still wearing the exosuit, so he deactivated the power source and slid it off, kicking it into a pile in the corner. Then he walked to the front of the ship and sat beside Sato.

"Thanks. I genuinely thought we were finished for a few minutes there" he told him.

"My pleasure. Where are Car'esh and Moga?" Sato replied.

"I'm not sure about Moga. Last time I saw him he was still alive. I'm not sure exactly what location in the facility he was being kept in, but it's hard to imagine he survived that destruction. Car'esh, is gone. Olan'ko shot him right in the face. It's an image I'll see every time I close my eyes from now on."

"He was a good man. They both were. It's a loss that will be felt by all who wear a uniform" Sato said as he bowed his head and closed his eyes for a moment.

"Where are we heading?" Isaac asked him.

"Magaly. It's the safest place we can go. Once there we can get Taretta the treatment she needs and then we will bring you to the Assembly leaders so we can try and expose Olan'ko to them."

Isaac looked out into the blackness as he reflected on what had just unfolded. Then he heard Sha'ala call his name from behind him.

"Isaac I need you back here please."

"How can I help?" he asked as he got up and walked back to where they were.

"I need you to help me remove this shard from her. Once I get it out you need to apply pressure around the area to stop the bleeding."

Isaac got down and placed his hands on her stomach.

"Are you not supposed to leave the thing in the stab hole so not to cause more bleeding?" he asked her.

"I can use this foam to cauterize the wounds, but it will only be a temporary solution. She will need urgent medical assistance once we land" she told him, holding up a small can she had taken from the med kit.

Sha'ala slowly began to extract the glass from Taretta. It was at least three inches deep and once it slid all the way out blood began to flow from the large gash, like a volcanic eruption. Isaac could see the meat under the skin as he pressed down. The two sides of the massive wound on her

317

stomach sliding up against each other and then separating constantly. His hands were soaked in blood and it became a much harder task to try and apply pressure, as they slipped across her skin. Taretta began to convulse.

"Hold her still Niers. Isaac keep that pressure on" Sha'ala ordered.

She reached forward and plunged the nozzle on the can into the bloody crevice, firing the foam inside. The substance expanded inside the laceration, then bubbled out over the skin. It looked like shaving foam at first, malleable, not very secure. Then it changed composition to be more rigid. Sha'ala fired an injection into her hand and Taretta's spasms subsided. Then Sha'ala lifted her eyelids and shone a light into her eyes, one at a time, before letting them slide closed again.

"Will she make it?" Niers asked her.

"I don't know. She has severe trauma to her head. There's no telling what that glass did to her internally. If we had access to the med bay, I could definitely tend to her successfully. The longer she goes without that type of treatment, the more likely she is to die" Sha'ala told him honestly.

Niers stood up and walked to the front of the ship to where Sato was sitting.

"I need to fly the ship. We need to get there soon" he told him.

"The ship is going as fast as it can, trust me. Go get some rest and we'll be there before you know it" Sato assured him.

"I said give me the ship" Niers shouted, grabbing Sato by the shoulder.

Sato slipped his arm around, twisting free of Niers' grip. He stood up, grabbing him by the collar and forcing him backwards, slamming him up against the side of the ship. Niers swung a left hook at him but Sato rolled under it and brought his other arm up, forcing his forearm under Niers' chin into his neck, holding him in place against the wall.

"The fuck is wrong with you two" Isaac shouted, jumping up and getting in between them, separating them from each other.

"He did this to her. He's responsible if Taretta dies" Niers shouted, pointing a finger in Sato's face.

"If it wasn't for him we'd all be dead by now" Isaac barked back at him.

"I'm sorry about Taretta Niers, I truly am. I had to do it. We needed to disrupt Olan'ko as much as possible. I had no idea the blast radius would be so big. But I make no apologies. It was a necessary risk that I needed to take" Sato told him.

Niers slumped onto the ground and placed his head in his hands. He began to weep uncontrollably. Isaac crouched down beside him and put his hand on Niers' shoulder to comfort him.

"I'm sorry about Moga and Car'esh" he said, before heading up to the front and sitting down beside Sato.

He looked out into the distance and began to reflect on all that had happened. He felt a deep sadness at the loss of Car'esh and Moga. Two people he had barely known but they seemed to have had an immense effect on him. It was strange. Like the type of feeling you get when a someone of great importance to society dies. People die every day and each one is a tragedy in their own right, but when exceptional people die in unnatural circumstances the loss just seems greater, because exceptional people are hard to find. His thoughts occupied him for a while as they headed for their destination.

"What do you make of all this stuff about the Karlal, ancient civilisations, building utopias and all that. Hiding secret plans and agendas from the Assembly for all that time and putting them in motion now. Seems a bit farfetched, no? How do you stay so secretive for so long?" Isaac asked the room, coming back to reality after some time in his own head.

No one answered immediately. They all seemed to be taking a minute to consider this question. Isaac was actually surprised that they hadn't done so before now.

"It's all a bit too much to believe" Sato finally offered in response.

"The idea that the ethos of a civilisation that disappeared before any of the Assembly races had mastered interstellar travel is still alive, having been lost for so long. It doesn't make any sense" Niers added.

"There are all the old stories, myths and legends about the Karlal. People have dedicated their lives to finding out who or what they were" Sha'ala said.

"Idiots have wasted their lives you mean. There's no truth to any of that. There's no solid evidence anywhere about them. Just remnants and ancient relics" Sato said.

They all took some time to quietly consider the idea of a shadow organisation trying to overthrow the Assembly.

"Either way it doesn't matter right now. We need to decide on our next steps after we get Taretta some help" Niers said.

"How far out from Magaly are we?" Isaac asked.

"Couple of minutes" Sato answered.

"What's the plan once we get there?" Isaac asked.

"We have a secure location where Sha'ala can treat Taretta's wounds. We can come up with a plan once we get there" Niers replied.

"Ok, were here. We can get into the detail later" Sato said interrupting them.

Isaac turned his attention back to the front window. As the ship emerged from sub space Magaly was right in front of them. Isaac was staggered by how similar it looked to Earth. The blue and green was almost identical. The land masses looked different. There were continents but they were obviously different shapes to the ones from Earth, but the general look of the planet was remarkably similar to home. It stirred a desire in him to see his world again. There was a constant stream of traffic coming and going too. Ships of all sizes were either entering or exiting the atmosphere of the planet. Their ship started to shake and rumble.

"Entering the atmosphere" Sato informed them.

Outside all Isaac could see was what looked like flames engulfing the ship. The heat from the ship passing through the atmosphere was causing this. After a few moments they broke through. Isaac was a little disappointed with what he saw. There were several buildings below them, maybe two dozen scattered around. That was it. It was a hardly a monument to what he had been led to believe was the greatest modern civilisation in the known universe.

"Overcast today," Sato said, "we'll be on the ground in a minute."

Then he realised that they were still above the clouds.

It took them a minute to make their way through the weather front. Below them was a city. This was a first for Isaac. All the planets he had been on so far were either uninhabited or were minor settlements. None of them had looked like this. To call it a metropolis was an understatement. There were buildings off in the distance as far as Isaac could see, and since they were high up, he could see pretty far. There were the ones that reached up into the clouds that they had just passed the top of. Others that were just below the cloud line. Smaller ones that filled the space between the high rises and everything else in between. They seemed to be heading to the outskirts, away from the sky scrapers.

"It's incredible" Isaac mumbled. Nobody seemed to hear him. They had too much on their minds. Ahead Isaac could see a platform. It looked to be a station for landing at.

"Is there like a customs or immigration place that we need to go through, because I don't have a passport on me" Isaac said glibly.

"Normally yes, but we've taken care of that through other channels. We just need to land and get indoors" Niers told him.

Sato approached the platform slowly and circled, until he found an appropriate spot to land in, out of the way of the main area where most people would be. He positioned the ship over the spot and gently placed it down on the ground. As soon as he did everyone stood up and started moving around getting ready to head out. Sato opened the back doors and rushed off away from them.

Where are you going?" Isaac asked.

"I need to get a vehicle. The safe house is twenty miles away. We can't fly this over and we're not carrying Taretta through a city full of people looking like that. I'll be back in a minute" Sato replied.

"Something discreet" Niers shouted after him.

Isaac looked down at Sha'ala, who was tending to Taretta. She was checking her vital signs and then she put what looked like a small gun to her arm and pressed a button.

"What's that?" Isaac asked.

322

"I'm keeping her in a coma for now. Her wounds are severe, and I don't want to put any undue stress on her body" Sha'ala replied softly and sadly.

Isaac stood up and moved to Niers at the front of the ship. "Anything I can do to help?" he asked.

Niers turned to respond but he didn't get a chance as there was an unexpected and enormous commotion outside. It started with a siren, or an alarm. Some sort of loud noise started to go off repeatedly. Then there were flashing lights. Red ones. They were almost blinding. Isaac got really disorientated and fell over backwards. As he got to his feet, he looked out the back of the ship. There were people everywhere. All dressed the same, wearing a uniform. It was armoured. Much more than the Olan'ko mercenaries were. Each one seemed to have a rifle type gun in their hand. They were all holding it butt to their shoulder, ready to aim in a second. They were surrounding the ship. Then the siren stopped and the lights died and there was a moment of silence.

"Surrender and exit the vehicle" a loud voice boomed from outside. It sounded like it was being broadcast rather than someone outside the ship speaking.

"MCDF!" Sha'ala exclaimed.

"What the fuck is that?" Isaac asked.

"Magaly Civil Defence Force" Niers replied.

"Like the police?" Isaac asked.

"Yes" Sha'ala answered.

"What do we do?" Isaac asked.

"Whatever they say if we want to live. Just put your hands behind your head" Niers replied.

Isaac did as he was instructed and then walked out the door behind Niers and Sha'ala. As he emerged he looked around. There were at least thirty armed guards

323

surrounding them. Each had their weapon cocked and aimed at the three of them as they exited the ship, ready to fire. Isaac followed Niers and when Niers got down on his knees Isaac did the same. A group of the MCDF broke away from the crowd and walked cautiously towards them, guns still drawn and cocked. Two of them walked to Sha'ala and brought her to her feet as she stumbled over trying to inform them of their wounded crew mate still in the back of the ship. Niers was next to be restrained. He was lifted up by two of the MCDF guards and lead away. Isaac knelt, his hands on his head, waiting to be arrested himself, realising Sato was nowhere to be seen. Where was he gone. Had he orchestrated this. Unlikely Isaac thought. Why would he do all he did and then turn them over now. That wouldn't make any sense. So, had he just abandoned them? That seemed unlikely too.

Isaac felt a hand on his shoulder and he looked up. There were two guards standing over him. One was pulling him to his feet while the other kept his rifle squarely aimed at him. There was no struggle from Isaac, and no aggression from the MCDF. It was quite an amicable arrest. He was led away and placed in the back of what looked like a mobile prison cell. His hands had been put in some type of restraint that were very similar to handcuffs from Earth. There were no windows in this particular prison bus. It was just a box and he had just enough room to sit down. The door was closed and he was alone. There was a light on so at least he wasn't in darkness. He sat there, contemplating again as he took another journey on his own to another unknown destination.

37

Isaac sat in the room. The same room he had been occupying for several hours now. No one had come to him. No one had interacted with him. It was just him in this room, alone. He was getting sick of the isolation that he constantly found himself having to endure every time someone captured him. He was also getting sick of being captured. The only sign of life was twice since he had been there, a little hatch in the wall had opened and there was a tray with some food on it. It was the same type of protein bar that he had eaten on the Sao'ise but it was sustenance, with a glass of water. The room was lit by a light that seemed to be putting a strain on his eyes after a while. That was probably the point of them. Isaac did wonder why he had been left here. It was a locked room, but it wasn't a cell. There was no bed for one thing. Instead there was a small table in the middle of the room, with a stool on either side. Isaac was currently occupying the one on the side of the table that was facing the door.

Then the door that had been locked made a noise and slid open. There was a Magalian standing on the other side. He was wearing what looked suspiciously like a shirt and tie, with a pair of slacks. On closer inspection that's exactly what they were. This took Isaac by surprise. He thought it was some kind of trick. That they had found out all they could about Earth and were going to use it to confuse him and get him to talk. Isaac sat there, looking as stoic as he could as the Magalian sat down on the chair opposite to him.

"My name is officer Val'han. I'm with the Magaly Civil Defence Force" he began.

"What are you wearing?" Isaac asked, interrupting him.

"Excuse me?" Val'han said, a little surprised by the question.

"Your clothes. What are you wearing? Where did you get them?"

"From a clothes shop" he responded, looking down at himself a little confused.

"I'm on to you?" Isaac said, shooting Val'han a look of suspicion.

Val'han looked back at Isaac befuddled, he even looked a little concerned about Isaac.

He peered down and made a note on his handheld device. A long note that took several minutes to complete. There was a silence in the room but Isaac just stared dead ahead at him, trying his best to show strength and determination and hide his fear and weakness. Val'han looked up from his notes and back at Isaac.

"Why are you here?" he asked.

"Because you people arrested me and brought me here" Isaac replied immediately.

"No why are you off your world, out here in the galaxy, consorting with terrorists?" Val'han clarified.

"Terrorists? I'm not consorting with terrorists."

"Your three companions that you were with when you were arrested. They are terrorists wanted by the Galactic Assembly."

Isaac wasn't sure how to take this. Had they always been terrorists, or had they just been classed as that recently since the Olan'ko facility incident he wondered. He needed more information. Then he suddenly remembered Taretta, how she was fifty-fifty on living or dying the last time he saw he.

"My friend Taretta, the one who was injured. Is she alive?" Isaac asked.

"She is. She was lucky. She's being treated at a facility not too far from here" Val'han informed him.

Isaac felt a weight lift off his chest with the relief of that news.

"So why are they terrorists? What have they done to be called that?" Isaac asked.

"They weren't until a few days ago. Then they seem to have decided to blow up an Ilian government institution for reasons that are yet to be determined" Val'han explained.

"Oh you mean Olan'ko's torture facility" Isaac said.

Val'han seemed to be taken aback by this. He wasn't prepared for Isaac to say that. He leaned back in his chair and took a moment to study Isaac. Isaac just sat opposite him, looking back, trying his best not to give anything away.

"What do you mean by that?" Val'han asked.

"It's pretty simple man. Olan'ko kept me in the facility your talking about for who knows how long and spent the entire time I was there running torturous experiments on me" Isaac told him.

"That's ridiculous. Olan'ko is one of the most respected generals in the Ilian military. Your accusations are preposterous" Val'han fired back disdainfully.

"If you say so" Isaac muttered.

"Why? Why would he do that?" Val'han asked.

"Well he told me it was to create a disease that would wipe out the sentient population of my planet" Isaac answered.

"Nonsense" Val'han snapped.

"If you say so" Isaac fired back sarcastically.

Val'han stood up abruptly knocking his chair over as he did. He moved to the door and pressed the button to open it.

"I am remanding you in custody for acts of terrorism against the Ilians. Since you are not a species that lives under Assembly law, I have no idea how you will be tried. All I can say is that you will remain in a prison cell until the Ilians come to claim you" he announced to Isaac.

"The Ilians are coming for me?" Isaac asked.

"Yes. Your crime was against them. Committed on one of their sovereign worlds. Maybe they will entertain your wild imaginings. I highly doubt it though."

"It's a true story."

"Yes well, the best of luck getting them to believe you."

"If you give me to the Ilians you might as well just put a bullet in me now."

"What's a bullet?"

"For the love of fucking God, how does nobody know what a bullet is. I mean you might as well just kill me now. Because they're going to. It just won't be as quick as shooting me in the head would be."

"Ninety two people died in the explosion you and your cohorts set off in that facility. If you are executed for that crime then so be it. That's their decision to make. I have no doubt that justice will be served though."

Isaac was a little shaken by this revelation. He hadn't even considered the death toll of what they had done. He wasn't prepared for it. It weighed heavily on him but he had no time to for guilt right now.

"If you knew the truth you wouldn't be calling it justice. You have no clue about what will be served" he said, a little less convinced in himself after hearing the repercussions of what he had been a part of.

A guard in a uniform came in the door and ordered Isaac to his feet. Isaac walked out the door and followed the guard down a corridor. At the end they walked through a door and descended a flight of stairs.

"Let me ask you something. Why would I make this shit up? Why would I leave my planet to come to a new one to start a fight with people I don't know for no reason. Does that seem like a logical course of action to you?" Isaac asked breaking the silence that was dominating their journey

"I'm not even sure you are from another planet. For all I know your genes have been modified to make you look this way. Once the test results come back, I'll have a clearer picture of what is going on" Val'han answered.

At the bottom the guard stopped at a sealed door and deactivated the lock. There was another long hallway on the other side. This one was lined on all the way down with prison cells. Not dissimilar to the ones in Olan'ko's facility, except instead of the fancy disappearing doors, this one seemed to have more traditional looking cells. The type with bars on them. Isaac looked in the ones he was walking past. There was one person in each of them. Most were lying down on the bed that was at the back against the wall. Some were standing up, leaning on the bars, looking out at Isaac as he walked post. The guard in front of him stopped at a cell where the door was open.

"Welcome to your new home for the foreseeable future" Val'han informed Isaac.

Isaac walked in to the cell and turned back around to look at Val'han, just as the door slammed closed in his face.

"Cosy" Isaac said, smiling at him.

"Good, I'm glad you like it. I'll be sending for you sometime soon. I have more questions to ask. But until then I would advise you to get comfortable. You won't be leaving this room until I do."

Isaac didn't say anything back. He just stood there looking at Val'han with a slightly crooked smile on his face. Val'han turned and walked away, the prison guard in tow. Isaac looked across the hall at the cell opposite from him. There was a Garian in it. Resting his arms on the bars looking back at Isaac silently.

"What's up?" Isaac said to him.

"Fuck off" the Garian replied.

"Ok" Isaac said, laughing involuntarily.

"What are you?" the Garian asked.

"I'm a human, you inbred fuck" Isaac replied as he turned his back to check out his new digs.

The cell was small. About eight feet by eight feet. The bed was at the back of the room. It was more of a shelf that was attached to the back wall. No blanket or pillow. Just a flat surface protruding from the concrete. He walked over to it and sat on the edge. Then he realised there was no toilet. He looked around until he spotted a small hole in the middle of the floor. He stood up and walked over to it, taking a moment to absorb it all.

"Now you have it" Isaac heard the Garian say.

He looked up at him and he was smiling back, with a contemptable look on his face. Isaac didn't say anything. He just gave him the finger.

"What's that supposed to mean?" the Garian asked confused.

Isaac didn't respond. He just turned around and walked back to his bed and sat on the end, looking up at the ceiling. He thought about his circumstances. It wasn't any better or worse than some of the scenarios he had found himself in most recently. Whatever happens now happens, no sense in worrying about it. He thought about the idea of being charged with a crime on a planet where he knew nothing about the laws or customs. How their trials took place and what were the possible outcomes of them. Would he be allowed to speak in his own defence? Would he need a solicitor? If he was found guilty would the death penalty be a possible outcome. How could he leverage the fact that he was an alien in his favour? So many questions began to swirl around in his mind. He snapped himself back to the present after a minute. The Garian was still leaning on his cell door looking over at him.

"Something you need?" Isaac asked sharply.

The Garian didn't say anything. He just kept looking.

"Is there something I can do for you? Or do you want to just keep gawking at me like some sort of pervert" Isaac snapped as he stood up and walked over to the cell door again, leaning on the bars. They both looked as menacingly as they could at each other, safe in the fact that neither of them would be able to do anything besides try to intimidate the other due to the bars restraining them.

Their eye contact was broken by a commotion in the cell to Isaacs left. The occupant seemed to burst into a coughing fit for a minute.

331

"The results of an occupational hazards sometimes make you wonder whether they are worth the effort" a voice from the cell said after the coughing had subsided.

Isaac recognised it. He couldn't place it, but it was familiar. Then he heard footsteps as his neighbour walked from the bed to his bars. Isaac saw arms come out through the bars and rest on them, but he couldn't see who it was.

"So," the voice began, "tell me more about this Santa Clause person."

Isaac smiled.